A BOXFUL OF IDEAS

Other anthologies from Paradise Press:

Queer Haunts (2003, expanded edition 2013)
Oysters and Pearls (2010)
People your Mother Warned You About (2011)
The Best of Gazebo (2012)
Eros at Large (2013)
Coming Clean (2014)

A BOXFUL OF IDEAS

Poetry and Prose
by LGBT Writers

Edited by John Dixon and Jeffrey Doorn

Foreword by Nicholas de Jongh

PARADISE PRESS

First published in Great Britain in 2016 by
Paradise Press, BM Box 5700, London WC1N 3XX.
www.paradisepress.org.uk

A CIP catalogue record for this book
is available from the British Library.

ISBN 978-1-904585-86-2

10 9 8 7 6 5 4 3 2 1

Printed and bound by CMP (UK) Limited, Poole.

Cover design by Russell Wilson.

Designed and typeset by Ross Burgess.
Set in Baskerville, with headings in Cabin.

Dedicated to

Michael Harth

1926–2016

BY THE BOOK

Don't play it by the book.
You can take a look –
at its regulations,
so long as they don't guide your destinations
too much.
A touch
should be as the spirit moves,
whether or not the book approves.
You'll not catch much on your hook
if you just play it by the book.

Don't play it by the book.
The ones who took
the highest prizes
didn't restrain their exercises
to the letter.
It's better
to suit the moment's need
if as a lover you'd succeed.
You'll get that sad lonesome look
if you will play it by the book.

Michael Harth

CONTENTS

FOREWORD

'Is the gay label necessary in these days of Acceptance?' the editors John Dixon and Jeffrey Doorn ask in their introduction to this fascinating LGBT anthology of original poems, short stories, excerpts from novels and non-fiction – nicely titled *A Boxful of Ideas*. The simple but provocative question startled me. I need to explain why.

The editors are raising an important question. Is it any longer necessary to make such a discrete Anthology today, today when Gay Marriage has crowned two decades of liberal legislation that have transformed gay lives for the infinitely better and brought us out of the cold? Have we not been welcomed into the ranks of the Accepting and Acceptable majority? Understandably Dixon and Doorn answer a resounding 'no' to their own question. 'Go tell that to gay people outside urban areas ... to bigots in the Mid-West and the Middle East,' they write, as they list just a few of the worlds where LGBT lives are still variously menaced by stigmatisation and even state execution.

Of course they are accurate. I, however, write from a rather different perspective than theirs. I welcome *A Boxful of Ideas* with its often retrospective and valuable impressions of what it has been to grow up and live in worlds where the designation LGBT was a curse. But it strikes me forcibly that here in the UK, while we are now given strong measures of equality with the heterosexual majority, we are still too often regarded as rare, exotic flowers cultivated in a special corner of the heterosexual garden and much of the time left to our separate selves.

We need, therefore, to go on writing about our gay lives, dramatise them, turn them into poetry and literature, to expose the ways in which we are still liable to be victims of forms of prejudice, hostility and even violence.

We need to do this also, partly because our lives, as many writers in *A Boxful of Ideas* make vividly apparent, are still and always have been somewhat different in various crucial ways. The hetero majority make appearances in our art. But heterosexual playwrights, film makers and novelists have shown scant eagerness to introduce LGBT characters and themes into their art work. Have you found anyone from LGBT ranks in the films of, say, Woody Allen or the plays of Alan Ayckbourn? We do not usually fit in with them as part of their family context. Think of a journalistic rather than artistic context: When it comes to Family, *The Guardian*'s weekly section that rejoices in that title is a throwback to the bad old homophobic days. It is caught in an unlovely, shameful 1960s time-warp. We as gay people are sons and daughters, uncles, aunts, cousins and increasingly parents but the so-called liberal *Guardian*, except on rare occasions, devotes itself exclusively to heterosexual members of the family.

As long as we are treated and regarded as separate and outsiders we need to record our own histories, experiences and life-themes in whatever art form. It's for this reason that I heartily welcome *A Boxful of Ideas*.

Nicholas de Jongh

INTRODUCTION

Gay Authors Workshop is a co-operative for LGBT writers. It meets regularly and is a forum for discussing work in progress. The work does not have to be gay; many of our members find writing a lonely business and feel at least initially more able to express themselves in the company of 'their own sort'.

Over the last ten years Gay Authors Workshop has produced several anthologies of short stories and of poetry. We decided this time on a fuller range of literary forms, with items unpublished or published, and drawn from our membership past, present and sadly deceased.

No theme was set for this anthology. We were surprised not only by the amount and quality of the material to select from, but by the variety of literary forms. In types of fiction we have selected short stories, excerpts from novels, flash fiction and a monologue. In non-fiction, several essays and confidences, and a diary. As in previous poetry anthologies we have not limited the number of lines in the way that many magazines and prizes insist on doing, and we include examples of haiku, a limerick, song lyrics, hymns, a villanelle, a sonnet sequence, concrete poems and much free verse.

Several themes or at least parallels surfaced, in particular the prose. The art of writing is touched upon several times. Jeff Doorn's title story 'A Boxful of Ideas' deals with ingenious ways of getting inspiration. Beth Lister's 'I Won't Be Writing Any More Novels' is about retiring from the fray. Michael Harth's 'Reading Group' is a wicked take-off of the supposedly 'real' reasons for attending reading and writing groups. Kathryn Bell's essay 'Hetty Garbage' doubts the necessity of love scenes in much popular literature. There are two revamps of classic stories: Henry James's *The Turn of the Screw* becomes Jeremy Kingston's 'The Twist of the Vice', and W. W. Jacobs's *The Monkey's Paw* becomes Leigh V. Twersky's 'The Monkey's Penis'. Love across the age 'barrier' is featured in Christopher Preston's 'A Daddies Diary' and in Beth Lister's 'Dog Minder's Monday Morning'. Underage sex features in Donald West's essay 'Facing up to Paedophilia', and in Joe Hucknall's 'Encounter in the Park'. Two stories, Tim Blackwell's 'A Night on the Rack' and Les Brookes's 'You Farzane, Me Duane', both set in living memory, evoke the variety of gay experience.

In the poetry there are similar cross-references. Rimbaud is the title of Zekria Ibrahimi's sonnet cycle; he also gets a mention in Chris Beckett's 'To the Teeming Bookshops of Addis Ababa'. Thunderstorms feature in Steve Ferris's 'Svantovit's Boy' and in Chris Beckett's 'Elegy'.

Though all the items chosen for this anthology are by members of the Gay Authors Workshop, not all the items are necessarily 'gay.' The members of the Workshop are, but they write as they please, often with some ambiguity. Take John Dixon's prize-winning story 'Comrades'. In a train accident an unknown woman dies in the arms of the narrator, a man. Would the story have sent more ripples, too many perhaps, if it had been an unknown man?

This perhaps begs the question – why nowadays have a writers group that is designated gay? Is it being exclusive? And then not always delivering the branded goods? A kind of breach of the Trade Descriptions Act? Is the gay label necessary in these days of Acceptance? Well, there are now several gay writing and reading groups, just as there are gay magazines, gay information and support groups, and websites, and LGBT sections in libraries and bookshops. As to the gay tag being redundant because of Acceptance – go tell that to gay people outside urban areas or in Northern Ireland. Tell it to bigots in the Mid-West and the Middle East, to Evangelicals in Africa and political leaders in Eastern Europe.

This volume is dedicated to the late Michael Harth. He was a founder member of Gay Authors Workshop, a writer of short stories, novels, song lyrics and reviews, and editor of the in-house magazine *Gazebo*. His wide knowledge and guiding hand from the formative years to the present will be greatly missed.

Opinions expressed in this book are those of the authors and not necessarily the editors or publishers.

The editors would like to thank everyone who has helped make this book possible, in particular Donald West, for first suggesting the anthology and doing so much in the initial stages to getting it off the ground, and to Ross Burgess for negotiating so skillfully the many pitfalls and intricacies involved in book production.

John Dixon
Jeffrey Doorn

A BOXFUL OF IDEAS
Jeffrey Doorn

He used to have a boxful of ideas. It started when he was working on his first novel. Extraneous plot lines or characters would occur to him, and he would start to get in a muddle. After writing himself into several corners, he hit upon a way to clear the decks and continue undistracted.

It was just a simple shoebox. He cut a slit in the lid; and every time an idea for a story or anything unrelated to his current work popped into his head, he would write it on a slip of paper and stick it into the box.

The practice stood him in good stead. He became a moderately successful writer, critics often remarking on his clear, uncluttered thinking. Whenever he needed something new or wanted a fresh start, he would open the box, close his eyes and rummage around inside. The piece of paper he withdrew formed the beginning of his next work.

It had been several months since his latest novel had appeared, and it was not selling well. The reviews had been poor. Come to think of it, his two previous publications had also received unenthusiastic notices.

Perhaps it was time to check his old ideas box, though he could not remember the last time he had inserted anything into it. When he extracted it from the bottom of the wardrobe in the spare room, it was dusty and a bit frayed. Carefully lifting the lid he found – nothing. It was empty.

Something must be done, but what? There was no point moping around the house. He began taking long walks, but nothing in the suburban streets or parks struck him as noteworthy. Then he remembered that some writers, Virginia Woolf in particular, and perhaps Joe Orton, had often sat on the top desk of a London bus with a notebook, jotting down bits of conversation and other observations. Would it work for him?

Journey after journey proved fruitless. His fellow passengers were either playing games on their iPads, sending text messages or babbling inanities into their mobile phones. How did life get so boring?

On one such bus ride through an unfamiliar part of town, he found himself listening not to conversations, but to the recorded bus stop announcements. When he heard the next stop was a library, he disembarked and stepped inside, hoping he would not be recognised. Apparently, no one noticed him.

He began browsing and came across some books on writing. Of course he did not need a book on how to write, but he idly took down a volume with a title something like *The Writer's Workshop*. Flipping through, he found hints and tips which he knew well, but also some exercises. One suggestion for reconstructing a sentence to create something fresh struck him as weird but worth a try. Take a sentence, it advised, and for every noun, find the word in a dictionary and count seven words ahead. Substitute that word, and if it isn't a noun, turn it into one. Later, one could take the verbs or adjectives and count a different number, or perhaps go backwards instead of forwards.

Hastily replacing the book on its shelf, he left the library and went home. He was not about to experiment with his own books, which he never reread or even looked at once they were out. There were plenty of classics to choose from. *A Tale of Two Cities*: 'It was the best of times, it was the worst of times, it was ...' Oh no, whatever he did, the pattern would be instantly recognised; and he did not want to be accused of mimicking Dickens.

1984: The famous first line could be rendered, 'It was a

brief, cocky deal in aquamarine and the closets were strewing thongs'. Fun, but yet another novel beginning, 'It was'. He always thought of Snoopy, the dog in the Peanuts cartoon typing out, 'It was a hot and sticky night,' a line lifted right out of an American Western.

How about good old Hardy, an early one, say *Under the Greenwood Tree*. 'To dwellers in a wood almost every species of tree has its voice as well as its feature.' After some minutes with the dictionary, he had altered it thus: 'To dynamos in a workshop, almost every spectacle of tremor has its volley as well as its feculence'. Hmmm. He did not recall ever using that word before. Its definition was 'dregs', 'scum'. How appropriate. It could be the title of his next novel.

SEVEN POEMS
Michael Harth

NARCISSUS

Johnny was a child
who never went wild,
but was early prone
to quiet games on his own.
And when he grew up
he showed no wish to sup
from the forbidden cup.
Or to swirl
any girl
to a play
in the hay.
Neither did boys
manage to ruffle his poise.
He didn't even seem keen to leap
on a sheep.

In fact, he was right on the shelf,
where he seemed inclined to stay,
He was quite content, for he had himself –
several times a day.

DYING-FOR-IT BLUES

I stay in waiting for you to call:
don't miss the scene: a pillow is all
that I need in the way of views:
I've got those dying-for-it blues.

It must be time you came off strike.
I've nearly forgotten what it's like.
Waiting for those size eight shoes
to cure my dying-for-it blues.

I'm a guy at the end of his tether,
so come on, buster, get your act together.
You can have me any way you choose:
I've got those dying-for-it blues.

I was happy to chase romance off
so just come round and get your pants off
before I finally blow a fuse:
I've got those dying-for-it blues.

Tell me that the jamboree's on
cos it's now the mating season.
Make me an offer: I won't refuse
cos I've got those dying-for-it blues.

Got the condoms, got the KY,
so there need be no delay. Why
don't you be the angel who's
gonna cure my need it blues?

THE LONG DAY

I never knew
the day could seem so long.
For without you
my ev'ry theme feels wrong.
My old ways of filling time
I've learnt were only killing time
now I could have a thrilling time
with you.
I never knew
the day would seem so long.

WEATHER SONG

The sun is bright, the sky is blue.
There's not a single cloud in view.
The touch of spring is in the air,
And birds are singing ev'rywhere.
Deer are gambolling in the heat,
The little lamb makes merry bleat.
Nature has never looked so well,
but I feel mis'rable as hell.

The sun goes in, the sky turns black:
Ev'ryone quickly dons a mac.
A freezing wind comes with the rain –
Winter's tough is back again.
In terror all these creatures flee
From such impartial cruelty.
Nature has never looked so fell,
but I'm still mis'rable as hell.

GUARANTEE BLUES

Manufacturers all try
to encourage us to buy
by persuading us that we can really trust 'em.
For everything they sell
they offer us as well
a promise, if there are faults, that they'll adjust 'em.

They've thrown in free repairs
on my new suite of chairs:
my electric fire has the same too.
A five-year guarantee
with my colour TV
so why can't I have one on you?

From chocolate bars
to the largest of cars
the same theme runs right the way through.
Any lack, small or large,
will be fixed without charge:
why can't it be like that with you?

Against theft, loss or fire
anyone can acquire
insurance for all they possess.
But you seem to make
the one risk they won't take,
however I argue and press.

Money back if I'm not
satisfied with the yacht,
or my hair doesn't like a shampoo.
Everything that I see
carries some guarantee
except where I need it most – you.

If a power transformer
proves a poorer performer
than it did when I had the preview,
write the makers a letter
they'll send me one better:
I do wish it was like that with you.

If my new murder story
's insufficiently gory,
or the video's only pale blue,
there's no doubt the shop's got a-
nother one rather hotter:
oh, why's it not like that with you?

When I bang on a nail
and it bends cos it's frail,
or a screwdriver won't drive a screw,
the shop will arrange
a straightforward exchange:
why can't I get one on you?

Something no good the shop
just refuses to swap
can always be flushed down the loo.
And I'd better confess
I can hardly repress
the desire to do that to you.

JOHNNY HAS GONE

I'm sitting here sighing, my heart is so sore.
Dull seem the things by which I used to set store.
Since forgetting the vows which once to me he swore,
Johnnie has gone for a soldier.

I'm sitting here sighing, my heart full of woe,
for though Johnnie came back, soon as he'd said 'Hello',
he slipped off again: now my tears overflow:
Johnnie has gone for a sailor.

I'm sitting here sighing: my sorrows won't mend,
for what is the use of a handsome boy-friend
if he's never here for a friendly weekend?
Johnnie's gone for a marine.

I'm sitting here sighing, left all on my own.
My one pleasure having a jolly good moan.
For, let's face it, darlings, I ought to have known
Johnnie just doesn't go for women.

LIMERICK

When Bill dropped his pants to the floor
And bent over outside the back door,
He explained, 'Course I'm straight,
Just obliging a mate.'
And then he obliged several more.

CARLA'S MOTHER
V. G. Lee

We have a stable-style back door. For most of the year we keep the top section open during the day so we can see the garden without our chickens wandering into the kitchen. This morning I sit at the littered breakfast table and watch you swing away from the house. Wearing the silk dressing gown your mother bought in Paris, you look like a rakish figure from an earlier century. Carla, I love your broad shoulders; your thick brown hair streaked 'heroically' with grey. You see? After more than three years together I'm still as foolishly in love with you.

You lift the latch of the gate dividing our garden from *her* garden. One day you will walk through that gate and never come back.

From the beginning of our relationship I accepted that your mother came first, that you loved her absolutely and unapologetically. At that time she was still living in France looking after her invalid sister. Each evening at some point, early or late, you rang her. No other calls were made from that cream-coloured phone on the coffee table in the living room of your Maida Vale flat. Instinctively I knew not even to touch it.

I always left the room during your phone calls.

'No need,' you insisted those first few times, your hand covering the mouthpiece, your eyes warm with affection.

But I wanted to show you how understanding I was – I would never be the one to make a jealous fuss. I appreciated that our relationship of mere weeks, then months, was like a grass seed blown on the breeze set against a lifetime of maternal solicitude and caring, but I hoped that while *she* continued her life abroad I would become indispensable to you.

'Let me tell you about my dream,' I'd said fifteen minutes earlier.

'Can we skip it?' You'd glanced up from the newspaper, giving me one of those fake smiles you imagine hides your irritation. 'Why not tell me tonight's dream tomorrow?'

'But it's only very short – about a snake.' I'd reached across the table for a slice of toast. The diamond in my ring you bought to celebrate our Civil Partnership caught a ray of sunshine and prisms danced across the table cloth.

'Snakes again,' you said. 'I'm getting tired of them. So what exactly did this snake do to you?'

'Nothing.'

'Snake saw you. You saw the snake. Nothing happened. That must have been exciting.'

'I killed it.'

You'd raised your eyebrows. '*You* killed a snake? Well done. So something did happen after all?'

I used to feel cherished. I thought we had everything we wanted, best of all we had each other. Together we chose this house.

'It's a happy house,' I said.

'I believe you're right.' You looked at me with such pleasure, as if I delighted you. Our lives have changed so much in the past year that sometimes I wonder if I imagined this.

Of course your cream telephone moved with us, taking up residence in the small single-storey home office you built in the garden.

The wire threaded back to the house, coming in under the windowsill of the spare room, along the skirting board and into one of two jack plugs – the other served the upstairs extension and our phone in the kitchen.

I've always spent a lot of time in the spare bedroom. I love the view from the window over our green and lush back garden and in a way it's my work room. I can keep an eye on the hens, I can watch for you while I iron, make lists, read books, day-dream.

That particular day, several months ago, started so well. After breakfast we'd taken our coffees outside. You'd wiped dew off the bench and we'd sat together making plans for the weekend. Later, I remember how completely content I'd felt running upstairs. Humming, I'd sorted through the pile of ironing, and then as I bent down to plug in the iron, the extension phone on the windowsill made a clicking sound. I picked up the receiver.

'Carla darling?' A woman's voice. Somehow I had plugged the extension lead into Carla's private line.

I should have quietly put the phone down but I didn't. I was curious.

'Hello, Mother,' you said. 'How's aunty?'

'Very frail. I could be Santa Claus as far as she's concerned. She doesn't recognise anybody but she's still very sweet-natured.'

Having listened once, I couldn't stop myself from listening in every day. You talked about the family I'd never met, childhood, people and idyllic times I knew nothing about, but neither of you ever mentioned me. It was as if I didn't exist!

Your mother with her, 'Carla darling, do you remember?' Never, 'Carla darling, tell me, how is Beth?'

And you, always saying 'I did this,' never 'we'.

The strain began to twist my feelings for you.

'What are you thinking?' I'd ask. 'Do you love me? How much do you love me?' I tried to keep my voice light but my constant need for reassurance began to annoy you.

One evening, you were washing your hands at the kitchen sink while I laid the table for dinner. I'd cooked skate, new potatoes and French beans from our garden. As you reached for the towel, you kissed my neck. 'Smells good,' you said.

I asked, 'Your mother does know about me, doesn't she?'

You looked surprised. 'Of course she does. She always sends Christmas cards to the two of us.'

'But never a birthday card to me.'

'I can ask her to send you a card in future.'

'Do you tell her about our life together?'

'Sometimes.'

'Only sometimes?'

'Beth, what is this all about?' You dried your hands on the towel far more vigorously than was necessary.

'I feel shut out. Your relationship with your mother is rather exclusive.' I'd tried to smile as if I wasn't really bothered but you knew I was upset.

'That's foolish,' you said, your eyes full of concern for me.

I rested my face against your shoulder. 'Carla darling, I'm sorry. Take no notice.'

'I love you so much, Beth,' you said and I believed you. Then and there I resolved to stop listening in to your conversations. We were together, we loved each other – I could well afford to be generous to your mother. I smiled up at you but you were frowning. You eased your body away from me.

'What is it?' I asked.

'Beth, you never call me Carla darling.'

'Don't I? I think I do.'

You knew immediately that I was lying. 'You've been listening in to our phone calls, haven't you? That's why you've been so weird – so needy.'

Being caught out frightened me, but I was also angry. ~~Angry and bloody needy!~~ 'OK. Yes, I did listen in. It was most interesting.'

'How many times?'

'Enough times to realise that I rate somewhere below the hens in importance — neither of you have ever said a word about me — not once, in months. I'm in the wrong but so are you. Don't I matter?'

You didn't answer me.

'Well? Cat got your tongue?' I snapped at you although I would have swallowed any excuse.

You walked out into the garden no doubt to ring your precious mother, although I doubt that, even then, you couldn't bring yourself to use my name.

That weekend your aunt died and off you rushed to France. When you came home ten days later, you made it clear that the subject was closed.

'Adorable.' Your mother must have been called that many times. Her figure is perfect in that old style of curves in the right places; her hair although unnaturally gold still seems glamorous. She has bright blue eyes in an unlined face, two pearly front teeth peeping *adorably* from under her full top lip.

The first time I saw her was at Waterloo Station, coming up on the escalator from Eurostar. Although I'd never seen photographs, I knew this was her. She knew me too. She raised her hand and fluttered gloved fingers at me.

I stepped forward. 'Mrs Adams, I'm Beth.'

'Of course you are,' she said, her lips brushing my cheek.

'Carla's waiting in the car.' I pointed to the Mephan Street exit. 'She couldn't find anywhere to park. You have a case?'

'I come with luggage. Ah, here it is.'

A tall elderly man struggled off the escalator with two large suitcases.

'You're too kind.' She touched his arm gratefully.

'My pleasure,' he said. 'Have a good holiday.'

'Not a holiday. I'm here for the duration.'

I picked up one of the suitcases. It was unbelievably heavy. I tried the other. I couldn't even lift it off the ground.

I said, 'I can only manage the one. I'll send Carla back for you and your other suitcase.'

'Surely they're not that heavy?' A shadow of annoyance crossed her face.

'Too heavy for me, I'm afraid.'

'But you're young. So sturdy.'

Again I apologised. 'I'll only be a matter of minutes.' I staggered away towards the automatic doors, my body listing under the weight of the suitcase.

As soon as you saw me you leapt out of the car. 'Beth, let me help.'

'Your mother's guarding the rest of her luggage which is even heavier than this!' Hesitantly, I smiled at you.

You opened the boot, picked up the suitcase. 'God, what's in here, half a dozen canteens of cutlery?'

'Probably.'

'Don't worry. I'll sort this out.' You kissed my cheek which was gratifying. It had been weeks since you'd shown me any affection. Which was why when you said, 'Better sit in the back,' it went unchallenged. I was happy to sit in the back if you would love me again.

At the kitchen table, I'd buttered my toast and spread honey. Had anyone been a fly on the wall they wouldn't have realised I was waiting for some further reaction to my dream.

Eventually you sighed deeply, 'So, why and how did you kill the snake?'

'I had to kill it before it had the chance to kill me.'

'But perhaps it had no intention of killing you. Perhaps it was basking in the sun just minding its own business ...'

I said quickly, 'That type of snake can't "just mind its own business". It's born to destroy. It has no alternative.'

'Couldn't you have avoided it?'

'No. *I* was born to be destroyed by a snake.'

With irritation you turned your gaze away and stared out across the garden. I could feel it – your desire to be in your mother's kitchen rather than your own.

'So Beth, how did you kill this poor bloody snake?'

'This is only a dream, understand?'

You nodded.

'I carried a stick. At one end was a triangular blade made from diamond glass.'

You stood up. Your shadow filled the kitchen, annihilating the prisms dancing on the white cloth. 'I don't quite believe in this stick with its diamond blade. It's rather complicated. I can't see you fashioning it or coming by such an item even in a dream. Am I the snake? Is my mother the snake? Perhaps after all, you – my sweet Beth – are the snake.'

'What do you think?' I asked.

'I think this melodrama has got to stop. I'm tired of it. You used to be so different; so funny and loving.'

'I know I did.' I'd bowed my head. 'But that was before. When I didn't know – because you didn't tell me – that your mother filled your heart leaving no room at all for me.'

'This is a nightmare,' you said. 'All on your own, you're driving me away.'

'Then make a choice.'

'I don't need to. You've made the choice for me.'

The garden is empty of you. It took months and your mother's ever-increasing presence in our lives for me to accept that the moment in the kitchen when you told me you loved me would be the final time. How could this old woman – for all her adorable qualities – have beaten me?

In my dreams I kill the snake and my enemy is removed

but reality is nowhere near as easy to control.

Is it, Carla my darling?

YOU FARZAN, ME DUANE
Les Brookes

All that summer he wore shorts. Brief cotton shorts, pale yellow and snug around the arse. His legs were the colour of charcoal and amazingly hairy. Too hairy, I thought at first – like shaggy black rugs. But within days they had worked their magic on me and I was devoted to them. He always sat next to me in English and rubbed his knee against mine. I still remember the tickle, the electrifying thrill of it. Miss Webber often smiled at us, I recall, as if she was in on the secret. His father was a visiting professor and they lived in a large house they were renting in Wood Lane.

When the holidays arrived he and the family went off to France for two weeks. It seemed an eternity. I felt dull, empty, forsaken. Were they planning other trips? Would they be away all summer? How would I survive until September? My family had no plans. I sat around indoors, reading a gloomy novel set in a death-haunted sanatorium. Then a postcard arrived, postmarked Rennes. *Too much bloody walking, the sea is freezing and we've been drenched by thunderstorms.* It seemed wrong to take delight in his misery, but my heart sang.

The day after their return there was a knock at the door. I was alone in the house and stuck my head through the upstairs window. It was a bright August morning. He grinned at me from the doorstep and pointed at his bicycle propped against the fence. I tore downstairs and yanked him in. We sat in the kitchen drinking thick brown coffee from giant mugs while he rattled on about the holiday. I didn't hear a word he said, though. I was too busy basking in the warmth of his big white smile.

I fetched my bike from the shed, checked the tyres and we

headed for the spinney up on the hill – always our first port of call. He rode a little ahead of me in his comically awkward fashion, head tilted slightly, feet splayed heavily on the pedals. Though athletic in other ways, he was ungainly on a bike – an effect of his height, I think. But awkward or not, his shaggy legs, his tensed muscles and taut buttocks were lovely to behold, and I drank in the view.

At the spinney we propped our bikes against a tree. No reason to chain them. Who would steal our jalopies? We followed a path to the pond, sat on a log and threw stones into the water. We did this in silence for some minutes, before I turned and glanced at him. Some bits of dry twig had fallen into his hair. I reached out, brushed them off and combed my fingers through his black curls. He laughed, pushed me backwards onto the grass and leaped astride my chest. He pinned my arms to the ground and I lay there giggling like a schoolgirl. Then he dug his fingers into my ribs until I shrieked.

'We should go away for a few days,' he yelled as we freewheeled downhill into Newton. 'I've got a tent.'

It had to be the coast, and Cromer was the obvious choice. Trains ran to Cromer and there was camping in the area. We stuffed clothes into panniers, a few provisions into rucksacks and strapped the tent and sleeping bags to the racks. On the day of departure we tore onto the platform just as the train was about to leave. It was no more than a couple of old wagons, but cosily picturesque. We threw our bikes into the guard's van and sat side by side in the carriage, munching apples and watching the sunlit fields roll past. We grinned at each other and his knee rubbed against mine.

The first site was full, but we were directed to another – a farmer's field with just a few tents and a primitive washroom in an old barn. The ground was rock hard. We smashed at the pegs with a small rubber mallet and fell about laughing. Eventually we crawled inside and lay there, hands behind heads, gazing at the dizzy blue canopy in a thrill of quiet delight at our snug little abode.

After a spot of lunch we rode into town, where the seafront was breezy – though baking in the sheltered places – and hordes were strolling the promenade and lazing on the beach. A Punch and Judy show had drawn a crowd of kids and their parents, and a sign above the entrance to the pier was advertising some variety entertainment at the Pavilion Theatre. We stared at it blankly, since the names of the performers meant nothing to us. But the pier itself, suspended over heaving brine and battered by strong waves, had a certain end-of-world appeal and we spent some time peering over the edge at the rusted, barnacled pillars. Then we polished off a couple of ice creams and lost money in the amusement arcade.

The cove that we found in the late afternoon, after a short cycle ride, was not quite ours. There were some other couples there, sunbathing on the rocks, and a family were paddling at the water's edge. The so-called beach was a thin strip of shingle. We changed into bathing gear beneath our towels and hobbled into the shallows, the cold making us shriek. 'Aaaaagh!' Farzan yelled. 'Worse than France!' But he was the first to take the plunge, diving headlong into the deep with a sudden thrash of disappearing legs and then leaping up again like an ecstatic dolphin, a halo of beads spinning from his wet hair. He gave a great gasp from the shock and then a bellow of laughter. I was standing up to my knees, shoulders hunched, shivering and hugging my chest. He beat the surface with his arms and sent a spray flying towards me. I shrieked and laughed and gazed in wonder – he looked so gorgeous, his eyes bright with elation, his hair plastered to his scalp, water cascading in torrents down his face and chest.

We pedalled into town for supper and found a steak bar in the high street, cheerful, bright, bustling, and just the ticket. We went for the mixed grill, and sat grinning at each other and playing hangman on a beer-mat while waiting for it to arrive. It came on a couple of large oval platters, accompanied by paper napkins and sachets of sauce. Our eyes flew open and we tucked in with ravenous delight. It was, quite simply, the best meal I've ever had. Nothing I've eaten in fancier places has ever come anywhere near. In my pantheon of great meals it holds a unique place, retaining an elusive magic that grows stronger with every year that passes.

The joke came to me as we were eating, by the way. It's a bit of a cheat, though. I mean, I'm not Duane, am I? I'm Greg. So I kept it secret at first, thinking it silly. Also, I wasn't sure he'd get the reference. But when, towards the end of the meal, I changed my mind, he was tickled pink. 'Oh yeah,' he hooted. 'Maureen O'Sullivan and Johnny Weissmuller.'

We returned to the tent with some bottled beer. The moon was full and bright, the sky clear and pricked with stars. A small group, sitting round a fire in a corner of the field, was singing softly to a couple of strummed guitars, but otherwise the deep quiet was broken only by the faint murmur of voices. We pulled our beds from the tent and squatted on them. And there we sat, lifting beer to our lips, listening to the sounds of the night, feeling no compulsion to speak. Secure and comfortable, we simply communed in silence. And shortly the singers switched to a new tune. The Bee Gees were big that year. We grinned and hummed along. *Ah, ha, ha, ha, stayin' alive.*

It was warm in the tent, so we left the flaps open, stripped off our shirts and lay on top of the beds in our shorts. Through the gap we could see the moon and the profile of trees against a pale sky. Moths and fireflies hovered round the entrance. I gazed at the scene for a while, my hands clasped behind my head. Then, drowsy from the beer, I must have drifted off because when I next looked the flaps of the tent were closed. I glanced at Farzan, who was sleeping. The air was still warm, though slightly cooler now. So I turned on my side and snuggled into the sweater I was using as a pillow.

I woke to the feel of his arm around me, his chest pressed to my back, his nose buried in the nape of my neck. Taken by surprise, I started. 'Hey, it's only me,' he whispered and licked my ear. I half-turned with a small gasp of delight and he drew me closer, hugging my waist. And there we lay, quite still, for several minutes, though my heart was beating wildly and I could feel the heave of his chest. Then his hand slipped into my shorts and grasped me firmly. I was rigid. As stiff as a guard on parade. I leaned back against him with a moan and he laughed quietly in my ear.

After a while, with sudden boldness, I turned on my back, slipped out of my shorts and smiled at him. He smiled back, then slowly removed his own shorts and knelt beside me. I stared at him, mesmerised. His body was not quite new to me – I'd seen him in the showers. But never this close, the thick hairs of his chest and groin almost brushing my face. Nor this big – in his present state, huge as a horse. He leaned forward and kissed my nipples. Then, kneeling astride my head, he gently swung his resplendent gear just inches above my spellbound eyes. I gazed up at his loins and arse and felt the dark growth of his fuzz tickling my nose.

When the moment came, he spat on his hand and smeared me with a gummy finger. The entry was painful, but after the initial thrusts I groaned with delight. Wriggling beneath him, I spread my legs wider with every push, riding hard with the motion, willing it to last for ever. But it was soon over. I watched his face buckle, felt the violent shudder of his release. Then, breathing deeply, he slowly withdrew and, leaning forward, massaged me with firm strokes. I responded instantly, bursting high over his chest in fulsome splendour, and breaking – or so it seemed to me in the lush technicolour of my imagination – like some great tropical flower from its pod.

He gazed at me in wonder for a few moments. Then, swaying a little, he fell forward onto my body and we rolled across the tent, glued together by jizz and rocking with deep laughter.

There would be no more summers together. And somehow, in some secret part of me, I knew. For all that autumn change was in the air and I sensed calamity long before the bombshell came.

It came on a Monday in early January. As I passed through the school gates I saw him sitting on the front steps. He looked serious, deep in thought, a bit dazed. I sat down beside him.

'We're going home,' he said. 'My father's been recalled.'

I nodded and stared at the ground. The news simply confirmed a long-held fear. For weeks our television screens had exploded with the austere face of someone called an ayatollah. Farzan had sometimes spoken about his country – its customs, politics, religion – but I had taken very little in. I was a dizzy creature and the place was just too far away. Ayatollahs meant nothing to me. Until then.

'I'll write,' he said. 'And we'll be back.'

'No you won't,' I said.

They were gone within a week. The house in Wood Lane was suddenly empty. In the raw winds of February I sometimes strolled past and gazed through the windows at the bare boards and walls. It was April before anyone moved in – a smart young couple with a flash new car. I watched the furniture arrive with seething resentment. Meanwhile there was school to think about, exams, the future. Everything was changing. The May elections, for instance, brought an insistent, half-familiar voice ringing over the airwaves. Until that moment, with next to no interest in politics, I had scarcely noticed the rise of Margaret Hilda Thatcher.

Not a word from Farzan. I grieved in secret. The summer came and I started to ride out to the spinney for old times' sake. Then an envelope flew through the letter-box. Inside, a postcard of the Azadi Tower and a photo of the lad himself in yellow shorts. *Hey, it's only me. How are you, buddy? Stayin' alive, I hope. I'm doing just fine. Going to university next year. Miss you and the rides. Drop me a line at the above address.* The above address was not too decipherable. I dropped a line, but nothing came back. Not sure about the post over there.

That was an age ago. I work for a London theatre now and live with Richard. And it's good, very good, don't get me wrong. But it remains an echo. An echo of rocks and coves and country lanes, of French fries and bottled beer and strummed guitars, of summer nights and the Bee Gees. I live, to be honest, in a kind of weird, buried hope. A hope that one day I'll just turn a corner and walk slap-bang into him. And he'll say 'Hi, buddy' and we'll stand there for ages just grinning at each other. And after that we'll dodge into the nearest place and order a mixed grill and shoot ketchup over everything and yak our silly heads off for hours and hours, his knees rubbing against mine.

The field at Cromer has changed, by the way. There's not a tent in sight now. Just a couple of chestnut horses that push their noses over the gate and nibble grass from your palm.

TONY'S YOUR MAN
Drew Payne

Even for Thursday night the talent was thin on the ground. Tony leant against the bar and surveyed the room before him. Mr Sloan's was Tony's local, the only gay bar in the area, even though it was a good twenty minutes' walk from his home – his cramped top floor flat.

He came here at least once a week, often twice if he could manage it. He was off to spend the weekend with his parents so this was his only chance to come to Mr Sloan's. He'd dressed in his usual cruising clothes, dark and slender jeans, white casual shirt and his battered old leather jacket; gel holding down his spiky hair, and made his way here, though never too early.

He was onto his second pint of beer, never more than two pints in a night because being pissed affected his perform-ance, when he saw the blond, out of the corner of his eye. The blond was slouched on one of the row of benches, against the right-hand wall, and was staring straight at Tony. Tony glanced down at his drink, breaking eye contact with the blond; so the game began.

When he glanced back, a second later, the young blond, eighteen or twenty, but trying to look older, was still watching him. He had a short goatee beard gracing his chin, his hair cut into a bristling style, he was wearing a black denim jacket over grey T-shirt and black combat pants. His posture was that of casual indifference but his eyes shone with interest.

Tony returned the blond's gaze, staring straight into the blond's face. He enjoyed this part the most, the game of eye contact with a new man. The glances towards the new man and then away, the check to see the other's interest; the changing of his position to present his body in its most flattering way; the communication through gestures and glances only.

Tony loved this part, this game, and he could happily play it all evening. Most of all he loved the boost it gave to his ego; someone else found him attractive, especially when it was someone so attractive. Sexual thrill boosting his confidence.

The blond pulled himself fully upright on the bench and patted the space next to him. Tony took a mouthful of beer, pulled himself off the bar and crossed the room, walking with just the right amount of macho swagger. Without a word he sat down next to the blond.

'Hi, I'm Cliff,' the blond said, his voice had the sharp edge of a North London accent – he was far from home, Tony thought.

'I'm Tony,' he replied as he shook Cliff's hand, a warm but still tight handshake.

'This your local?' Cliff asked.

'Yes. I haven't seen you around here before,' he answered.

'I've just moved here, you know how it is, I fancied some company, you know,' Cliff said as his face broke into a smile.

'Me, too,' Tony replied.

Cliff slipped his hand onto Tony's thigh and squeezed the firm muscle there. Tony enjoyed this attention, the physical caress of another man, the thrill of another's touch.

Then Cliff kissed him. Without a word Cliff's mouth closed over his, Cliff's tongue stroked over his lips before slipping inside his mouth. A slow and almost leisurely kiss, Cliff's tongue building up a head of passion inside of him, Cliff's lips caressing his own. God, he really knows how to kiss, Tony thought.

Then the kiss was over and Cliff was leaning back, on the bench, though his hand remained firmly on Tony's thigh. Cliff's face was almost creased with a broad smile.

'I like you,' Cliff said as his hand began to slide up Tony's thigh.

'I like you too, but I don't go any further than this,' Tony told him as he quickly put his hand over Cliff's hand stopping Cliff's movement up his thigh.

'What?'

'I've got someone at home and this is as far as I go,' he told Cliff.

'You've got a fucking lover!' Cliff's hand shot off his thigh and his face almost exploded into anger. 'You get me all revved up and then drop me flat. It's fucking bastards like you that mean I'm single. You should fucking stay at home!'

Without looking at him, Cliff leapt up from the bench and stomped across the bar. Tony watched the back of Cliff's blond head, until it disappeared around the corner of the bar, but Cliff didn't look back.

With his usual sigh of disappointment, Tony stood up from the bench and headed for the door.

As he passed the bar, on his way out, Jerry the barman called out:

'Night, Tony.'

'Goodnight,' he replied.

On the street outside Tony felt the cold night air sting at his cheeks. It was a clear sky, he could see the stars scattered across the heavens; there was probably going to be a frost tonight. Tony turned up the High Street and began his walk home.

He hardly thought about his route home, he could walk it on automatic pilot, and soon he was at the front door of his own building, though the cold was now making his eyes water and his cheeks glow. Still without thinking about it, he climbed the three flights of stairs to his flat. His mind was still buzzing with the events of the evening, still buzzing with a few hours he'd had to really be himself. He wouldn't get another chance now for over a week. That seemed such a long time away.

Inside his flat, without turning on the light, he quickly walked into his bedroom and began to undress. Once he'd shed his jacket, jeans, shirt and boots he finally turned the lights on. There, in the room's mirror, was a reflection of that vile and ugly body, that unnatural thing.

He reached up and undid the tight bindings around his breasts, then he pulled off the high topped control pants he was wearing, with the sock filled with cotton wool pushed inside it (his 'cock'). Then he stared into the mirror, again.

The image that stared back was always unsettling. Small and flat breasts, that hung limply off an equally thin chest; down to the groin that was a flat, wire-haired thing, that ugly and pathetic thing of a cunt, not the glorious appendage of a fine shaped cock and balls. Gone was Tony, the real person inside of her, to be replaced by Antonia, the person she had been born.

For the next week she'd have to be Antonia, with her soft clothes and body that was so wrong, until she could have that heaven of being Tony again, even if it was only for a few hours.

Turning away from the mirror Antonia reached for her plain, cotton pyjamas.

TWO POEMS
Gregory Woods

EVEN NOW

When with men's eyes and fortune in disgrace,
I reassure myself that to the wise
a body is a gaudy commonplace,
mere parts: throat, torso, navel, belly, thighs ...

Behind a surface we expect surprise,
as in a palace: part each veil of lace
in hope of penetrating to the prize,
the place within the place within the place.

Even your nakedness is a disguise:
when you deploy your undissembling mace,
the mark of your authority, it lies.

For all your artlessness, when we embrace,
your most uncomplicated sigh denies
the face behind the face behind the face.

TAKING PICTURES

He wants me to buy a
camera. I buy one. He
says I didn't warn him
I was going to take
pictures. I ask why he
needed warning. He shrugs
and starts to sulk. He lights
another cigarette
and starts browsing the T
V listings. I go out
to the hall and put the
camera away in the
sideboard, next to the good
glasses. I hear him switch the
telly on. It sounds like
cartoon music. I go
and sit on the edge of
my bed and open a
book. I don't read a word
of it. I can hear him
coughing in the next room.
I picture him naked.

HETTY GARBAGE
Kathryn Bell

The picture her name produces in my mind's eye is plump, middle-aged, wearing a flowery apron and headscarf, looking like Andy Capp's wife Flo. But Hetty doesn't look like that really; she's blonde and beautiful, like Eva Marie Saint or Grace Kelly in their prime. Because, among other things, she's the 'love interest' that ruins so many otherwise excellent action/adventure films. *North by North West* and *Rear Window* are just two out of hundreds. Television programmes, too, suffer from her intrusion; she has wrecked *Doctor Who*, for instance. And remember *All Creatures Great and Small?* The series about the country vets – mildly amusing and enjoyable until Hetty turned up, when it went rapidly downhill. And *Only Fools and Horses* – that sharp, clever comedy destroyed by the two women, Cassandra and Rachel, who turned it into a soppy unwatchable puddle. Even the brilliant American comedy *Frasier* died soon after Niles and Daphne got together. Niles's mooning over Miss Moon was funny as long as it was unrequited and Daphne oblivious. When that changed, the whole thing was doomed. Then there's *The X-Files*: to be fair, that series was on the skids before Hetty arrived; she only hastened its end. If I win the Lottery (unlikely as I don't buy a ticket) there will be a prize for the reader who can think of the biggest number of films and TV programmes that Hetty has mangled.

And books ... it's almost inevitable that Hetty will turn up in books, even when you think you're safe. *Hitchhiker's Guide to the Galaxy* is a brilliant book; funny, inventive, zany genius, and untouched by Hetty for its whole length and that of its sequels *The Restaurant at the End of the Universe* and *Life, the*

Universe and Everything. Then comes the fourth book, *So Long, and Thanks For All the Fish.* Why Douglas Adams allowed Hetty, in the shape of Fenchurch, to lay her clammy hand on that book will never be known, so there is nothing to say except that if you haven't read *So Long* ..., don't. Keep the first three wonderful books unsullied.

What's variously described as 'serious', mainstream, or non-genre literature is, of course, mainly Garbage-centred. It's not always a bad thing. To the people Jane Austen wrote for and about, marriage was the only respectable career open to women and so her tales of how her characters achieved that goal can't fairly be described as Hetty Garbage. Hetty is not, here, intruding into the plot; she *is* the plot. Fair enough. More often, though, she is neither use nor ornament. In *The Brothers Karamazov*, Dmitri/Grushenka is important to the plot. Ivan/Katerina – not important, could profitably have been omitted. But let us not take on the classics, or we'll be here all day.

One might think that the area of children's literature, at least, would be Hetty-free. And one would be wrong. Not so in the past. Enid Blyton, whatever her shortcomings, had no dealings with Hetty. Richmal Crompton – yes, but only in fun. Capt. W. E. Johns – Hetty? Who she? But in the 21st century – oh, dear. I refused to read Phillip Pullman's *Dark Materials* because I read that its main characters, Will and Lyra, are in love at the end of the final book. I don't want to read about teenagers in love, I thought, I'll stick to *Harry Potter*. How's that for irony? The first five *Potter* books are, indeed, Hettyless except for a few short passages written with a light, humorous touch appropriate to their setting. But in Books 6 and 7 Hetty runs riot. Harry, Ron, Hermione, several other Hogwarts students and Ron's brother Bill all acquire 'love interest', none of it particularly interesting and, except for Bill, all irrelevant to the plot. Worst of all, the werewolf

Lupin, who was shaping up as a perfectly good closet gay in Books 3 and 5, is lumbered with a tiresome girlfriend – later wife – for no other reason, apparently, than that both may die and leave an orphan for purposes of symmetry (the series began with an orphan so it must end with one. Why? No one knows). Not content with burdening the two final books with unnecessary Hetty, J. K. Rowling has, since publication of Book 7, been giving interviews in which she reveals the eventual marital status of nearly all the main characters and some minor ones, even introducing 'characters' who do not appear in the books at all, purely to provide spouses for the book characters who remain unattached at the end of Volume 7. This is all doubtless well-intentioned; the information is given in response to questions from readers and perhaps the author feels that by supplying it she is giving good value for money. She is surely misguided. Some readers are unquestionably interested in the personal lives of the characters, but they could have been left to speculate on them without having a lid placed on their imaginations. *Harry Potter* is a tale of magical adventure, a chapter in the eternal epic battle of Good and Evil. Ending it bogged down in mundane detail of who married whom, how many children they had and what their names were, only diminishes its power.

For a time I thought the relentless heterosexuality of the series might be mitigated when Rowling announced that she considered Professor Dumbledore, a major character in the books, to be gay. The announcement was made at a book reading in Carnegie Hall, New York, three months after the publication of the final book. Dumbledore apparently had one 'tragic infatuation' in his youth (Toronto Press Conference, October 2007) after which he led 'a celibate and a bookish life'. 'Whether they physically consummated this infatuation or not is not the issue' according to Rowling (interview in *The Student*, March 2008). Not terribly gay, then;

scarcely denting the inexorable accumulation of Hetty Garbage in the books.

I am not trying to claim that love and romance have no place in literature, art and entertainment. The 'romantic comedy', like any other genre, has its excellent as well as its bad examples. The novels of Barbara Cartland and the like are still popular, and I have no wish to put down these works nor the readers and viewers who like them. My objection is only to Hetty's tentacles reaching into every other area of artistic expression, so that it's scarcely possible to find a book, play or film that does not incorporate the obligatory 'love scene'. After all, we don't expect to find a saloon-bar fight in *every* film, nor a visit by aliens from space in *every* novel. As a child in the forties, I went to cinema matinees where a roar of disapproval would rise from the audience whenever the hero and heroine got within groping distance of one another. A few roars of disapproval wouldn't go amiss today.

COMRADES
John Dixon

I don't remember the crash itself. Nor any screams. Or sirens. Only that a woman, a total stranger, died in my arms.

I was too stunned – by whatever it was that had happened – to call for help. A paramedic came up. I looked pleadingly into his eyes.

'Can't you help her?'

He shook his head.

Her head lolled on my chest and her glazing, unfocused eyes stared up at me.

'Someone'll be back for the details,' the medic said, and left.

I couldn't leave. I couldn't leave her. I was accountable, as never before, to a fellow human being. She had almost made an offering of herself, a gesture no-one could refuse.

The ambulances and emergency services began to arrive. All the space was needed. The other bodies were taken away. We were left till last. I heard someone say, 'They can't have been married long.'

I assumed her details were in her handbag. I didn't want to open it. I wasn't sure I wanted to know. As it was I felt like a looter.

I took a visiting card out of my wallet and wrote, 'So very sorry.' I tucked it into her hand and walked off in the general direction of home.

I had a frantic text message from the hanger-on who calls herself My Partner. I didn't reply – and unthinkingly turned into a side road, then turned right, and right again and again, then left and found myself back at the scene of the event. The whole area had been cordoned off. There were no ambulances, just hoists and cutting machines working by arc-light. A crowd had gathered round the barriers, not relatives or friends, just ghouls, craning their necks, hovering round the film crews, moving forward every time a workman in protective gear arrived or left. There was nothing to see. The real players had moved on. The bodies had gone. She'd been taken. I had left. There was no point in staying.

I went straight home and looked at the report on television. An in-yer-face journalist was shrilling up-to-date snippets. 'Professional counsellors are on their way to help the bereaved. Even now as I stand here ...'

The phone rang. It was an official from the scene.

'We got your details from your card. You didn't come to our Information Desk?'

'I didn't know there was one. Anyway I've little to tell. I didn't know the lady.'

'I'm sure,' he said quietly, 'but we'd like to talk about it. Not just the woman. We need to know as much as we can. There's to be an Official Enquiry.'

'I can't remember much,' I protested. 'Anything at all – really.'

What have I to tell them? What's he accusing me of? I'd never noticed her until it happened. She must have been standing next to me on the train, gripping the hand rail. I didn't touch her. If she'd bumped into me I'd've recoiled at the touch. Muttered an audible apology. Without meaning it. Possibly even mouthed an expletive.

'You're entitled to counselling help,' the voice said and rang off.

The woman who calls herself My Intended rushed in, thanked God, and smothered me with solicitous questions.

'The moment I heard I knew you'd been involved. I just knew.'

I didn't respond.

'I can quite understand you don't want to talk – yet.' She paused, presumably hoping I might blurt something out. 'Well, at least, have a bite to eat.'

I shook my head. The news bulletin said that information about the victims couldn't be released till all the bodies had been identified and the relatives informed.

I felt a pang of resentment. Please say she cannot be identified. Let her be a total unknown. Then I can give her an identity.

The phone rang again. My Erstwhile Partner answered it. 'It's a man. He wants to talk to you.'

It was her husband.

She did not live far away, quite near the train station after mine. I dreaded I'd see a more domestic background to her. The semi-detached was undistinguished, drab almost. The front garden was crazy-paved in a very tight-lipped way, with hardly any cement between the stones, several of which were buckling.

A middle-aged woman answered the door. She looked too young to be the mother or mother-in-law, possibly an older sister. I was shown into the front room and introduced to a horseshoe of relatives, all women, who sat on the sofa and armchairs, like items of furniture themselves.

'So,' one of them muttered. 'So. You were the last person to see her alive?'

They stared at me, as if I'd done something wrong. I didn't answer and looked round the room, wondering if the décor reflected her taste. I attributed all the kitsch to the husband,

and the few good pieces to her. There was no other evidence of her existence but a small photo on the mantelpiece. He must have dominated her, stifled her with these relatives – his relatives, almost certainly not hers. How she must have hated him! She was looking for someone else. She did choose me. She did single me out. Do not pretend that In Extremis she didn't know her own mind.

'I'll get her husband,' said the slightly older woman. 'He's in the garden.'

They all hung their heads. At the thought of him grieving? What did he know of grief?

'He says he'd be pleased to see you. It might be better if you met – outside.'

She took me via a conservatory to the patio.

The husband was about my age, the same build, same colour hair. He had tired, swollen eyes. He looked drawn and cadaverous. I suspect he always looked like that, even before the accident.

'Thank you for coming,' he said. 'I just wanted to ask – if I might – if you don't mind, that is – well, not ask, no prepared questions, of course – really for you – to tell – to tell me – if ...'

How could I not help despising him? He was unworthy of her. He hadn't protected her when she needed it. And it was me he seemed concerned for!

'It must've been very harrowing for you – not knowing this person – this ... my wife.'

Was he implying she'd been forward and familiar? Wanton, deliberate even, in latching onto me as the last person she was ever to see?

'Bit surprised that she was ... actually on that train.'

'Well, funnily enough, as it happens,' I said. 'I was on it only by chance. An announcement said there were delays and changes of platform. Yet there was a train waiting. I ignored it at first, but when I heard the whistle I instinctively ran – before even checking the destination. It turned out OK. I would normally have got a later one.'

'That's interesting,' he said. 'She usually went – earlier. It's a pity she wasn't on the usual one or ...' He looked wistfully into the darkened garden. Perhaps he wanted to say 'Why couldn't it have been you who died?'

He shifted position and stared at me. 'In your arms, you say?'

I hadn't mentioned this. I assume he'd found out from the paramedic or the Information Desk.

'She must've been standing very close to me,' I said. 'Then – before we reached the next station – it all happened.'

There was a long pause. I really wanted to say to him – I'd seen her from the start. So close, so tender, trusting, she came to my arms, without asking my permission – still less yours. She knew I'd accept. She was not a total stranger. She was in my arms long before she died.

'We had difficulty tracing you,' he said. 'The police said someone had disappeared without reporting properly.'

'Not exactly true. I left my card.'

'Oh, yes, indeed. So you did. I forgot. The police gave it to me.' He handed it back. 'I'm glad we met. Despite the circumstances.'

You mean despite the fact she died in my arms.

We shook hands.

So, he wants me to hand her back to his arms, does he? No, I will lay her gently in the earth.

'May I come to the funeral?' I asked.

He looked on the point of asking another question. I think it might have been – 'Did she call out my name? With her dying breath?'

The woman who keeps calling me Her Soul-Mate is getting

on my nerves. I can't bear to touch her anymore. There's nothing there. She suggested I get counselling.

'Oh,' I said. 'You mean – talk about it, relive it, then get on the next crowded train?'

'I'm serious,' she insisted, and phoned to invite a counsellor to the house. He was there within the hour. He looked like one of the ghouls.

'You're one of the lucky ones,' he assured me. 'Near the worst fatalities. Miraculously you survived. Not bereaved either. Nonetheless, we have enough counsellors to deal with your case as well. We'll need an hour for the first session, half an hour thereafter. It's a free service.'

His questions were endless. I sighed.

'This is for your Peace of Mind,' he said. 'Do you get flashbacks?'

'No.'

'What? None at all?'

'No. Not even of your questions.'

'My questions? Flashbacks of my questions? You mean my questions dwell in your mind? You hear them echo and resonate?'

'No. I think my hearing was damaged in the blast.'

'You can't hear what I'm saying! I hadn't thought of that possibility.'

He summoned my Would-be Partner. He spoke to her quite loudly. 'Typical. Seen it all before. In denial.' He patted her gently on the shoulder. 'Not to worry. I've no doubt my services will be called on again.'

From that moment till the day of the funeral was the most motivated time of my life. I conducted an investigation parallel to and surpassing the Official Tribunal. Once all the victims had been identified and the relatives informed, a list of names appeared in the newspapers. She looked much younger in the photo. It helped me reconstruct her life on a more than conjectural basis. I photocopied all the reports; newsprint tends to turn brown. They became Exhibit A in my dossier, which I hoped soon to laminate.

Her name surprised me. The husband, so-called, had not mentioned it. He just said My Wife or She. And in a way I was grateful for this. A name ties one down. The surname – his name – was easily forgettable. Her first name was not the one I would have chosen for her. I have yet to decide how I'll address her.

Her age did not surprise me. She was my age. She could have been a lost twin. I checked the exact birth date in the Public Record Office. A few days separated us – even more a chance. Twins are Ordinary Fate. But we – we could have married, without incest.

The newspaper reports did not give the date she had married – not long ago I would have thought, but long enough for her to have regretted it. There were no children, which, with him as her husband, came as no surprise.

She had worked in the City. I checked the firm, and went to the wine bar nearest to the office. I spent lunchtime and evening eaves-dropping on her former colleagues, occasionally catching her name above the hubbub, trying to establish her role at work. I sat there for hours drinking, slowly. At closing time, I took the journey she'd have taken home.

I was careful not to be seen waiting outside her house at night. I had an unimpeded view through open windows, undrawn curtains with the lights full on. The slightly older woman – the one I'd thought could be a sister – seemed very close to the husband. In times of grief there is much hugging. But to that extent?

It was clear they were going through all the cupboards, having a turnout. The dustbins were full. I sifted through them, hoping for a keepsake. I was surprised they had chucked the newspapers. They couldn't have been keeping a scrapbook.

These investigations took up my waking hours. They helped put in perspective a recurrent dream, which even sleeping by day and waking at night could not dispel. It was a peaceful setting, in the eye of the storm. I drowned in the gaze of her eyes. They encompassed horizon after horizon. I couldn't close the lids. Even when I awoke from the dream, her eyes were still there, still open. Not even the coffin lid could close them. I wanted to look at her again in her entirety; uncorrupted, enhanced, fleshed out by the facts I'd learnt.

The funeral service was dull. The relatives I'd seen were there, some work colleagues from the wine bar, and several other people who seemed to think they had some right to attend. I could hardly wait for them all to go.

I stayed at the graveside all night. The flowers were beginning to fade. I pushed them on one side. The earth was fresh. I could easily have dislodged it. I sat at the end of the grave, like a faithful dog on a tomb top.

Her immediate family dropped in intermittently over the next few weeks. Their numbers soon dwindled, and their stay was progressively shorter. I, myself, was forced to return home on occasion.

The woman who says she is soon to be My Wife is becoming utterly insufferable. So is the doctor who gave me the certificate. So are the people from the job I had. But she is the worst. Every half hour she says, 'Are you alright?' She shows me pictures of wipe clean show-houses, travel brochures, bright sunny places, meals out. She seems to be wearing a new outfit every time I bother to look at her.

'It must've been awful. It could've been you. It was a miracle. Don't you see ... Someone – Up There – wanted us to remain together.'

I laughed and almost replied ... Someone – Down Here – had other plans.

I will not go to the cemetery on her birthday or the anniversary of her death. When the Investigating Tribunal finally reports, the whole issue will be brought to life again, like Judgment Day itself. There'll be a resurgence of grief. The family will make a special pilgrimage.

I need not fear them. We are all beyond recognition now. They cannot take anything away from me. She is not in the coffin anyway. She is out there. Waiting for me. Looking like her double. Waiting for another calamity. I can meet her only in an extreme situation.

I frequent crowded, enclosed, vulnerable places – full trains, buses with standing room only, sale queues, capacity audiences.

A DADDIES DIARY
Christopher Preston

Yesterday it hurt. I slept without dreaming for a change and woke in the morning missing his warm presence in my bed – the first man there in four and a half years. His smell lingered on the side where he had lain the night before. I don't think either of us slept that well, although we both declared we had. It all came back to me, the tricky geography of sharing a bed, what to do with arms and where do the legs fit? We started off on our sides both facing the same direction. My knees slid neatly under his buttocks and my arm draped over his thirty-inch waist to cradle his now flaccid cock in my hand. It's a familiar position from the past, which now seems centuries ago. We changed positions throughout the night, just like the time lapse images of sleeping people in scientific studies, but half waking on every turn. He set the alarm on his phone so he could take his mum out for a coffee on her birthday but we woke early and found him rock hard.

'Do you need to pee?' I said.

'No, it's always like this, and it's fine, we don't have to do anything about it.'

It was a mistake really, or rather, an omission. There was no age on Toby's profile, but he dutifully sent a picture of his 'smiling face' – a flattering black and white photo of a dark haired, clean shaven young man with a winning grin. *He's read my profile properly, probably another one, mid-to-late twenties.* I always reply (except to the now persistent computer generated scams) because you never know what entertainment and conversations might occur. At this time in my life, almost every opportunity is to be seized. Attracting much younger

men is new to me and had I known his age, I might well have
politely answered, 'Thank you, Toby, you're lovely, but are a
bit too young for me.' Aware of approbation around age gaps
in relationships, including my own views, I'm trying to under-
stand why everyone older wants younger and that we are now
seen by the young as 'hot' or 'cool'.

The location finder showed him on the Island and our chat
revealed that he was on holiday with parents, bored to death
with no Wi-Fi.

'Do you know a beach where I can get naked?'

I replied cautiously, texting that I often went there, and
agreed to meet.

'Thanks,' he replied. 'I do find you attractive, but I
wouldn't have any expectations.'

It was messy, our meeting at the beach. His message said he
was on the left hand end, wearing a white baseball cap and
grey tee shirt, but I found no one. *What if he is already naked,
how will I recognise him?* A text sorted it. He'd not crossed the
pass over the rocky promontory which, at high tide, divides
the nudist beach from the rest of the bay. I retraced my steps,
almost colliding with an elderly woman and daughter, recog-
nised from a Christmas Day party. They were looking for a
path up the cliff to the road above. At almost the same time a
young man in a white baseball cap followed hard on their
heels, grinning in recognition. I had a dilemma, should I
introduce this young man, who I had never met before, to
these women who I had only met once? Somehow I stumbled
through that moment, and pointed along the beach to a path
up the cliff.

'It's just past that tree.'

The Mother, with a wicked twinkle in her eye, said, 'We
will avert our eyes.'

I laughed. 'That's not really necessary.'

I turned my full attention to the youth in the white cap. He looked nothing like his black and white photo. *Oh, fuck, he's much younger than I imagined.* Tall, pale and rangy his dark blond hair escaped from under his cap to frame English rose cheeks. His jaw and neck sprouted a scruffy week-old red beard, his upper lip, blond fuzz. I threw him a friendly smile and as we walked along the beach I asked him, 'How young are you?'

'Twenty.'

That's a forty-four year age gap. My mind raced. *What do I say to him? He surely can't be into men my age. Nothing more than a pleasant hour on the beach and a cooling swim will occur.* He appeared supremely confident as we negotiated our way through the sun-bathers, looked for a spot to plant the sun umbrella and laid out our towels, mine in the shade and his in the sun. We undressed and I watched him remove three skimpy items of shapeless clothing to reveal what seemed to me perfection.

He looked down at himself. 'I've never been naked on a beach before, I hope my cock behaves itself.'

I offered factor 50+ sun-block but he wanted to get his bum tanned for the first time ever.

He got out his phone. 'I thought I put my age on.'

Maybe he's just saying that, now that we're here. But he seemed sincere.

He looked on his profile and immediately made the correction. 'Would it have made a difference?'

'Possibly, I don't know.' *I don't want to hurt his feelings.*

We fell into easy conversation getting to know each other sentence by sentence, lapsing into paragraphs. My expectation of monosyllabic teenage grunting disappeared along with the notion that youth don't know much these days. I liked this young man, more confident about his sexuality than

I was at twenty. Pleased that his cock had behaved, he turned over onto his front to reveal my favourite part of male anatomy – that curve of the spine as it descends to meet rounded buttocks.

The sea was rough with surf that dumped on the beach, full of drifting seaweed. We swam out with strong strokes. Toby did Water Polo style with head out of the water. In the deep we trod water, and showed off, attempting synchronised swimming.

Back on our towels, I wondered where to take this. 'You saw my age?'

'Yes, I like older and you are very sexy.'

I blushed, flattered. 'Thank you. Don't you have a boy-friend?'

'My ex is only nineteen; I can't really talk to people my own age.'

I threw caution to the wind. *It's only sex so why not try it?* 'Do you want to come back to my place?'

He turned on his side and looked at me, his eyes alive. 'Yes,' he replied with a vigorous nod of the head.

There's no mistaking that signal. His cock stirred at the expect-ation and mine followed suit. The sun disappeared behind clouds; we shivered and packed up the umbrella.

On the drive back, he talked about his parents and siblings. 'They're all cool with my being gay.'

I envy you. When I was twenty we were still illegal in New Zealand. We fought for what you've got now. 'Do they know you like older men?'

'No.' There is a moment, the first, of uncertainty. 'I don't know how they would take that.'

'How do you feel about your father and me being a similar age?'

'I don't fancy my dad and you are nothing like him.' I calmed down inside, relieved by his answer and smiled back.

Facing each other naked at home, I worried again about the age gap, but he took my hand and gently led me to the bedroom. Later, after sex and lying close together, he picked flaky skin off me, plucked some irrelevant hairs off my chest and inspected various parts of my body which made me laugh.

'I wish I had grey hair, and I really love your chest, mine is so flat.'

'No, it's beautiful,' I said.

He talked in a focussed way about his university studies and hopes for the future – not the hair-brained shite one might have expected – and joked about managing his female flatmates. 'They have no clues about cooking and cleaning.'

'I remember living with untidy women. How do you manage?'

'I do a lot of washing up. It avoids arguments.'

So, he's domesticated, his mum has taught him survival skills.

He looked at his phone. 'Is that the time? How did that happen?'

I shrugged.

'We have a family dinner booked. Can I go to a restaurant here in a tee shirt and shorts?'

'Probably, depends which one.'

He texted his mum and she replied immediately.

'It's OK, they haven't left yet. I'll tell her something about meeting up with friends.'

'Won't she want details?' I ask.

'I'll make something up.'

'Best to be non-specific and a bit mysterious, then you don't have to lie. She'll get the hint that it's private.'

As we neared the family rent-a-batch he asked me to drop him around the corner from the bus stop. 'They might just see us if you stop outside.'

He still has a problem, but it's not for me to force the issue and anyway, I'll probably never see him again.

Today is a bit better but not much. Last night, his long text, saying that he'd told his mum about liking older men and how she was cool with that, got an equally long reply from me. *Yeah, right. She's thinking guys in their thirties.* Maybe it was a mistake to reply. The blue towel he used for our frequent showers together, still hangs on the rail, as if expecting his return. I sniff it, but there is no trace of him there, just vivid memories.

That night I went to sleep dreaming of 'What if?' *I've around twenty years left alive and the sex will fade out at some stage along the way. He would be forty – still up for it – perhaps a good age to start again. I'd have to send him out for extra sex though. Banish all thoughts, it's just impractical. But he's good company. I could show him the world, though he's pretty well-educated already. Dad's an investment advisor, so he doesn't need support and in any case, he's got to make his own way. Nah, forget it.*

I woke to an unexpected text. 'Good morning, handsome,' which encouraged further delusions. *He fits into my life so easily, adapting to my routines, suggesting but not insisting, on small changes. I like that. Older men can be so inflexible, ensconced in their own immaculate homes, devoted to cherished furnishings. What madness are these thoughts – after only one evening?*

I had things to do that morning and after a considered hesitation, asked him if he had plans.

'No, not really.'

'The beach, later?' *A tentative suggestion allowing him to opt out.*

'Yeah, why not?'

A casual and uncommitted reply.

Not wanting to seem desperate, I waited until mid-afternoon before offering to pick him up on my way to the beach.

'Yeah, come and get me, please – this is a bore.'

Now he sounds desperate.

At the bus stop, he texted me that he'd be five minutes.

'Sorry about that, my parents decided to go for a walk in this direction – just had to wait until they passed.'

'Did you tell them anything?'

'Just that I'd been out with friends and meeting up again today.'

'OK.'

The sea was colder, but the sun hotter and the wind stronger, blowing the sun umbrella inside out, so we moved to partial shade. Going back to my place was this time, taken for granted. We fucked. I cooked – new potatoes, garlic prawns in avocado salad and coleslaw. He poured us white wine to the correct level in each glass – the widest part.

I would drink less if I lived with Toby. Just as well I did extra potatoes as the prawn and avocado salad didn't have enough calories for a young man. *I would put on weight cooking for two, again. He'd need larger portions.*

After dinner, I found his page on facebook and sent a friend request. He seemed surprised that I could manage that technically.

'You don't have to accept. I won't be offended.' *But I really hope you do, except that I hate facebook and how people live their lives on it.*

'Can I stay the night?' he asked.

'Yes.' *I wonder if that's wise.* 'You are the youngest man I've been with, I mean the age gap.'

'This is the age of the "Daddy". It's all cool and I've been with a few older guys.'

I resisted the urge to ask their ages or how they compared with me. 'I would have been terrified at the thought of having sex with a much older man.'

'It's fun and more interesting, you missed out.'

I nod. 'Yes, I can see that now, but men went to jail or had to flee the country.' *There is also that label of the 'dirty old man' preying on young flesh, at least there was in those days.*

He texted his mum, 'I'm staying over at friends.'

She texted back, 'Goodnight'.

Do I have any spare toothbrushes in the cabinet ...

'I hope you don't mind, but I brought my toothbrush just in case.'

I laughed. *Not only can he read my thoughts but he thinks ahead – unusual.* We brushed together as if we'd been doing it for years.

The next morning over breakfast, with great care he picked 'a piece of sleep' out of the corner of my eye.

'You are very good at intimacy,' I said.

He looked surprised and pleased.

'I noticed that yesterday. Humans need to touch and be touched.'

It was his last day on the Island and later at the beach, our routine was the same; we lay on towels, swam then went home. This time we fucked outside on the deck, miraculously avoiding the mosquitoes. We drove in silence on the way back to the bus stop. *I can't say anything that puts pressure on him. Any move has to come from him ... be his decision. What is he feeling? I can't ask him. What if he wants something more? No, that would not be sensible. But ...*

'Mum saw that I had a friend request last night.'

'Was that OK?'

'Yes, I think so. I'll wait for a bit before I accept, until she has forgotten about it.'

'You don't have to accept.'

'I'd like to be friends.'

'That would be good.'

'We can text for now.'

'Yes.' We drove again in silence.

'It's only just started and now it's over,' he sighed.

That's the first time he's spoken about our three day affair. But it is over.

'Let's just find somewhere to park,' he said as we approached the bus stop. 'We can have a cuddle.'

We did that, kissing in the still broad daylight on an elevated point off the main road, visible to all.

As he opened the door, there was a 'Goodbye ...' with an almost imperceptible endearment attached. It might have been a 'darling' or a 'dear' – difficult to tell. I replied just as quietly and caught myself adding a similar endearment, which died away as soon as it was spoken. I drove away, glancing in the rear vision mirror at his receding figure to check if he turned back. He didn't and I continued home in a dream.

THREE POEMS
Alice F. Wickham

LOVE FLOWERS

Love flowers
In Apple Blossom time
Time moves swiftly, softly down
Minds unfettered
Spirits entwined
Stay awhile
Let's shilly shally in the moonlight
Birds sing
Dreaming
Begins
(*I Remember You*)
I haven't forgotten, you know
That smile
Luscious walk
Lethal style
Your words left no room for doubt
And still I doubted
More fool me.

COMPLAINER

You have pared it to the bone
This life
Sold your home
Divorced your wife
You read the news
It scares you to think
The more you absorb
The further you shrink
You say that life is unfair
But what on earth can you do?
You are just a cog in the wheel
You hold no political view
You cannot bear politicians
And despise celebrities too
Your opinions are many and varied
Just as your friends are few
When you were young you had answers
To poverty, war, and greed
Now you shunt off to M and S
To grab the things you don't need
Your working days are over
Retirement has begun
If only you lived in the South of France
Life would be much more fun
But you note that the immigrant crisis
Is hurting the red, white and blue
You watch them invading the NHS
Stealing your place in the queue
You complain about our miserable world
But have no solutions to offer
If only you'd learn how to shut your beak
The rest of us might not suffer

INTO THE BLUE

We've awoken
Our lives now are broken
And from that chaos we remain
Forever lost
The 'human cost'

Into the sea
There is no 'me'
No job
No kids
No family

Money gone
Passports shorn
Hands
Heads
Clothing
Torn

Into the blue
Our time remembered
Baggage sunk
Limbs dismembered

We won't accept
And yet we must
That what we were
Has turned to dust

Still

The light is clear
We ride the storm
Freed from here
Spirits born

FRIDAY NIGHT

Ross Burgess

'How was the drive?' Mike had just arrived to spend the weekend with Andrew and me in our little terraced house in Kent.

'Traffic not too bad for a Friday evening; the M1 was a bit congested, though. Can I smell cooking?' Mike had come alone; it seemed he'd split up with the boyfriend (or 'affair', as we said in those days) who'd come with him on previous visits. Over a leisurely meal, with a bottle of red wine, he updated us on the latest gossip and scandal from the Wolverhampton crowd. I couldn't contribute much to this conversation, having only briefly met the people they were talking about, but the other two enjoyed chattering away. Andrew's slight Black Country accent seemed to get a bit broader talking to Mike, and they both occasionally lapsed into the gay Polari that had never quite caught on in the circles I'd moved in.

Eventually we all agreed it had been a tiring day, and it was time for bed. Mike was to have the guest room on the first floor, and Andrew and I would be in our bedroom immediately above.

'OK, I'll go on up then.' So saying, Mike kissed me on the lips and gave me a hug. Was it a coincidence, I wondered, that he'd waited until Andrew was out of the room? He definitely seemed to be holding me closer, and for longer, and with more enthusiasm, than might have been expected – certainly I was getting more than the 'sisterly' embrace he'd given Andrew. Mike was not bad looking, and his work in the factory kept him in reasonable shape, but he had never struck me as being what I'd call my type; however he suddenly seemed quite a bit more fanciable as a result of this unexpected attention. But just then Andrew reappeared, and Mike went up to bed. Andrew and I finished putting the dishes away, and went up to bed ourselves.

Andrew fell asleep pretty quickly. I had lain beside him for a while, wondering what to think about Mike's approach, when I heard a cough from the room below. Clearly Mike was still awake, and a wicked thought came into my mind. What if I were to go down and join him? But could I have misread the signals? Would he be offended and cause a scene? Somehow I thought not. But could I get away with it? What if Mike had already had a wank and was no longer in the mood? What if Andrew woke up and discovered what was going on? Could we keep it secret? And most of all how could I even think of cheating on my boyfriend with one of his oldest friends? And there was a practical difficulty: the use of condoms had not yet become as essential as it is today, but some lubrication would certainly help things along. So could I retrieve the tube of KY from the cabinet on Andrew's side of the bed, in the dark, without making a noise? This question at least could be resolved, one way or the other, by trying it out. I very gently moved Andrew's arm, which had been lying across me, got out of bed, crept as quietly as I could round the bed, stumbling briefly on a shoe or something lying on the floor, and slid the drawer open. I felt around inside, and there was the tube amongst a pile of handkerchiefs. I took it out, and very quietly closed the drawer again. Andrew seemed to stir in his sleep, so I remained quite still until I was sure that his breathing was deep and even. So, having answered the practical question, somehow the other questions, about cheating and consequences and suchlike, no longer seemed quite so pressing. Still it was with my heart pounding that I opened the bedroom door, went out, and pulled the door to after me.

I was shivering a bit as I walked naked down the stairs,

holding the tube. As I went into Mike's room the squeak from the door hinges was followed by a sound of movement from the bed, but I quickly slipped under the duvet beside him.

'Well, this is a surprise!'

'Ssh,' I replied.

It was warm in the bed. Mike gave off a slight smell of sweat from the long drive, with a taste of wine mixed with toothpaste on his breath. He flinched as I put my cold hands on his body. I soon established that he too slept in the nude. 'Let me warm you up a bit,' he whispered. I could feel his prick against me beginning to harden, and mine was starting to come to life again after having shrivelled up with the cold and the fear of being discovered. He held me tight, and it became pretty clear what he wanted.

'I think you might need this,' I whispered, putting the KY into his hand. He was bigger than I'd expected, and despite the lubrication I had to grit my teeth as he started to enter me. Soon however I relaxed, he was fully inside me, and I squeezed a bit to encourage him – not that he needed much encouragement. It felt good, no doubt all the better for the element of risk. The moan when he came was loud enough that I worried we could have been heard upstairs, but there was no sound from above. We were lying there together, both satisfied, with his prick gently softening inside me, and I was starting to doze off, when I heard a bed creak from upstairs. Fortunately there were no sounds of footsteps, but I thought I'd better get back where I belonged. I gave Mike a quick kiss and slipped out of the room. I stopped off at the loo, and it occurred to me that this could be my alibi if necessary, so I didn't take quite so much care as before to avoid making a noise on the stairs. As I got into bed Andrew roused slightly, and put his hand on my prick, but I pretended to be asleep.

In the morning we all slept late. Eventually I put on a

dressing gown and went down to make three cups of tea. This time I knocked before going into Mike's room. He was yawning and stretching. 'Did you sleep well?' I asked.

'Very well,' he replied, with the widest of grins. At this point I noticed the KY tube and put it in my dressing gown pocket.

Andrew was awake by the time I got upstairs with his tea. 'That's funny,' he said, 'I could have sworn we'd got a tube of KY in this drawer.'

'Let me have a look,' I said. ... 'Why, here it is.'

ANOTHER GAY ANTHOLOGY
Ivor Treby

The editor, a modern lad,
asked 'Was I writing?' He'd be glad
to see what new work I'd select.
(Some piece might suit, if not too bad,
politically was correct,
and had all suspect syntax checked.)

I should have known I'd waste my time
submitting words that spring and chime,
spark unexpected melody
that owed *some* debt to prosody:
but old obsessions will not die.
I sent him metre, form, and rhyme.

Back came the script: and, at the foot
a line or two of kind advice –
'Such tortured grammar may seem nice
(though what a strange unnatural vice!)
to your ear, pleasing maybe – but
up with these quirks I dare not put.'

My corseted, outmoded lays
would only consternation spread,
had stood no chance to win his praise:
'I don't believe that nowadays
you'll get away with that,' he said.
(I think he hoped I'd hang my head.)

No matter. I will not despair.
Throughout my life I've had to wear
the stigma of inversion, bear
with such my 'problem', weave and duck.
If you don't like it, pet, tough luck!
I could not give a parrot's fuck.

THE TENTH CHAUFFEUR
Elsa Wallace

All chauffeurs look the same, reflected Poppy when picked up for the Board meeting. But is this possible and if so why? The uniform was a factor. The cap hid the face a little if they all acted as this one did, turning away and ducking the head as he opened the door, perhaps embarrassed by his service task.

They were all burly, all had the same compact body just contained by the dark green coat and trousers. They could not be clones, they only varied as to race.

She was 28. With the turnover of staff she calculated there had been at least seven drivers so far. With each changeover her father sent her a message: 'Your driver now is Kearner.' Or Clovian or Tindett.

She thought they were on a rota at first but once a driver had completed a spell with her she did not see him again.

It was courteous of her father to let her know but quite unnecessary, for they were interchangeable. They were not personalities, they did not chat like the commercial cabbies in the City.

She raised their taciturnity with her father.

'I just think a little conversation would be pleasant – and make the drive less boring for them.'

'There is a boredom allowance built into their salary,' he said. 'They are instructed not to be friendly. We don't want gossip. It's for our security. Who knows what contacts they have through their work, rival companies, the media. They're vetted of course, but we can't cover every contingency. Be thankful they are silent. I always find it useful reading time.'

She thought there could be discretion without silence. She was unlikely to divulge company secrets. A little talk about the weather, books, films, TV, current news could hardly be dangerous.

'They must concentrate on the road,' said her father. 'The traffic is chaotic.'

She persisted in her efforts.

'Good morning, Partell. A lovely day again. Let's hope it lasts into the weekend.'

'Yes, madam.'

'Have you anything planned?'

'No, madam.'

'Oh, do you work this weekend?'

'No, madam.'

And so it went. She could elicit no more. Their voices were similar in tone and accent.

But there is a chink in all armour.

One day as she settled in the back with a soft green rug over her legs (it was mid-autumn) she heard before the engine was switched on:

> By car, by bike
> I take you where you like.
> By bike, by car
> We may go too far.
> Wherever you want to go
> I can't say no.
> But our next jaunt
> May not be what you want.

'What's that, Vetterley?' she asked, startled.

'The radio, madam. I apologise.'

But it had not been. And the voice had been the usual except it had a drawling quality.

In the coffee break at the meeting she approached her father.

'Vetterley may be a poet, or he likes poetry. He recited to

me some lines. I didn't recognise them. He seemed too embarrassed to continue.'

Her father laughed. 'Did it scan?'

'No, I don't believe it did.'

'Then it wasn't poetry.'

'It did rhyme.'

'That isn't enough.'

'You know, Dad, there's no need to tell me who is driving me each time. They're so similar! Do they come from the same agency?'

'Yes, a very reliable one.' He looked stern. 'You don't imagine I'd leave it to chance? Once something satisfies me I stick with it.'

Her mother did not satisfy him and was paid well to remove herself. At twelve Poppy had opted to remain in the family home, saying she disliked her mother's associates.

'Now I must make a phone call,' he said, 'but the meeting must resume on time so please, Poppy, make notes for me. That minute-taker doesn't catch the nuances.'

Poppy reviewed her reasons for choosing to stay with her father. He was no more affectionate or kindly than her mother had been. When it came down to it she loved her large primrose coloured room with its handsome ironwork balcony which in summer draped in vines let her pretend she was in Italy. I am like a cat, she thought, I have my territory.

Colwain was her driver to go home.

He also drove her to the airport for her winter holiday in Marrakesh.

Her father said, 'Strictly speaking, you shouldn't have a company car for that. You really must learn to drive. I don't accept this nonsense of slow reflexes. It's lack of application.'

'But I crashed the Citroen, and I was only doing forty.'

'Oh, it was second-hand. That didn't matter.'

Colwain was helpful with her case and, to her surprise,

with an answer. She had altered her conversational technique.

'Colwain, what did you do before driving for the Agency?'

'I was a bouncer, for a nightclub, madam.'

'And this is better?'

'Much better.' He smiled showing even teeth in his round fresh face.

Perhaps they were all ex-bouncers. That would explain the formulaic physique. Only Vetterley was a little different, smelling faintly of lemon.

Colwain added he would be meeting her on her return, but a change in her plans prevented this. The woman she met in her hotel enchanted her so much that she did not want to stay on without her. Candace's holiday ended two days before her own. Every hour together was precious and she managed to get on the same flight home. They would meet at a hotel next day.

Her father had told her several times, 'Poppy, you can always bring people back here, you know. The spare room's always available. You realise, don't you, that I'd welcome any friend of yours? So long as it's not your mother, ha ha.'

She toyed with the idea but was practical. Like a cat she could not have sex *sotto voce*. Some months her hotel bills impacted severely on her finances.

When she let herself in she slipped off her shoes. Her mother always refused to do so but Poppy and her father liked the hygienic Japanese custom.

Upstairs she was disturbed to notice the door to the master bedroom was ajar and the lights on. He was never home this early, not even on such a dark January afternoon.

Burglars? She should ring 999 but feline curiosity made her creep up and peep in.

Colwain, deshabillé, lounged in an armchair frowning over a crossword. Three gold rings shone on his dark muscular hand.

What a cheek! Well, she thought, if he proved difficult she could easily fell him, her karate training paying off at last. There was nothing wrong with her reflexes, Father was right. She just did not care to drive. Who would, when they could be driven.

Subdued notes of Monteverdi impinged on her ear. She gave the door a gentle push to reveal, disposed about the lofty green and gold room, eight other chauffeurs partly clothed, playing cards, reading, or drinking red wine from the best glasses.

On the bed, loosely entwined, were her father and the tenth chauffeur, possibly Vetterley. Unmemorable faces turned toward her.

Hospitality had been drummed into her by her un-satisfactory mother.

'Who wants tea and coffee?' she said, 'I'm just making. Hands up, teas first.'

When at length they had the house to themselves and were washing up cups and saucers, Poppy asked, 'Seriously, Dad, do you never think you would like a little variety?' thinking of her own inclusive repertoire.

Her father laughed. 'To you they all look the same, as you said, but I know the difference, even in the dark.'

THE WORM BOY
Simon Dessloch

THE TRICK

I liked him from the first, the filthy whore. He was different. Not just different from the other whores but different from the type of boy I prefer: skinny, cute and none too tall.

Well no, he was all of those things but unlike the cute, petite, *flat-tummied* boys I usually go for, the Worm Boy had a pot belly.

Normally I like to stroke those lean, hard boy bodies, feel the sharpness of the bone, tease that sexy spot inside and see them quiver when I fuck them, *feeling myself through them.*

I still see him in my dreams: stork-like; an *inhuman* part of me.

The Worm Boy was a little dude, his thighs so thin they made his legs look longer, and he was pliable like a girl.

The first time I saw him I was taking a short cut from work. I do the accounts for *Totally Queer* and *Queer Sphere*. I took the back streets to avoid the tourist scrum on my way to the gym. He was leaning against a brick wall in the freak show, side show part of the West End. I thought he was a pregnant girl and I was disgusted. Disgusted with myself. Because she turned me on. And if the thing really was a girl, then my arousal would have to stay a wank fantasy. For the first time in my life I was jerking off to the idea of doing girl.

THE PIMP

Timmy barely knew anything when I first met him. A cute, little thing he was, pixie-faced, *like a girl but not a girl*, you know what I mean.

I taught him blow-jobs, like, *don't scrape your teeth on my dick, baby*. He was different after that, like, now he can't say *don't* any longer, just sort of says *doat*, and when he sneezes it's not *hatschi* just *schi*.

I had to remind him to collect the money first. Not that thinking was his strong point. He really needed someone to do that for him. And that someone was me.

I realised roundabout then that I'd sort of gotten used to having him around. The place was always reasonably neat. Every day there was a warm meal to be had.

And I liked it when we were close. First I'd thought he had a pretty face, shame about the rest, but I'd gotten fond of his disproportionate, gangling features. I liked the way his body gave when I lay down on him. I liked touching that belly. Once or twice I fell asleep on top of him and dreamed of being sucked into the belly of a whale.

THE TRICK

I'd never paid for sex in my life and I cursed myself for being a coward. Scared of a pregnant girl. Scared of the possibility of, the very idea of, a pregnant girl whore. How pathetic. How could she possibly harm me?

I walked past her every day, and every day I was more curious. What did she do with her customers? Perhaps she only did hand and blow jobs. Would fucking her kill the unborn child? Did she even want this baby? Or was she banking on losing it? Hoping some brutal client would relieve her of it?

Was I that client?

The thought stopped me dead in my tracks. Heat filled my head, exploding into sweat. I was so painfully hard, I wanted to scream. Instead I hid in the shadows of Floral Street, biting my nails, just staring at her.

Or him. *Him*, I told myself, *him*. My knees were twitching. I needed to sit down.

I lit a fag, sat on a stone step before a boarded up doorway. I couldn't act on this, could I? I would never have my answers. I would never know the identity, the *true story* of this creature.

She was negotiating with a customer now, and I felt relieved, the tension ebbing away. The moment was lost. I'd had my chance, but I was never going to take that step, was I?

You're a coward, I smiled to myself, *a fucking coward. But that's alright.*

You're going to die in ignorance. I nodded to myself, examining the unevenness of the cobble stones, their never-ending beauty, stone I could almost see myself reflected in. I imagined my ancestors paving a street for the very first time.

A scream and a shout came from the direction of the girl-boy. She was fighting with that Trick. There was no one near except me. He smacked her one. Shit! I figured I was marginally bigger and taller than the guy, but I'd never been much of a street-fighter or pub-brawler. I always thought that macho posturing rather silly. There were better ways to get rid of your aggressive feelings, better ways to show you were a man.

I was striding towards them. She saw me, and maybe sensing that help was on the way made her brave, or perhaps she thought I was the guy's accomplice, and that she better fight for her life. She kicked him twice with those stork-legs. He punched her in the belly. I was close enough to hear the strange sound it made. She collapsed and he put the boot in. 'Hey!' He looked at me, expression like a little boy caught wanking, and fled. I imagined him hiding in the next dark corner, relieving himself of the pressure in his balls.

The girl was vomiting stringy puke that looked like vermicelli. She was hugging her belly, and I feared a more terrible calamity might be upon me. I knelt on the stones and saw her body clearly. Saw a wispy pale moustache, an Adam's apple. I saw a crotch bulge too, not like he was well-endowed in any of those places, but unless she was a Victor Victoria, *she* was definitely a *he*.

I touched him, and he felt familiar, felt like a boy.

He was crying. I gave him a tissue. He dried his eyes, but didn't wipe the vomit off his chin, like he hadn't noticed or didn't care. I pulled another hanky from my leathers and cleaned his face.

The boy's eyes were dim and I wondered whether he was just too stupid, in an intellectually subnormal sort of way, to notice or care whether he had sick on his face. I asked, 'Are you badly hurt?' He shook his head. I rested my hands on his shoulder, not quite daring to move it to where I wanted to touch him. He shook it off. 'Are you sure?' He shrugged, and well, I had a feeling that perhaps I was overstaying my welcome. It's not like he was making an attempt to thank me. And what the fuck was I doing here? Was this boy a mute as well as an imbecile? It was obscene and disgusting and – why did monsters like this have to be born into the world?

'It's 25 quid for a blow-job.' He whispered, and I noticed he was on his knees, while I had by now stood up.

I needed privacy for this.

I reached out my hand like a chivalrous knight helping a damsel in distress and I kinda liked it. Half of me was still stuck in the fantasy of the little pregnant girl whore.

'You have to give me the money first.'

I gave him twice that and took him to a hotel where you pay by the hour. I asked him how much he charged for a fuck, and he didn't answer. I didn't know why. Maybe he had a different baby-moron-word for it. I decided that I had to take control of the situation. There was little point in conversation.

In the room he unzipped me with unexpected haste, would

have gulped me down in that dumb mouth and finished me in record time, I'm sure.

'We've got an hour. Let's not waste it.' I made him lie down, and he didn't seem to understand what I wanted and finally I laid a hand on his belly. He removed it, looking at me. I re-attached it and he gave in. After all I'd paid him 50 quid. I had a right to touch him. He looked away, and I reached beneath his T-shirt, found soft, smooth skin. Squeegee. No muscle. Like – *tit*.

I coughed and swallowed and squeezed. He squirmed and I let go, remembering that half an hour ago the boy had been violently attacked. 'Sorry.' He didn't acknowledge my apology.

I put a finger in his ass. He gripped it like a frightened child might hold its mother's hand. I fucked him and it felt like eavesdropping on his insides. I wasn't wearing a condom, when I'm usually so diligent about that kind of thing. I had two in the back pocket of my leathers.

I didn't want to kiss him but riding him like this, the way his body gave, was a revelation to me. But I don't think *he* liked it, or maybe he just didn't like *me*.

There was only one time that I ever did girl. I'd taken too much of the wrong thing and most of that night is a blur. I remember vomiting into her kitchen sink. I remember diving into her slippery cleft. She'd been a little ragdoll waif. I got hard for her and I came. She was happy one moment and sad the next, then angry and hysterical. I never knew why.

Someone was knocking on the door. My time was up. 'You have to stop now,' the boy said. I ground him into the mattress. He squeaked. Five sharp thrusts and it was over. I pulled out of him. Saw something wriggling on the pink bedsheet. Good sex can get messy. That's the risk you take if you don't want to be reduced to sterile dildos and phone sex. But this boy's shit was alive. What else did he have inside him?

What was it that was wrong with him?

I fled into a dingy bathroom. The light bulb socket seemed to have a loose connection, creating an on-off effect. I jumped into the shower and turned the taps. Cold water hit me. I rubbed frantically at myself, fished for the soap and found some girly stink shower lotion. I sluiced the filth off my dick and in the semi-darkness I saw a shower bowl crawling with worms. Felt them invading me.

Slowly the water heated and the light flickered on. My breathing and heartbeat slowed. I switched off the shower, towelled myself dry, returned to the room and found the Worm Boy gone. He'd left the door open. From the stairway a fat woman saw me and giggled. I shut the door. Went to the bed, found ruffled sheets, messy, yes, but there was nothing left alive on or in them.

I got dressed and told myself I'd imagined the whole thing. I'd seen creepy-crawlies in the shadows before, when I overdid the dope, saw phantoms, spiders, things that weren't there, optical illusions. This was a civilised country, for fuck's sake, things like that didn't happen here.

I checked the shower basin and found it filled with nothing but bursting soap bubbles.

I left the hotel and went to a place I'd never been to before – a café-bar called The Out Side. I hid inside, sitting at a tiny coffee table shielded by a window, drank vodka and coke, then espresso, then vodka and ice, alternating between booze and caffeine, hot and cold, till my teeth hurt like they were going to crack.

That boy. He didn't know any better. But he'd ripped open a tiny wound inside me. Now I had to stitch it up somehow. I would live, bearing an ugly scar. Intoxication took hold. The tension ebbing away. My mind dissipated into the techno-pop, the incomprehensible chit-chat, and looking at the club-crowd starting their evening, I was able to stop imagining what it was like to be him.

The Out Side played *Sexy Boy* and I ran away again, worming a path through the crowd, brushing against beautiful bodies. I bashed into someone. Took a moment to recognise him. He was the man that had beaten up the Worm Boy. Our eyes locked. We understood each other.

I passed a row of taxis. I needed to walk this off. But before I left the nightlife behind and headed for the deserted residential district that was my home, I paid a brief visit to a 24-hour pharmacy.

THE PIMP

I knew about the worms. Found some in Timmy's shit, when the toilet hadn't flushed properly. I asked him did he want medicine for it. He shook his head and hugged his belly proudly, looking sort of all maternal.

Fair enough, I thought, it's his choice. If he wants to keep 'em, who am I to say *no*? They were, like, his pets, I suppose. It never bothered me that they were there, living inside him, somehow a part of Timmy.

'Just don't do any anal with the customers,' I told him and he nodded vigorously.

THE TRICK

The next day I went back to the street where the Worm Boy plied his trade. I hid in the shadows, not wanting him to see me just yet. Then back-tracked and bought two take-away hot chocolates from the nearest coffee bar. I made sure I took a wooden stirrer.

I returned to my dark hiding place and dumped the powder into one of the drinks. It wasn't precisely dosed but this would probably be my only chance.

He looked anxious when he saw me approaching. I was afraid he might run, so I waved and performed a huge smile.

He looked at me, then away, at me, away. When I was in range I thrust out the drugged chocolate, as though to shake his hand, making sure he took it.

'It's 25 quid for a blow-job.'

'I just came to say *sorry*, for yesterday, it was –' I fished three tenners out of my Levi's. I wanted to make sure I had bought half an hour of his life. 'I just want to talk, OK?'

I sat down on a stone step and sipped my chocolate. He sat beside me. I tried to touch him but he pulled away. Looking sideways at him, I thought of a figure in a cartoon – sticks for arms poking out of the sleeves of a too tight T-shirt, like he was a child growing out of it, the belly only half-concealed. I wanted to fuck him so badly. That moron. That *monster*. Thin legs in pants tight as stockings.

He spilled chocolate on himself and his hands got sticky. I half expected him to start salivating like a baby. He wasn't looking at me.

I imagined introducing him to my friends. He'd never get past the front door of The Out Side. Taking him to dinner would be a major embarrassment. At parties I'd have to pass him off as my adopted sponsored victim, or tell everyone he was off his head on Ketamine. And I didn't think I'd like him spending a lot of time at my flat and getting too cosy there. But I'd miss the sex.

He drank quickly. The chocolate was lukewarm. When he finished, I stood my half full cup against the wall, thanked the Worm Boy for his time and left.

THE PIMP

It was the hot chocolate, Timmy said. He'd got home that day feeling sick, clutching his belly, spent the next hour crapping and puking. It didn't make any sense. Timmy'd had hot chocolate before, many times. I asked him had someone roughed him up, and he didn't answer. I took him to the doctor, who said it was an allergic reaction to the de-wormer, and that it would pass, and that the main thing was that the worms were dead. Timmy cried, and the doctor said that surely the pain wasn't that bad.

I took the boy home, and he cried mostly for the next few days. He crapped more than usual for two weeks. He'd had quite a lot of them packed in there. All dead now. His body flattened out. Timmy's a lean machine now, angular and well-proportioned. He's making more money too.

But he was miserable all the time, brushed my hand away when I touched him.

The flat became a tip and he stopped doing the cooking. We had a bit more money, so I hired a cleaner for a day a week. When her cat had kittens I persuaded her to let me have one for Timmy. And finally Timmy stopped crying and being sad. It was a little tortoiseshell kitten, barely old enough to leave its mother. He called it Tommy, and I said *It's a girl-cat*, but he ignored me. Whenever Timmy sat down or lay down, Tommy climbed onto him. She took up sphinx-position on his chest, purring proudly, or curled up on his sunken belly and went to sleep. In profile sometimes Timmy looked as if his belly had returned.

He let me love him again.

For a while everything went back to normal, but then the kitten got run over by a truck, and Timmy started crying again. I don't know what to do now. I don't dare get him another pet. I guess I just have to be there for him now more than ever.

THE TRICK

I'm dating fat guys now. None are quite like the Worm Boy, of course – their bellies less soft, often they've got more fat on the rest of them, or they're squat, chubby, but also more intelligent, educated, discerning and economically secure, more grateful too. It seems they can't believe that a fit and gorgeous guy like me would fancy them.

The other day I walked through that street for the first time since I poisoned the Worm Boy. I expected him to be gone, but he's still there, leaning against the wall, much more clearly male now, and slim like the boys I used to like.

He no longer holds any interest for me.

WHEN NIGHT REVEALED THE HEAVENS
Ramon Gonzales

The view from the top of the cliff by the sea-shore revealed a flat and barren landscape devoid of any human habitation that stretched as far as the eye could see. It had turned dusk and across the sea a few orange-stained clouds revealed the spot where the disk of the sun had just retreated beyond the horizon. Caressed by a gentle summer breeze I lay on the ground and almost instantly I fell into a slumber.

When I awoke it was night and all around me was enveloped in the deadness and silence of darkness, but high above there was a firmament of flickering stars. Scanning the sky I delighted in gazing at the constellations; amongst them I spotted the planet Venus, disguised as the Evening Star and the brightest amongst the real ones – its disguise betrayed by its almost imperceptible journey across the heavens.

Right above me was the Milky Way, that luminous trail which gave the name to our galaxy, also known in Spain as 'Camino de Santiago' as it was thought to have guided Christian pilgrims from all over Europe to the tomb of Saint James in Santiago de Compostela. As a small child, as in a flash of revelation, I believed that God had put it there for that purpose and thus confirming his existence. I now know that it simply points to the centre of our galaxy and its orientation is no guidance to us mortals anywhere on this Earth, no longer the centre of the Universe.

I knew that all the stars that I could see were only a fraction amongst some two hundred billion that formed our galaxy in a Cosmos of countless trillions of others, perhaps the number was infinite. The idea of infinity filled me with incomprehension, astonishment, awe and some kind of terror; indeed, I was experiencing the sublime.

Could it be that in the immensity of the Universe, ours was the only living planet? The idea seemed absurd. I imagined countless other worlds where life had evolved into rational beings who shared with us a free will and a moral sense, also an aesthetic sense which might have allowed another being in another planet to look into the night-sky and in that moment in time, share with me the beauty in the wonder of Creation.

I could only be sure that in the eternity of time, my life was transitory and ephemeral, that the matter which made my body would soon be no more, but would continue in its perpetual transformation and become part of other bodies, other lives, and the soul's treacherous desire for immortality without the body would not be fulfilled, for the soul needs the body – the life giver, the prison, the paradox – to make the person.

I awoke from my reverie disconcerted by the disappearance of a part of the starry-sky which had earlier reached the horizon. I then watched as the stars were enveloped by a mantle of black velvet which spread across the sky plunging it into darkness. It then liquefied colourless and descended on an earth as dark and invisible as myself.

THREE POEMS
Daniel Clements

HAIKU ONE

A summery smile
our eyes meet for a moment
we both walk on by

HAIKU TWO

A chill in the night
his scent in the winter air
his breath on my neck

UNTITLED

We had spent so many evenings talking into the night; politics, people, love
I devoured every word that came out of your perfect mouth
I knew that I cared about you more than I could say
That first night for us, last of my childhood
You were waiting for me with a smile
We didn't speak, only in actions
You took me to your room
You held me tightly
You laid me down
You undressed
We kissed.
Kissed
Licked
Sucked
Gasped
And breathe.
You were warm
I was just breathless
Wondering if I had changed
Or if everything was the same
I wanted it to always be this way
Believed we would be together forever.
I cried on the day that you left the last time
Chest heaving, tears streaming, heart breaking
If only you had known how much you meant to me then.
I wonder if you ever think back to the evening talks, the smile, the first night.

JULIE AND CAROL
Alice F. Wickham

Julie Brocklehurst woke up one day with a splitting headache. A single thought reverberated through her brain. 'I'm fifty'. She took two painkillers and swallowed them with a glass of tap water. 'Fifty.' A second thought filtered through her mind as she put the coffee pot on the burner. 'Carol's pregnant.'

The first thought had an excuse, it was rational, after all, she had turned fifty. It had taken three bottles of wine, ten cigarettes, and one calorie-infested four-cheese pizza but turned she had, and there was no going back. The second thought was odd. It hovered there in front of her eyes like an escaped bat. What right did it have to exist? Carol had been trying for five years to have a baby. Five solid, mid-life crisis years. There was no way, in her mid-forties, she was suddenly turning up pregnant.

Julie laughed at her image in the mirror. 'What brought that thought to my mind?' She tried to recall any strange dreams. Something that might have implanted such an odd thought in her brain – but her dreams were non-existent.

It occurred to Julie, as she stepped under the shower, that if Carol had been pregnant, it would put their friendship in jeopardy. She looked down at her bloated tummy and tried to remember the last time she had seen pubic hair from that angle. To her surprise, a red rivulet trickled down her thigh. She put a finger into her vagina and felt the old slippery sensation. A left-over egg? Her finger, when she extracted it, was drenched in blood. The final thought that Julie Brocklehurst had that morning was 'Wow, I could still get pregnant'. When Julie reached for a towel hanging on the shower screen, she slithered onto her spine, cracking two of her lower neck vertebrae. She lay semi-conscious for about ten seconds before her breathing slowed to zero. It was a tragic end, but relatively stress-free, when one considers how life can play out. Julie Brocklehurst wasn't to know about the cancerous tumour lurking in her ovaries, predestined to grow to the size of an apple, and then to a melon. Julie was spared that journey, at least.

Carol was standing on the tube station platform in Waterloo, waiting for a train and thinking about how much she had drunk the night before. Far too much. It was Julie's fault. OK, she was fresh into her fifties, and she had the right to celebrate but did they have to drink so much?

It was kind of sad, Carol thought, that Julie should have had no 'special person' with whom to share her fiftieth birthday, but did women really need men? She and Julie had had a whale of a time, recalling old adventures in their twenties and thirties. Two failed marriages later, they both relied on one another for emotional support in an increasingly harsh young world.

Strap hanging her way to Baker Street, Carol thought she could detect a faint whiff of pre-menstrual hormone coming from her body, and the thought mortified her. A man turned and gave her a brutal stare. Pulling her iPod from her bag and wheeling through two hundred tracks, at last, she found a melody appropriate for the circumstances and she plugged a set of earphones into her ears. The Buddhist mantra cooled her anxiety about her body's strange smell.

When she reached the office, Carol went straight to the bathroom where she discovered she was not yet bleeding, but the hormonal odour persisted. Was it her imagination? Or did the scent of her body permeate the office?

The thought came to check on her friend Julie to see how she was faring. Julie was bound to have a bad hangover – they were not as young as they once were. Gone were the days when they could stay out until 3 a.m., return home steaming drunk, and still wake up bright-eyed and bushy-tailed for work the next day. Carol made a mental note to text her friend at lunchtime.

The new fee earner was a psychopath – like so many of these young lawyers, fresh out of law school, she had too much in the way of balls and not enough humanity. A chit of a girl, she knew less about legal process than Carol herself did. The girl's youthful ambition and impatient manner grated on Carol's nerves, but she was not about to tarnish her reputation as the unflappable PA, and she was certainly not going to allow this young harpy to disturb the pleasant working environment that had taken her years to cultivate.

Carol swallowed the humiliation of attending to the little madam. At around 11 a.m. a bizarre thought entered her consciousness. 'Julie's dead'. Naturally, she dismissed the idea. It had flickered into her mind and was gone, like a cinema scene.

At 12.30 p.m. Carol looked at her face in the bathroom mirror at work. She saw dark rings under her blue eyes, and she felt she had to own up to the fact that her eyelids were starting to sag, a little. She saw lines etching themselves into her nasolabial folds, but according to her latest wonder cream, with SPF dual protection, this problem could be easily fixed. Her hair was holding out, considering she hadn't treated it in over a month, but underneath the dark blonde highlights, Carol knew the truth. She was mostly grey. 'And yet,' she told herself, 'I'm still getting my period, so I could still get pregnant.'

But what sort of creature would she produce at forty-five years of age? It was anyone's guess. Didn't she know about the danger of deteriorating eggs? Having a baby would be madness, the cells would be weak, not robust, and one could expect to produce a child with a flaw of some sort. Besides, what baby would wish to be born in the womb of an older woman? The foetus would be about as fresh as a week-old lettuce. She and Julie were old enough to be grandmothers.

At 5 p.m., she applied lipstick and dabbed shadow on her lids. She told her image in the mirror. 'I'm still tasty and nutritious, good enough to eat, if a little curled at the edges.' She sent Julie another text. 'Hi Julie, hope your head hurts as much as mine! I'm meeting Lysander at the NT tonight to discuss our "relationship".' Julie didn't reply. Probably at home sleeping off her hangover, thought Carol.

Carol arrived at the National Theatre at 6 p.m. She hadn't seen Lysander since the night she had caught him shagging a younger woman and she was feeling nervous and insecure. Lysander was half-an-hour late, as usual. His prerogative, Carol decided as she sipped more of her wine. Lysander's height, boyish charm, and the fact that he was only forty-one gave him certain inalienable rights. He arrived, flustered and apologetic. They made up over a second bottle of Sauvignon. Lysander shed a tear. He told Carol he loved her. She accepted, what choice did she have?

They returned to her flat above the Art Gallery in Teddington. Carol's hangover still bothered her but she felt it her duty to oblige. After all, she was the one who had called the meeting.

Lysander undressed and hung his jacket and trousers in the wardrobe, and then he folded his smalls and placed them in the armoire.

Naked and aroused, he took Julie in his arms and began kissing the top of her head.

'You're my woman,' he told her. 'I don't want to lose you.'

Pressed to his chest, barely reaching his shoulders, Carol felt more like Lysander's child than his woman. She snuggled into his broadness and allowed herself to float off as he stroked her hair. Lysander was eager to make love. They lay on Carol's bed and kissed, if not passionately, then enough to inspire a solid sense of togetherness. Lysander soon entered her and Carol concentrated on the task at hand. When Lysander climaxed, she felt a peculiar tug in her womb. A voice deep down insisted that he had somehow managed to impregnate her, despite her precautions. Nonsense, she told herself, but she held on tighter than usual to her lover.

Julie woke up in the tub. She gazed down at the inactive form, the mouth half-opened in a grimace. She stared at it in wonder. 'Was that me?' She stepped out of the tub and into a white light. 'So this is it, the final curtain.' There was no hesitation, she walked straight into the tunnel. Halfway along, Julie met her mother – the schoolteacher – who said in gentle tones for once, 'Julie, my love, what are you doing here?' The look on her mother's face took Julie by surprise. Her mother was clearly smiling.

'Mum, I could say the same about you,' Julie said.

'It's not time yet dear,' Julie's mother said. 'Go back, you have a life to live.'

Julie felt the usual irritation at her mother's interference. 'No, I don't, my life is over.'

'That life, yes,' her mother said.

The perspective Julie had of her mother changed. The figure was now off in the far distance, a speck, but it was not her mother who had moved, it was she, Julie, who was spinning back through time. As the light faded, Julie was caught in darkness, shrinking, shrinking, shrinking to the size of a pea, then to a grain of rice, then smaller still. She was an atom, folding in on itself, lost in a black sea of particles, and then her mind collapsed and she was gone.

At first, Lysander's reaction was predictable. 'I'm not sure I'm ready for fatherhood, and isn't it rather dangerous, having a child at your age?'

Carol looked him in the eye. 'If you are not prepared to

support me on this journey, fine, I'll go it alone, but I'm having this baby, Lysander, and you're going to be a father, whether you like it or not.'

Her words sounded brave, but inside she was quaking with fear. With Julie gone, who could she now lean on in her time of need? Julie had been like a mother, a sister, a companion, all rolled into one.

Lysander's long elegant fingers toyed with the coffee cup. His words took her by surprise. 'Look, Carol, I love you and I'm not about to abandon you. Isn't it time we moved in together?'

Carol felt elated. Good old co-dependency, you could always depend on it. As they walked hand-in-hand along the embankment, gazing at the boats cruising up and down the river, Carol felt joy tinged with sadness. She was thinking of her friend again. 'Where is she now, I wonder?'

And a voice inside seemed to say, 'I'm right here, Carol.'

RESTORATIVE JUSTICE
Donald West

In his silent, deserted bungalow, Daniel woke up to some unhappy thoughts. He regretted letting his wife persuade him to move to a place by the sea on his retirement. He had lost contact with friends and work colleagues. To make matters worse she had developed a rapidly progressing paralysis. Confined to the house, looking after her single-handed until her death, he had lost the habit of socialising. Their only child, a family man living in Australia, had been no help. Now nearly eighty, he was spending his days glued to the television. He dreaded a monotonous future, inevitable decline, loss of independence and being put into a home for the aged and decrepit. He had already spent several uncomfortable months immobilised following hip replacement operations, when he was at the mercy of a series of strangers, social workers less concerned with his welfare than completing forms and telephoning their office. At the moment his general health wasn't too bad, but walking was tiring and he was prone to breathlessness, which he thought bad signs.

Trying to shake off his depressed mood, he got up and was crossing the living room. At first glance he noticed nothing, but feeling a draft he saw one window was open, a curtain dangling outside and fragments of window pane on the floor below. The room was undisturbed, but a pair of old silver candlesticks and a carriage clock, the only antiques he possessed, were gone from the mantel piece. A burglar must have broken through the window while he was asleep, grabbed the most obvious things, and departed.

In shock, Daniel gazed at the empty spaces on the mantel. Rousing himself, he began sweeping up the broken window glass. The thought came to him that a more desperate criminal could have murdered him and ransacked the place. He sat down, fear overcoming the idea that he really had nothing left to live for. He knew he ought to ring 999 and, still trembling, was about to do so when the doorbell rang and he saw a policeman on the porch.

By chance, an off-duty policeman, walking by during the night, had spotted a young man with a parcel coming out of the gate of Daniel's bungalow, looking up and down before hurrying away. His suspicions were confirmed when he noticed the broken window with the curtain flapping. He caught up with the young man, showed his badge, asked his name and demanded to see what was in the parcel. Harold knew he was trapped and offered no resistance as he was led away to the police station. Next morning a policeman, forestalling Daniel's 999 call, visited the bungalow to tell him his burglar had been apprehended and he should come to the police station to identify his property. Weeks went by, with Daniel still worrying about the possibility of further intrusions, when he had an unexpected caller.

'I'm Vernon Harrison a social worker for the magistrates. I have news about your burglar. He's called Harold Eastman and he's on bail awaiting sentence. We'd like your co-operation.'

'What do you mean, what do you want from me?'

'He's twenty-four, has no previous convictions, with a good character reference from his employer and a history of recent domestic trouble. The court thought he might be a suitable candidate for their experiment in restorative justice. He would need to meet you, apologise for the upset he has caused, and agree to a plan of restitution. It could be a hundred hours of voluntary unpaid work, helping you for three months, doing gardening, shopping, cleaning, painting, or whatever you think might be useful.'

'I don't know about that. I think anyone who breaks in at night should go to prison. Having him around is the last thing I expected. It's frightening.'

'People often feel like that at first, but I would be his supervisor. I've been trained in mediation and would be in close touch with you in case of any problems. He would be on conditional caution and discharge, which means that if he defaulted or behaved badly he would be brought back to court and sentenced accordingly. You would be doing a generous act for society, to rescue a young man from imprisonment, loss of job prospects and pressure towards a life of crime.' Despite misgivings, Daniel found it difficult to refuse in the face of persistent reassurance.

As the day came for Daniel to attend the social worker's office and be introduced to Harold Eastman, his anxieties returned. He feared meeting an ugly, aggressive brute, but found instead a clean-looking, neatly dressed and quite handsome young man of athletic build, pleasantly filling out a neat, sober suit. Harold was soft spoken and polite, advancing sincere apologies and a wish to be of service. He had lost his job after his arrest, so he could work whenever convenient, but if he found another job he would put in hours during evenings and week-ends. If the judge approved the plan at the forthcoming trial, he could start immediately.

When Harold appeared at the bungalow for the first time, Daniel felt awkward about assigning tasks, although there was no lack of things to do. He had long ceased trying to keep up appearances. The bungalow was shabby, with curtains and upholstery unkempt, paintwork grubby, outside hedges sprawling, flower beds overrun with nettles and grass full of moss and weeds. Harold smiled and said there were things he might help with. It was settled that the one hundred hour contract over three months would be fulfilled by two and a half hours Tuesday and Friday, three on Sunday, beginning the following Tuesday, and always starting at nine-thirty. Before leaving, Harold asked 'Is there anything I can do now, while I am here?' Daniel pointed to a burnt-out ceiling light. Replacing the bulb required unscrewing the shade and Daniel was shaky on stepladders. Harold saw to it at once.

A honeymoon phase followed. Harold proved cheerful, friendly and willing. Soon the parting cup of tea produced by Harold at twelve-thirty became a snack. Then the mid-day snack became a lunch and Harold started finding extra things to do and staying on. One morning, when Daniel was still trying to cut his toenails and finding it a struggle, Harold soon took charge. He was swiftly becoming indispensable. Far from worrying about a criminal being around, Daniel was beginning to wonder how he was going to manage when the three months were over.

One day Daniel remarked that he missed being able to soak in a hot bath. He could stand up under the shower overhanging the bath, but climbing out of the bath from a lying position had become difficult. Harold insisted on helping. Harold ran the bath and when Daniel had undressed Harold helped him lower himself into the bath. 'Call me when you want to get out,' he said. When Daniel called he was surprised to find Harold stripped off and stepping into the bath. 'Let me help you stand up.' After that was accomplished he said, 'Let me soap you down before drying.' Daniel felt firm, well-soaped hands passing over his chest and back, flanks and thighs and finally over his genitals. He felt sensations he had not had for a long time and was embarrassed by the beginnings of an erection. Harold gave no sign of embarrassment. He finished the drying off without comment, and let Daniel dress himself.

The incident left an impression. Daniel kept recalling Harold's attractive young physique and his own reactions and wondered if it was wise to encourage a repetition of the bathing routine. He felt more strongly than ever that he was going to miss Harold. When the completion of the three month court order was approaching Daniel tripped over and was badly bruised. Harold rushed to his assistance.

'You really need someone to look after you all the time,' he chided.

'That's as maybe, but I don't fancy social services carers, and I can't afford expensive private help.'

'Why don't you employ me living in? Much cheaper than visiting carers. We get on fine and I enjoy being of help.'

When the court order expired, Harold took up occupancy of the spare bedroom and a new phase began. Having found no other work, he became a full-time housekeeper. Except on his days off, he did the cooking and they took meals together. He liked spending time tidying the garden and demonstrating his handyman skills, repainting the shabby walls and mending the leaking conservatory. Before long they were taking outings together, their formal master-servant status fading away. The bath-soaping ritual continued, but not quite as before, Harold usually not bothering to strip off or step into the bath himself, so that propriety was preserved, and Daniel's involuntary responses on some occasions were never referred to.

Despite spending as much time together as a married couple, their conversations generally avoided the topic of Harold's crime, but from occasional references to it Daniel pieced together a rough, exculpatory version. Harold was the product of a violent and abusive home from which he escaped by finding work and lodgings at an early age. Lacking education he was condemned to poor pay and short-term posts. He had acquired a girlfriend and they were saving up to buy a flat, but she was impatient and he needed to get money quickly. She had a friend with a market junk stall and encouraged him to risk occasional break-ins to obtain goods to sell on this stall. She had deserted him when he was arrested. Daniel believed this and sympathised, though he did not much like Harold excusing his behaviour with the adage 'Desperate situations make for desperate measures'.

As Daniel's attachment and dependence increased, he realised that young Harold needed some life of his own, so he made no demur when Harold announced that he had found another girlfriend and would like to have her back to sleep with him sometimes. Daniel had to admit that the sounds of their noisy love-making made him jealous, especially as gradually increasing involvement with the girl meant rather less devotion to him. However, after an emotional conversation, when Daniel remarked on a lessening of their time together, Harold swore he would never give up his caring role, and Daniel was reassured.

Soon after this Daniel received a rare visit from Edwin, one of the few friends from his working days who kept in touch. Harold made them an excellent dinner and Daniel was able to tell Edwin how his life had been transformed by Harold's presence. As Edwin was due to leave Harold's girlfriend arrived. With the briefest of greetings she disappeared into Harold's bedroom. As Edwin was leaving he remarked to Daniel 'I hope she won't make a difference'.

The decline with age that Daniel had feared was coming about and he was using a wheelchair and needing Harold's help to push him. The situation eased with the acquisition of a motorised chair that Daniel learned to manoeuvre unaided. Harold would accompany him sometimes, walking alongside on the favourite routes they had enjoyed when Daniel was able to walk unaided. One of these was a hilly path following the shoreline, with lovely views across the bay. It was there that the accident happened. For some reason, perhaps because Daniel pressed the wrong lever, the chair made a quick jerk forward, veered to one side and toppled down the steep slope to the shore. It was not a long fall, but Daniel was flung from the chair and broke a leg. The shock precipitated a fatal heart attack.

At the inquest Harold testified that because at that point the path was narrow and he was walking behind, he failed to grab the chair when it suddenly lurched beyond his reach. In the absence of any witness, misadventure was the inevitable verdict. It was no surprise that Daniel's will gave the bungalow and the small remainder of his savings to his dear friend 'in recognition of loyal service'.

When attending Daniel's funeral his old friend Edwin muttered the insinuating remark: 'One hopes Daniel's fear of being killed by an intruder hasn't finally come to pass'. The person sitting next nudged him and silently pointed to the royal coat of arms on the wall bearing the motto 'Honi soit qui mal y pense'. On hearing of some spiteful gossip following the funeral Harold did not let it disturb him. He was in possession of a comfortable residence, greatly improved by his years of 'restorative' effort, and much appreciated by his young bride.

THE TWIST OF THE VICE
Jeremy Kingston

When it became known that I am not a man, despite the evidence of the author's name printed on the title page of my books, I was soon the recipient of letters forwarded from my publishers asking 'Mr Quintin Jessel' if that particular name possessed a resonance that I should have chosen to conceal my sex behind it.

I would reply that two persons bearing names much like those had played significant roles in my childhood. At that I would leave it, although of course much more could have been said, and in my latest book *The Twist of the Vice* I give in coded form a fuller account.

I do not know if the Misses Charlotte, Emily and Anne Brontë received letters asking why they submitted their books under the particular names of Currer, Ellis and Acton Bell; but the reason that, like myself, they chose a man's name was because we wished to write of stresses concerning which we, as women, were supposed (by men) to have no knowledge. I mean, to cut it shortly, the frenzy of erotic desire, the ecstasy this can bring when it is satisfied, but when suppressed becomes a mania that can hurtle its stubborn sufferer towards murder.

Attempts are being made to identify the original of the place I name Spigh Hall and I do not expect, nor indeed do I wish, those attempts to be unsuccessful. *The Twist of the Vice* was written because I could not do otherwise: the death of my twelve-year-old brother Miles at the hands – I should say in the hands – of our wicked governess has darkened my life; and while the work of recalling and recreating those terrible last weeks at Bly brought grief anew, the prospect that she might at last be identified, exposed and ruined brought to me at the least a possibility of heartsease.

I choose not to give the creature her actual name, nor even hint at it in a punning manner; but Squawky is indeed the nickname my brother gave to her, for she was a pathetic sort of human hen, frantic to become a mother, aware that no cockerel would ever be enticed by her, and reduced to snatching at other people's chicks in the evil desire to make them hers.

She was reared in a small and superstitious Hampshire village where the vicar was her father, an impecunious and lackadaisical person who of course burdened his wife with a quiverfull of offspring. Squawky was the youngest of five daughters, all but the eldest – of whom she was insanely jealous – destined to become governesses and remain spinsters their whole life through.

There is a sort of desperate woman who will throw herself at any man, and when deprived of him, and in the absence of a successor, throw herself at his memory. From the rage felt at her deprivation she will create an enemy in whom her desire, perverted into revulsion, can be embodied.

Such a woman was the she-devil Squawky, foisted upon us by our uncle who cannot be exonerated of blame for blinding himself to the danger to which, by appointing her our governess, he was thereby exposing us. He was a man of considerable charm, a confirmed bachelor, expressing no interest in women, though his manner captivated them when he wished for this. I later came to see him as supremely selfish, although in his defence it must be said that he had never expected to become guardian to two young orphaned relatives.

Mr Quint had been his valet, much indulged by him, and together they had journeyed throughout Europe and even beyond. When Mr Quint became enamoured of Jessel this did not, my uncle was to tell me, anger him but he could see no place for Jessel in his immediate household. The solution he seized upon was to give Mr Quint supreme authority in the running of Bly, with Jessel appointed our governess, while he exchanged the position of reluctant country squire for a city life he found more congenial to his tastes.

That halcyon period in our lives was cut short by Mr Quint's fatal accident, which plunged poor sweet Jessel into inconsolable grief. Much though she loved us she could not endure to stay. So it was that she was replaced by Squawky and our lives became irreparably disordered.

Oh, how she fussed over us! took every opportunity to claw us into her embrace! called us constantly her little angels, her precious ones, her darlings, her sweetest of the sweet, her dearests — How we endured her slobberings I can hardly say, though I believe we took our endurance as a sort of challenge. Miles said to me, on one of the increasingly rare occasions when she had left us alone in each other's company, 'It will be interesting, will it not, if we let her continue this slobberiness, just to see where it will lead her?'

Alas that a course determined in a spirit of enquiry should have brought about such terrible consequences.

She pretended to see ghosts, and perhaps did see them, for her mind can never have been securely hinged. First it was the ghost of Mr Quint, staring at her from the North Tower; she was entirely certain it was he, she told Mrs Grose, the housekeeper at that time, even though she had never cast eyes upon him in life, and he would have been, on the battlements of the tower, a hundred yards distant from her. Then she saw him prowling outside the house and on the terrace. After this came a ghost she 'knew' to be Jessel's, and this presented Grose with the evidence that she was lying because, though she had foolishly told Squawky that Jessel was dead, she was still alive, and is to this day.

Grose was sworn to secrecy but of course she told Agnes,

the housemaid, who told Luke, the groom, and everyone, including Miles and myself. The ghosts kept popping out of the woodwork, and she was regularly to be found, though I only became witness to this the once, hurling abuse and cursing at the vacant air.

Of course Grose should have reported these outbursts but she was a simple woman, awed by authority, and Squawky was a ruthless bully. She refused to accept that Miles and I did not share her visions, and made herself believe we only pretended blindness because of some infernal pact we had already entered into with them. Her habit was to question us shrilly, and before we had assembled our bewildered thoughts she would put, like a witch-hunter, into the air between us the answer she required, demanding that we then affirm it. In the days when Miles and I could still treat her ravings as an amusement we would deliberately leave half-finished our answer to a question in order to see what new nonsense she would inevitably put into our mouth.

At last I had had enough of her tirades. On that last afternoon, beside the lake, when she could persuade neither Mrs Grose nor I to say we saw Jessel striding along the far shore, I turned upon her, called her a mad virgin and a harlot – thus showing how much I had yet to learn about the ways of the world, even though Mr Quint had entertained us often enough with tales of his foreign adventures. I told her I hated the sight of her foul face, and I can see as clearly as if she stood before me now her expression of appalled astonishment. No one had ever before possessed the strength of mind to confront her in this manner. Her mouth sagged open, she fell howling to the ground, and we left her writhing at the water's edge. Had she then cast herself into it how much happier our lives would have been. Early the next morning Grose conveyed me to London, to the security of my uncle's house in Harley Street.

Next day came the dreadful news that she had killed Miles. Luke had been a horror-struck eavesdropper outside the dining-room where she was shouting at my poor brother to make him say he saw Mr Quint outside the window. She was ordered to London and dismissed the moment she presented herself. The proper course would have been to have her arrested on a charge of murder but my uncle chose to have her conveyed to an asylum. From here she managed to extricate herself and when, years later, Jessel and I located her she was a governess again, in a family named Douglas (Duncan in my book). She was trying her seductive tricks on her young charge's older brother, at that time a student at Cambridge.

We managed to terminate her employment there, whereupon she once again disappeared from view. Now that we have run her down for what will prove to be the last time I am sending a copy of *Vice* to her employer, an industrialist's widow too deaf to have marked the ramblings of the creature serving as her companion. Jessel and I will then present ourselves to Squawky, and if my reappearance does not strip out the last vestiges of her sanity then the sight of Jessel, no longer wraith but fleshly flesh and blood, should bang the coffin lid down upon her for good and all.

And my dear brother, who gave such delight to everyone permitted to enjoy his charms, will be avenged.

FIVE POEMS
Chris Beckett

LEMON FOR LOVE

Today Mahmoud Ahmed is singing again
wailing out of Abebe's radio

> *lemon for love! lemon for love!*
> *lemon you are so sweet*

his voice is long and stringy as a branch
it throws the lemon down at his girlfriend's feet

lemon for love! lemon you are so tasty!
if she picks it up, it means she will marry him

now the chorus is shouting *hohohohoho!*
clapping all its hands, stamping its fifty feet

now Abebe's fingers are jumping and clicking
his shoulders shaking! his knees popping!

because the girl in the song is beautiful as Makda,
                                    Queen of Sheba
and yes! she has bent to pick up the lemon

Mahmoud Ahmed, you must never stop singing
your voice can make anything happen

it twists round my brain like the roots of a tree
it opens a fresh leaf in my heart

Mahmoud Ahmed, if I sit here by Abebe's window
will you throw my lemon for me?

WHEN I WAS TEN, I STARTED WATCHING MEN

Early morning, sun still cool, a young man stops
outside our gate and burns my eyes

   be my boy wife!

he says, but not in words

an old and honourable role in goldmines, coalmines
so why not in a city high enough to take your breath away?

the young man smiles over his shoulder
as he starts to piss

years later, in a book, I hear the voice of a Kikuyu boy
who also started watching men when he was ten

he watched them going quickly into public toilets
one day he went into a public toilet too

   ayeeee! it was disgusting!

he'd never *ever* do again, what he did
inside that filthy toilet with a man

but soon, his hunger back, more like a storm than sunshine
he did it once again, again, again

and there he was bewildered! rubbing his wide eyes
then rushing home to brush his teeth *like all eternity*

THREE SLAVES OF SODOM
GO TO THE MERCATO

(for Robel Hailu)

A trinity of cursed boys
two short, one tall, their hair in corkscrews
so the air must feel it

sit in Tomoco's
sipping three small lions of coffee
from Harar

before they sally out again
freely but together, like a small fleet of lake-dhows
into the deep souks of the Mercato

where all admire the width
of their smiles, how warmly their boat-fingers praise
a cotton or the fish-buckle of a belt

and one stallholder, whom they call *Gashay!*
(meaning *My Shield!* to express affection for the sort of older man
who plays an uncle figure lightly, but with seriousness)

out-spreads his sails
as you would too – how we thirst for tolerance, a little keg of
colour to nurture the flame!

shouting

> *welcome, citizens!*
> *my brave-chinned zegas*

and everything his stall possesses
of traditional shirts and shawls, and cheerful prices
gets up on its feet and sings

To the Teeming Bookshops
of Addis Ababa

A thirst for knowledge being one
of the most urgent

do you see this brush-stroke of a boy sprinting
from Arat Kilo
                    down the length of Wingate

                                        into Piassa?

if stopped, either by his shirttails (flying)
or a hand on his athlete's shoulder
even on his athlete thoughts (also flying)

he would say a rumour just reached him
too insistent for day-dream

that a new translation of Rimbaud's *Bateau Ivre* is hitting
the milky surface of your shelves

though he already owns a tattered copy in the French
and two or three in English, plus one of almost holy status

in Amharic

   Yesekere Merkeb!

knowing he will see the same loved, breathing body of the

                                                    poem

behind the gauze of each re-working

only adds to his excitement   the knowledge he craves
not in facts

but in the energy of words racing
on their bare feet
from language to language, bookshop, laptop
getting fitter and faster
the more they are taken into the thin air of the mountains
                                                    and stretched

ELEGY FOR A THUNDERSTORM

What is a storm if not weeping?
and the boy washing
himself in the storm
with a rough hand and rough soap
is he not a great trunk of water
attracting thirsty looks of men on the track?

rain grieves when our loved-ones
suffer from drought
it fills our ears with its sadness
so how can we not cry
when rain weakens
and the storm is put out?

one restless afternoon
a thunderstorm
like a stampede of buffalos
like the hide of a panther thrown over the earth
still roaring and hissing
like a colossal road traffic accident

on the muddiest section
of motorway between Addis Ababa
and the underworld
when everyone rats into their holes
and the town sags
and starts to break apart

the possibilities for great
naughtiness dawn
amongst wet bodies of children
even rainbuckets lick their lips
as another crash
of thunder unties a row of small houses

and the storm looks at itself, amazed
by its own strength
frightened even, maybe it knows
this is too much water
in a land of historical famines
too purple this shower

for people with such clean noses
and a religion washed
in Nile-water
so it looks all-round for a tap
somewhere up there
in the metal-grey clouds

and turns itself off
leaving memories
of great bell-drops banging
on roofs that cause even the roofs
them-tin-selves
and the boy scrubbing his arms

to sing this elegy
for the unforgettable
thunderstorm
of their life
seeing that none of us is as strong
as our desires

DOG MINDER'S MONDAY MORNING
Elizabeth J. Lister

Jeez! The mud washed down by last night's storm-rain! Where to go? Scottish Border country and I only know the path through the Loaning and up round the fields. I squelch in my wellies and take my hands out of my pockets in case I stagger and need to break my fall. God help my arthritic wrist if I do! The dog's feet! Wash them in the bath when we get back? I'll walk up the hill where the farmer's track is firmer ground.

Oh good, the sun has opened the tips of the rose-bay willow-herb flowers! What a bank of beauty that will be in a day or two; takes one's mind off the fact that dog walks are a daily round of poo-pick-ups in black plastic bags. Tomorrow I'll bring my camera. I captured the wild roses on film last week, huge cascades of pink flowers in the ten-foot high hedgerow, tumbling right down to eye level; and I got a good shot of buttercups but their time is over and now hogweed stands tall. I lose sight of the dog when he sniffs in amongst the tall grasses (and like it when he poos where I can't locate the deposit). I can't feel any affection for hogweed. Did we once make peashooters out of the stalks? I remember they didn't taste nice. Fancy that no one told us that hemlock is a similar plant!

I'll enter my two photos in the *Countryfile Calendar* competition because they're pretty; though probably not at all the standard the judges are looking for – and if I won I wouldn't know what to do with the advanced photographic equipment that is the prize. Might not bother.

Neighbour Wendy came at half-past eight, as she said she would. How anyone manages to be organised enough to come for a cuppa and chat before leaving at ten to catch a plane to Madeira I don't know. Last night she came with a left-over tub of chick peas and a bag full of fresh veg and salad stuffs and gave me an idea for an evening meal. And on Saturday she got married to Portuguese Eduardo! She arranged the details of the wedding herself, down to the last 'favour'.

'Did Eduardo help you?' my feminist hackles threaten to rise.

'Oh, we work together, you know what I mean?'

No, I don't! It would seem to me that you do the lion's share.

I took Wendy into town on Friday afternoon, to collect Eduardo's hired kilt for the wedding. A Portuguese Scot! On Sunday we returned the kilt, called at the art gallery to see the current exhibition, bought lavender and hebe plants at the nursery gardens and ended up in the village pub with beer and crisps. I don't know when I've had so much fun! I couldn't get the hang of this lovely girl, Wendy; her eyes shine, she's charged with energy and she laughs. I couldn't help wondering what her need was for my eighty-year old company and why she seemed to take pleasure in it. Then I noticed how frequently she mentions Grace who died at the age of ninety-three last November; evidently she cared for Grace for years. This morning Wendy confided that she was closer to her granny than her parents and it all came out about her having meningitis when she was a baby and not being 'normal'.

'My sister's normal,' she said, 'and my parents were fonder of her than they were of me. I think I was a worry to them and they were a bit ashamed of me, you know what I mean? They liked to keep an eye on me and I stayed at home until I was twenty-one. I didn't have a teenage, you know. But on

Saturday at the wedding my sister said she was sad because she hadn't got to know me better.'

'There's the rest of your lives,' I said.

'Mm, aye, but I do get on better with older people. I think my granny cared for me more than she did my sister; happen she felt for me because I wasn't quite right in my head. I went to special school with all the other ... you know, er ... children but I was lucky, wasn't I, because I was transferred to High School? I had to have a special teacher, you know what I mean? She kept an eye on which lessons I could do. I was bullied and the other kids made fun of me but I was good at woodwork. I made my own bookcase and I was good at domestic science but I can't stand pressure. I can't do with anyone watching over me but I can cook. I manage all right, don't I?'

'You manage very well,' I say with fervour.

'I worked at a chicken factory for my first job' (she says, rolling her Scottish Borders' Rs) 'but I had to count the rows of eggs and I could nae do that, you know what I mean? So I went to the fish factory and I've been there for twenty-one years. If there's anything I need to remember the supervisor writes it down and puts the bit of paper in front of me and then I do everything right. I'm a bit slow, you know what I mean? I have the dyslexia.'

Is it dyslexia I wonder? Are all reading difficulties branded with the label dyslexia? I would say you have difficulties coping with the written word, Wendy, and what the hell does it matter when you work, shop, book holidays abroad, take pride in your garden and help other people? What a woman! You, Wendy, are a tonic.

After the pub yesterday I was invited to the upstairs flat to meet Eduardo.

'You'll see he does nae speak the English well but we understand each other fine, you know what I mean?'

'How do you expect him to learn English when he has to listen to the broad Scottish-Borders accent spoken by you, your friends and your workmates?' I ask, and she laughs.

Eduardo, a smallish man who also works at the fish factory, says he came here from Portugal for work. He made me a cup coffee. How is it that continental folk make such a good cup of coffee? I have beans and a grinder at home but my coffee is anaemic by comparison. Could it be because of their Dolce Gusto machine which Wendy looked up for me in the Argos catalogue? Wendy is pleased because I admire the wedding presents and the copious number of greeting cards. Eduardo and Wendy have lived together for eleven years.

'You haven't exactly hurried into marriage,' her game-keeper father says.

But Wendy was married before, as a young woman. Her husband died, drunk, swallowed his false teeth and choked to death! Could you make up a story like that? Wistful, she says, 'The doctor said I'll probably never get over it, you know what I mean?'

I can imagine.

'And no children?'

'I had two miscarriages. Eduardo was upset when we lost the baby, but I had nae bought anything, you know. It's bad luck to buy too soon. I've a blocked tube and it's no use bothering because I cannae have a baby. We have a good life and we enjoy our holidays, you know what I mean?'

Wendy, you are so sensible and beautiful! And if I could get hold of the woman who calls herself a hairdresser and who hacked at your fair, curly hair, making it into such a straggly mess, I would sack her. But your trust is childlike and you don't expect better.

'I'm more confident now. I did nae dare to go anywhere by myself at one time,' she says.

And confident you should be! Do you know that you are

the warmest, most genuine shining personality that I think I have ever met? I have only read about people like you and then it was the fictional. And I am one of those older women with whom you like to relate and it brings tears to my eyes because you want to be in my company, because you care about how I feel and repeatedly urge me not to do too much.

Forgive me that I wondered when we first met if I could cope with what I thought was 'your thrusting presence'; you have a kind, enthusiastic nature and you confuse my boundaries. I have a tendency to draw back and be cautious but you make it easy to be open with you and love you. In one week you have made an effortless transition from neighbour to friend, to joyful companion and it has nothing to do with gender and sexuality ... or has it?

I find I'm thinking about gerontophilia now you're not here; of loving and living with a partner who is years younger than oneself. I have never entertained the idea as I can't imagine that I would abandon my independence in favour of co-habitation at my late age or that a young person would choose to live with an elderly woman. It has always embarrassed me to imagine life with any of the young women I meet. I cringe and wonder whatever they would feel if they knew a woman like me had loving thoughts about them! But this is not the case with you, Wendy. You have enabled me to live the possibility in my thoughts without feeling shy. I can see that there would be warmth in loving and being loved by you, and enjoyment and happiness. It almost seems that choice doesn't enter the equation because love happens ... you know what I mean? Both of us free and willing to make new memories. Age doesn't seem to worry male/female relationships or a few of my 'mature' male friends who live happily with partners that are thirty years younger than themselves.

But you see I need so much time to myself in order to write

my stories and paint my paintings; could you cope with that, Wendy? You did say that you like to do things by yourself, so perhaps there would not be a problem and you would be out at work in the early mornings, which is when I write. But there is no fish factory where I live. Where would you work? We would have to live a little meanly if our only income was my state and teacher's pensions.

I've never had anyone to help me in the garden; that would be great and you would love my garden. There's the wooden swing by the tree paeony (the flowers are double pink) and it has a resting place each end for our mugs of tea, or glasses of wine; it's nicely screened by the minarette plum and green-gage trees. And the bench by the honeysuckle is for two, so are the corner seats under the silver birch tree. I would be glad to hand over the growing of tomatoes and cucumber in my little greenhouse to you and become your overseer.

I enjoy cooking; you say you like to eat well and it is much more interesting to make meals for two and sit together at the table or lounge in front of the telly. Ah ... but I can't see us choosing to watch the same programmes ... but you would have your own room with a telly. Enjoy films together? Oh, and the decorating! I haven't to move heavy things and can only paint small sections of wall at a time but I'd hold the ladder for you even if I couldn't climb it.

What would people say? That it was pleasant for me to have a young companion who could be of help as I deteriorated? Would they query whether we make love once the door is shut on the outside world but say, 'Na, they're not likely to be together for the sex, ha ha! Look how old she is; she wears hearing aids, you know, and all her teeth are not her own.' Because they wouldn't realise that it is your radiant face, comely body and the soft smooth skin of your shoulders which attract and which you offer willingly to be caressed by my experienced lover's hands.

You needn't know about this notion of mine, Wendy, in fact you must not know that your blithe self has engendered these thoughts. You are married and your idea of caring for older women is as a friend and nothing more. I must fit in, and be grateful for, a small place in your generous nature.

It's noon. The sun may have dried the paths a little. It's time to walk the dog or for the dog to walk me.

You will be boarding a plane to Madeira and I won't be here when you return because my dog-minding days end on Saturday. I was pleased that you wanted to know when I would be back.

GROUP READING
Michael Harth

Quentin was at last coming to the end of the passage he had been reading; and as Simon glanced surreptitiously once more at their new member, or rather potential member, for he hadn't yet actually joined the group, he noticed that the fellow looked even more fidgety than when the reading had started. It reinforced the feeling he had had, when he first saw him: the crumpled jeans and check shirt hardly betokened literary abilities, and were distinctly at odds with the more decorous attire of the rest of the group.

On the other hand, they did suggest a more physical attitude to life than seemed to be the case with the other members, who didn't, up till then, include a single person with whom Simon could have contemplated any intimate contact, even in his usual fairly desperate state. He had hoped that, by moving to London, he would be able to get regular sex, or at least more regular than had been the case in Basildon, where his score averaged somewhere around three times a year. Unfortunately, being too shy to make friends easily or to go out cruising, and too fastidious to cottage, he found London little better, with the added irritation that he knew it was there all over the place, if only he could screw himself up to go out and get it.

But though he regularly promised himself he would, when it came to crunch time he always chickened out, so he did what he could to relieve his frustration by writing stories which, he assured himself, were erotic rather than pornographic, though even so it was an activity he made sure to keep entirely secret from the group. Admittedly he stayed faithful to the first principle he had imbibed from them, that there are no happy endings in anything with pretensions to being literature, so that the stories always ended, after an enthusiastic, if not very realistic, description of a sexual encounter, in the protagonist being left once more on his own, for one reason or another.

Simon viewed the newcomer – Godfrey had introduced him as Matt – with mixed feelings: he hardly seemed likely to fit in with the group, but on the other hand he was solidly built and could almost have come off a building site, so taking him near enough to the type of guy that peopled Simon's fantasies to set his pulse racing. There was an aura about him that suggested he got it regularly, too, he thought enviously, something that seemed highly unlikely with the other group members, who did their best to make it quite clear that they were only interested in the life of the mind. Though he strove mightily to emulate their example, Simon could not manage to expunge the constant stream of sexual thoughts and desires that tormented him, and which, at times like this, prevented him from concentrating properly on the literary feast being spread in front of him.

So he was guiltily conscious of some slight sympathy with Matt, especially as he himself experienced a considerable degree of difficulty in following Quentin's long sentences and somewhat convoluted style. He knew it was literature, so he persevered, but caught himself continually casting surreptitious glances at Matt, and even wondering what he liked doing, though each time he would redirect his attention to the reading with a mental slap.

When it finally stopped, the Convener immediately rushed in with his judgment.

'Excellent, my dear Quentin,' he approved. 'I confess to having become a trifle apprehensive when I realised you were about to deal with the coarser side of life, but in the event you handled what could have been a distasteful subject without any taint of carnality, and I am sure no one could have taken offence.'

Simon was much the youngest of the group, and still rather over-awed by the high literary level of the other members, particularly Quentin, whose regular use of such terms as 'semiotics' and 'post-structuralist' made it clear to Simon that he operated at a stratospheric level which Simon himself was unlikely ever to attain. He racked his brains desperately for something intelligent to say about this latest offering, but as he hadn't even been able to work out why what Quentin had been describing merited such discretion, he felt at something of a disadvantage.

'Your similes were so well chosen,' Penelope, a long-standing woman member, remarked. 'I particularly liked the part where the butcher glances at him as he asks for half-a-pound of skinless sausages: that image will stay with me for a long time.'

'Skinless!' Terence rhapsodised. 'So subtle!'

'No one else could put so much meaning into a meaning-less glance,' Claude enthused.

'Then the scene where he serves the sausages to Emily!' Miles was not to be outdone in appreciation. 'The underlying tensions were so brilliantly not expressed.'

'Your metaphoric deformations at the very end were simply superb,' pronounced Jocelyn, who, by dint of having published a monograph on *The aesthetics of the semi-colon* was their acknowledged literary expert. 'I fear the subtlety will be wasted on most readers but, even with the hoi polloi, it must make an effect on the subliminal level.'

'I didn't understand a word of it,' the new arrival, Matt, finally expostulated. The fact that his vowels betrayed his proletarian origins went some way towards explaining his obtuseness, though they could hardly excuse it. So there was an appalled silence at such crass insensitivity, while Miles thought to himself that it confirmed his impression that Godfrey had made an error of judgment in allowing him to attend their gathering.

'You might find it easier if you saw it on the printed page,' Clarence, more kind-hearted than the others, offered helpfully. 'I'm sure Quentin would be happy to lend you a copy.'

Quentin inclined his head gracefully.

Matt's outburst had caused Godfrey acute embarrassment. The Convener was realising that he should have checked the fellow's credentials more carefully before he allowed such an uncouth specimen to enter their little enclave, but on the phone the wretch had sounded perfectly acceptable to his sensitive ear, and when he had said that he was interested in the technique of fiction-writing, Godfrey had assumed a certain basic standard of culture. The fact that he had now revealed his proletarian status was hardly sufficient excuse to ask him to leave, so he overlooked his behaviour for the once, and called on Patrice to restore the tone of the meeting.

After a certain amount of searching among the masses of sheets in his folder, Patrice finally managed to extract what, he informed them, was the next chapter in the novel he was currently engaged on, and from which he had read sections at previous meetings.

'You will remember,' he began, 'that Julian has just been introduced to the new deacon, Basil Clanricarde, at a tea-party held to welcome him by the Vicar's wife, and finds something familiar about him. Then that evening he recalls why he thought he recognised him: he had once caught him cheating at Ludo when they were boys. We left him wrestling with his conscience over whether he should inform the Vicar. I take up the narrative at the point where –'

But it was all too much for the new arrival. 'What's gay about that?' he demanded truculently.

'I beg your pardon?' the Convener said a trifle coldly.

'This is supposed to be a gay writing group, isn't it?' Matt went on.

The Convener inclined his head. 'It is,' he answered.

'Well, where's the gay bits?' the intruder wanted to know.

'What do you mean, gay bits?' the Convener asked, his tone growing more and more frosty by the second.

'You know what I mean, sport,' Matt said, compounding his offensiveness with an increasingly plebeian intonation. 'When do they have it off?'

'If you are referring to smut, that is not the sort of thing we encourage,' Godfrey said, his voice positively dripping ice.

'Not much point in my staying, then,' Matt declared, heaving himself up from the chair. 'Call yourselves gay writers! I reckon you got me here under false pretences.'

Everyone maintained a disapproving silence as he made his way to the door, dislodging several charming little pieces of North Korean Art Deco in the process, one of which didn't survive its journey.

Godfrey had been thinking of trying it at the *Antiques Roadshow*, but it was worth the loss to be rid of that crude fellow.

'What a disgusting brute,' Mervyn said, as they heard the front door slam. 'Does he imagine we have nothing better to do than pander to his vulgar cravings?'

'Perhaps now we can get back to literature,' Miles declaimed fervently.

There was a murmur of agreement round the room in which Simon joined abstractedly, after a last disappointed glance at the back of Matt's jeans. 'They might be very clever, but none of them has a rear view worth a damn,' he thought, with a flash of rebelliousness. But then his full attention was required to work out how to remove any carnal taint from the relationship between the protagonists in the story he had brought to read. It was perhaps fortunate that the discussion on some of the finer points arising from Mervyn's fascinating evocation of the spirit of the woodland, as seen from the point of view of one of the younger trees, a technical tour de force written entirely without the use of verbs, took up so much time that they didn't get round to his piece.

It was when he was walking home that Simon allowed himself to regret that they hadn't heard any of Matt's writing. It might have been quite amusing, he thought wistfully. Of course it was a literary group and not a pick-up joint, but he did wonder whether Matt would have extended him an invitation to come back for coffee, and he let his mind dwell on the possible consequences. Then, when he got home and was emptying his briefcase, he found a visiting card among the papers with the name Matthew Hutchings, and a phone number.

The fellow must have slipped it in as he left, he supposed: it was a nifty bit of sleight-of-hand, for he certainly hadn't seen it being done. He rather doubted if he could use it: should the group ever get to hear about it, they'd probably freeze him out. But it did start him off again, and soon he was seated at his word-processor, letting his imagination run riot. 'This one,' he thought, 'is going to be really steamy.'

And indeed it was: he became so over-heated that he had three wanks over the scenes conjured up, only finishing it by working on into the small hours. Lying there after he had switched off his computer, he reflected that there probably wouldn't be much point in actually contacting Matt now: after the degree of excitement his imagination had engendered, any actual encounter that took place couldn't possibly come anywhere near it.

THREE POEMS
Steve Ferris

SVANTOVIT'S BOY

The sun had baked the ground for weeks.
The weatherman had given up conjuring.
Honeycomb cracks crazed the fields.
The hardiest crop had withered to grey stem.
Rivers and reservoirs had shrunk.
There was talk of rationing.
Wits had conferred humour upon the events
Suggesting each citizen bathed with a friend.

Finally, the Slavic gods of storm and thunder
Capitulated to pagan prayers and rolled out
Their drastic canvases in the theatre of the sky.
The countryside held collective breath.
Out with black dog I watched cloud pile,
Monstrous staging, a baroque palazzo ceiling.
And as the first globules started to fall
The air grew thick as though with plasmolysis.

The crossbred ignored the pelting but
Leapt at the wounds of electrical discharge.
I saw the waif in the field ahead,
Tiny, dancing like a recipient of convulsive therapy.
He must have tracked my approach,
Along gravelled path on boundary sides,
But reacted not at my presence and witnessing,
Tearing off his clothes as if they burned like sun.

He was as white as bone in the garish gloom.
The interference of dust driven up,
Fragmentation on impact with solid earth,
Haze around his body as drops broke into spray.
His dance had no rhyme or rhythm,
Just the frantic ecstasy of a neophyte trance.
He whirled and leapt and fell in mud,
And rolled and stood, transformed to clay.

I would transpose him to the market square,
A sudden lull in traffic and passenger transit,
People sheltering from the half-forgotten orgy
Of the elemental shower of refreshing beauty.
If the dog had not sat and seen,
Inclined his head, this way and that, shook excess
From his floppy ears, I would have believed him
Invisible, not there, a mere harbinger.

PLAZA REAL

I was here in this precise place twenty years ago,
Almost to the day and it hasn't changed much.
The traffic's gone and they've put cannonballs
As pavement punctuation, pedestrianising.
And there's a kebaberie and a bank of vending machines
Instead of taxis, but the palms don't seem any bigger
And the fountain's a tiny thing, shrunk and shrivelled,

Isolated in the middle of the rectangular square –
They're never square, Squares – and the hostel
We stayed in when I was still almost a boy
Is called an hotel now. It retains the rest of its name,
Though the entrance is aggrandised and marmoreal.
The snail-roast still rotates on the corner,
Its golden, well-oiled carcasses

In the alley that trails into the architectural crevices.
Tourists flock here now and the prices reflect it;
Menus come in multiplied languages
And the world-weary waiters chirrup
In tourist-speak tailored for the international itinerant.
Behind the marble, twenty years ago to the day,
I shared a room with Paul and was struck

By the radiant dazzle of his brilliant
White Y-fronts,
The palace of privacy in Easter hols.
(And when I casually mentioned I hadn't seen him
Naked, he said it wasn't for want of trying.)
I looked into that well that so many hotels possess,
Rising to a quadrilateral of Spain's sky,

Falling to a skylight roof above the dining hall below,
Steamy odours wafting up from hidden kitchens,
Piping and cabling lacing the funnel like spider web.
And in the room diagonally across,
Two Fifth-formers whose faces I still have,
But whose names have slipped into obscurity,
Cut short.

MINOR TRAGEDY

One of my kids came straight
Up to me to bleat
About the hair down my chin,
And the hooves on my feet.

The kid came to me
Scampering, bold as brass,
To try to count the bristles on my face
And the lines on my arse.

This kid didn't care,
Far bolder than the timid rest,
Counting the curls lower down,
Then the curls higher up my chest.

Frolicking kid in the glaring sun,
On the verge of starting to melt,
Poking stubby fingers into my tufted ears,
Matting them inextricably in my carpet pelt.

Each time butting in, the recalcitrant kid:
I tried to make him quit.
'You stink, Mister,' he shouted.
'You stinky, caprovine git!'

He tried to imply, this headstrong,
Springy kid, that I was an old goat.
He claimed he saw the lozenge in my eyes
And the grizzle of my coat.

In my flesh the jarring kid
Grew like a festering thorn.
He made so bold as to grab at my face,
And search for some horn.

'Where's nanny?' he inquisitively nosed,
Altering the timbre of his voice to mock-gruff,
And on his ten digits made lists of confirmation,
Adding up my teeth and all other stuff.

'If you think that of me,' I said
To the capering kid close by,
'Follow me up this mountain scree.
Stick to me, or daren't you even try?'

In green, in green, the kids romp round,
A bunch of billies,
But their stupid questions succeed
In giving sundry the willies.

LIONELLA
Elsa Wallace

Lionella Strijdom regretted, resented, her father being named Lionel; she felt it detracted from her own name, making it merely derivative, or an apology for her not being male.

She liked to think of herself as a lion woman, a lion lady, and when she was eleven during the school craze for foreign pen-friends (linked to stamp collecting) she sometimes styled herself 'Lionessa'.

She was seven when brother Jeremy was born. Warned by her mother of the dangers of touching his fontanelle she was wary of him until he reached his fourth year with a full head of brown hair and therefore seeming less fragile.

She was blonde and sturdy, he thin and unassertive. Mr Strijdom sought to build him up physically and mentally for boxing lessons when he was nine. He was indifferent to the bright red gloves which fascinated Lionella. She put them on and her father playfully made a feint at her, to be surprised by the force and speed of the punch she delivered to his ribs.

He said, 'Now I understand the value of primogeniture. Jeremy will never catch up. She's had a seven-year headstart on him, our undivided attention. All the power of the first-born is hers, and can't be taken from her. No wonder some tribes take care their firstborns are male.'

'What tribes?' scoffed his wife, 'you do talk piffle.'

'Oh, Arabs. Berbers.'

'Rubbish. If it could be done without infanticide we'd know all about it. Just be glad Nella is strong and healthy.'

'Oh I am,' said Mr Strijdom hastily.

She was strong. When Jeremy was being picked on she beat

up the bully on school grounds, to the headmaster's displeasure.

'She's getting to be a bit of a tomboy,' said Mrs Strijdom. 'She ought to have gone to boarding school to mix with suitable girls.'

'Government school is good enough,' said Mr Strijdom.

Lionella had always associated with younger children, giving the twin boys next door rides on her bike or making wigwams for the family of little girls across the road, but her chief playmates were her cats of whom Jeremy was afraid.

Until Augusta's advent the only girl her own age whom she brought home was the myopic Patsy who suffered from nervous tics and was having to re-sit Standard Four. Lionella was perfectly satisfied with this 'lame duck' as Mrs Strijdom called her, and would read to her *Children of the New Forest* and Raphael Sabatini as they had sandwiches and cool drinks in the pergola.

Patsy was succeeded by a lanky boy, silent due to a severe stutter, with whom Lionella would cycle idly up and down the avenues, she holding forth on her future plans: working with wild animals, or on trains or boats, until he was siphoned off to Peterhouse, to Mrs Strijdom's relief.

She was no better pleased with Augusta Strydom whom Lionella met at commercial class. The two girls were similar, heavy-boned, square blunt faces and straight thick hair. They liked the shared name and called each other by it in an unfeminine manner: 'Hey, Strydom, how goes it, man?' Private jokes were their treasure and sometimes they only had to look at each other to burst out laughing. As much as they could they dressed alike and as Mrs Strijdom said 'got themselves talked about'.

Augusta got her to play netball (which previously she'd found boring) and they looked even more alike in their whites.

But Mr Strydom was nomadic and eighteen months on the Copperbelt was enough for him. He was returning to the Transvaal where he thought he'd once been happy, though his wife and children could recall no such period of content.

Hearing her deserted daughter's sobs at night Mrs Strijdom almost felt sorry for her.

Her husband said, 'She bawled like that when that cat died. She'll get over it.'

'She should have gone to University, then she'd have more friends than just the one.'

'No, that's for Jeremy as he can't go down the mine.'

Lionella continued playing netball but so aggressively she had to be dropped from the team. She completed her commercial course and got a job in the mine office.

In Jo'burg Augusta had also finished her studies and was working for a secretarial agency. Letters between them became more frequent but in shorthand, to Mrs Strijdom's frustration.

At last came the invitation from Augusta for Lionella to join her for a holiday in Durban. Lionella couldn't get to Ndola Station fast enough and hardly waved to her parents and brother, so anxious was she for the train to start.

She never came back.

Mrs Strijdom was disgusted. 'Why that agency took her on before they even got her references is beyond me. Of course she's a good speller, you can't fault her on that. You remember the spelling test? She could even spell haemorrhage.'

'I don't see why she needs to spell haemorrhage,' said Mr Strijdom.

'Well, I'm glad Jeremy will be at Wits. He can keep an eye on her. It's a violent city.'

So it was. A business man, Louis Mulroy, was deprived of his valued secretary when her house was burgled and her husband shot dead. She fled to safety in Cape Town and Mr

Mulroy had to apply to an agency, urgently, for a replacement. The two took it in turns and for a short while he thought there was only one of them as they had adopted almost as a uniform a blue skirt and jacket with a tailored white blouse.

Mr Mulroy was small, fifty and ill with a chronic bowel complaint. Occasionally it was only one or other of them holding the fort in his office. He was much impressed and learning of their ambition to start their own agency he offered a property he had at a very low rent.

'This is all very well,' said Mrs Strijdom, 'but I wish she'd meet a nice man and get married.'

Jeremy met the men in the Strydom circle and reported that all they talked about was cars and fishing.

Mrs Strijdom came down to 'see for myself' and was annoyed to find the sofa in their sitting room occupied by a large young woman, Melanie, who had been kicked out by her family.

Mrs Strijdom expostulated, 'She didn't "find herself pregnant", Nella! She did something obvious for this to happen. Just because she's one of your girls doesn't mean you're responsible for her. Another lame duck!'

'Not at all. Her work is excellent and she'll be back after.'

'And the baby?'

'We'll sort out something.'

After that visit, from Mrs Strijdom's point of view worse befell. Mr Mulroy, who had formed a habit of dropping in to their office to see how they were doing and to put business their way, somehow learned about Melanie and was full of sympathy.

'The same happened to a friend of my aunt's. To this day – and she's ninety now – some of her people don't talk to her. She lives in Brakpan,' he added as though that were punishment enough.

He gave some thought to the situation and presented a solution.

'You can live in the annex to my house. I built it for my parents. They're long gone to the Lord. It's got four rooms and the garden's right there. A kiddie needs a garden.'

The Strijdoms now had a phone and Jeremy reported to them, 'The garden's so big he has a full-time gardener. There's a pool but he's having it covered because of the baby. He's got a grand piano. I'm going every Sunday to play for him, he likes my music if no one else does. Poor bloke, he's got this gut thing – sometimes he has to go to the jacksi three times in an hour.'

Mrs Strijdom said to her husband, 'I don't know about this Mulroy, why's he doing all this for them? What's he getting out of it? Where's his wife? Or wives, come to that – he could have had several by now. What do we know about him?'

'He's got money.'

'And that's good enough for you? I'll have to go down again, see what's what.'

He made her wait until he himself was going south to visit his sister.

She found what Jeremy had described. A too-large house in extensive grounds, a cook, two maids and a chauffeur. In the car from Jan Smuts she was apprised of the fact that Mr Mulroy, who had never married, had now offered it to them (either one of them would do) as he had no one close to whom he could leave his property.

'Just a formality,' said Augusta, 'a marriage of paper, no strings attached, no goes in the bedroom. Those days are over for him, poor chap.'

Mrs Strijdom was shocked.

'You're not going to do it?'

'Not I,' said Lionella.

'I might,' said Augusta, 'It'd be a laugh.'

'Marriage isn't a laugh, my girl.'

'You said it,' observed Lionella.

Lunch was served on the back verandah overlooking the garden where three muscular tabbies stalked something minute and Melanie played with her baby on the grass.

At the other end of the verandah Mr Mulroy lay on a sun-lounger, his special food and drink to hand and Jeremy's music tinkling over him from the French windows.

In a low voice Mrs Strijdom said, 'If you do marry him you'll change the name of your business.'

'No,' said Augusta, 'we'll always be Strijdom and Strydom. Aren't I right, Strijdom?' and laughed.

Mrs Strijdom winced. She glanced towards his slight form, flat as a board on his lounger. She felt she could never esteem a man who looked hungrily at a water biscuit and then shook his head.

As if he was aware of her censure, Mr Mulroy groaned and sat up. At once the women ran to him and assisted him indoors.

'For goodness sake, Nella, are you his nurses now?' Mrs Strijdom said when they rejoined her.

'Oh, he can make it on his own but a bit of help doesn't come amiss.'

'Well, and you've still got that Melanie round your necks.' She groaned. 'I really can't see what's in this for you, Nella.'

Augusta grinned at her mate and said, 'Territory!'

Perhaps it was so: Lionella's gaze encompassed garden and occupants in blazing sun, penetrating shrubs, trees, tall walls, passing over suburbs and bush, paths, streams to where her counterpart was sprawled among the members of her pride, golden eyes half closed, yawning, lazily swatting a romping cub in the Kruger National Park.

THE MONKEY'S PENIS
Leigh V. Twersky

Brenda remembers the hands. Rifling through her pockets. Did they take it? The question knocks on her head louder and harder each time, but she doesn't know the answer. Only that she has to warn Kira.

Warn Kira. Warn Kira. That refrain. Like a constant gong.

'Who's this Kira?' The young doctor yawns to the night nurse in the intensive care unit. 'Must be delirious. She's hit 41 degrees. Increase the antibiotics. And check on her every five minutes.'

A beautiful December morning: the sun rising in a rhubarb and custard sky. In his Victorian conversion flat, Kurt Beaupierre was having the non-smoker's equivalent of a post-coital cigarette.

Tyler. The travel writer. Been all over the world and docked at Kurt's. Now they were locked together in a sleepy embrace, bodies clammy as new-born pups. Kurt watched Tyler's neck throb, and relished the breezy out-breaths on his shoulder. Tyler had wanted to talk. Kurt, no. Not even to learn his name and job. Too much information. He just wanted sex. He also wanted a piss.

Sliding out of the sheets, so as not to disturb Tyler, he shivered in the cold and slithered into a pair of jeans. Realising from the feel that he'd put Tyler's on by mistake, he groped his way to the toilet, aware of something in the pocket. Being in another guy's clothes made him horny as if he were in new skin. When he finished weeing, he put his hand into the pocket and pulled out what appeared to be a furry sausage with mange.

It was getting lighter now. Kurt looked at the thing. For a second it seemed to vibrate in his fist. He dismissed that idea and went into the kitchenette.

Time to arouse Tyler. Nicely. The real stuff. Cafetières – no instant shite.

He put the cup on the bedside table and ran the sausage down Tyler's cheek. 'Coffee?' he whispered.

Tyler groaned and opened one eye, and then both, when he realised what shirtless Kurt in *his* jeans was doing. He sat up with a start. 'What are you playing at?'

Kurt brandished the object. 'This your dildo?'

Tyler leapt out of bed and shook his shaved head. 'No, you idiot. You don't understand. It's a lucky charm. But evil.'

Kurt sneered. 'You don't believe that crap, do you? Just drink your coffee.'

Tyler said nothing.

'Oh, you do. Well, I dread to think what the rest of the rabbit looked like.'

Tyler took a sip of his coffee and stared at the threadbare grey carpet. 'It's not from a rabbit,' he said. 'It's from a monkey. It's a monkey's ... er ... penis.'

Kurt burst out laughing. 'No wonder you don't like me playing with it. You want it all for yourself.' He gulped his coffee.

An awkward pause followed. Tyler broke the silence. 'I got it from this guy in Rio. We shagged all night, five, six times. I saw the penis on his bedside table and picked it up. He told me it grants three wishes of a sexual nature. I made fun, too. He said, "You'll have to keep it now you've taken it, but promise you'll never wish for anything." "Don't be ridiculous," I said. "I'm not taking it." He said, "OK, but it will find you." I asked him if he'd used it. "Oh, yes," he said. "If only I hadn't." So I haven't tried it.'

'Why not? No harm in trying.'

'I had a date with him the next day, but he stood me up. I went to his apartment. He didn't answer the door but it was open. I went in. He was at home all right. I found him in his bedroom. Hanging from the ceiling.

'The penis was still there. I know this sounds weird but it seemed to be winking at me. I grabbed it and have kept it ever since.'

Kurt shuddered and thought for a bit. 'You really think there's a connection?'

Tyler shrugged. 'It's yours now.'

Kurt examined it. 'So, how's it supposed to work?'

Tyler stalled. 'All right, but promise you won't do this.'

Kurt nodded.

'You hold it in your hand and tell it your wish.'

Kurt winced at the musty smell and the tickly hairs. 'Cool. I wish David Beckham would come here and shag me senseless.'

Nothing happened.

'See?' said Kurt after David Beckham's no-show. 'Superstitious nonsense.'

'The wish has to be genuine. Deeply felt.'

Kurt laughed again. 'So, that's its get-out-of-jail-free card,' he said, stroking the ruddy fur in his palm. 'Shit! Is that the time? Gotta go.'

He got rid of Tyler, flung on a coat and ran most of the way to work. When he arrived at the fringe theatre, where he was a kitchen-hand, he realised he'd forgotten to change back into his own jeans and still had the penis. He was going to call Tyler but stopped.

As he said, it belongs to me now, and if his jeans fit me, mine'll fit him.

He thought about Tyler wearing his jeans and felt a twinge of arousal at the image of that bruised V-shaped body. He recalled with a smile their games, the mock strangling, the tiny cuts he'd made on that lean torso, the pre-coital fight and his domination of those pretty-boy looks. He'd put his best friend Janine off at the last minute, blown her out by text as soon as Tyler caught his eye in the bar. He'd had to have him.

Sorry Janine. A fuck 2 kill 4. L8rs.

He'd hoped, as always, that this would be his last sordid one-night stand, but addiction is never satisfied.

Why couldn't he have liked Janine in that way, been *normal* instead of lonely, childless and marginal? His parents would turn in their graves if they knew their son was one of those 'she-men' he shamefully remembered them mocking.

Coming out for him had been a huge door slamming shut, but in his face or behind his back he could never tell.

He shook his head, took a deep breath and grasped the penis. Some of the bristly hairs prickled his palm, and he said, 'I wish I was straight.'

His mind turned to Janine. Nothing.

He was thinking, 'Load of bollocks,' when the penis hardened and expanded. He saw it protrude from the gap between his thumb and index finger. 'It's getting a ... stiffy!' he cried, startled, incredulous. A spurt of whitish liquid oozed from a tiny slit at the end he'd not noticed before.

The opaque cum dribbled down the base of his thumb onto his wrist, and a strong smell of stale semen made him gag. But he still had the hots for Tyler and his twilight world.

Must be a trick mechanism triggered by body heat to secrete a lotion and make it seem realistic. And there are plants that smell like cum.

He kicked himself for even thinking there might be something in it, and pocketed the penis.

The next day Janine came for dinner. Kurt wanted to make it up to her. Plus, he'd be a shoulder to cry on if her social-worker boyfriend Randy had been up to his tricks again — sleeping around or beating her up after a hard day.

'Leave the bastard,' Kurt would say. 'Or at least report him.'

'Not that easy.' Janine would wring her hands and avoid his eyes, knowing he was right but too scared to make the break, and unwilling to admit it.

They'd met ten years before at Kurt's first job in a West End theatre and bonded immediately. Janine was always cuddling him or touching him in some way, which made him wonder whether she fancied him or saw him as a safe haven away from her abusive man, who, however, every time Kurt saw him, behaved impeccably.

Janine was wearing a tight black mini-dress with a pink chiffon scarf round her neck and her blonde-streaked hair in a ponytail. Her latest black eye was fading.

'I followed your advice,' she said, her hand on Kurt's arm. 'I've dumped him.'

'Hallelujah!' He pecked her cheek. 'Make sure it's for real this time.'

'Don't worry. Just hope he doesn't come after me.' She nodded and sipped her white wine. 'Anyway, I'm single again. And available.' She looked at him.

And the look exploded in Kurt's brain.

Without thinking, he stroked her shoulder, and to his shock, a frisson of pleasure ignited his groin, like a lit fuse. He stared at Janine and put his hand on her left breast. In a flash he remembered the monkey's penis and his cock ballooned.

Janine made some sound and moved his hand away, but he replaced it and squeezed.

'No,' she was saying, 'don't,' but the words had lost their meaning for him. So had everything else he'd ever known.

She was slapping his face and backing away. It hurt. Rage filled his loins.

'Let me, Janine. I want you. Like you want me. Stop shaking your head, you stupid bitch, coming on to me with that tight dress. What do you expect? I'll fucking show you, making me feel this way, playing games. Ssh. Dress ain't much protection now, is it, eh? You deserved everything Randy did. Bet you even enjoyed it. Stop screaming. Feel that meat injection inside you. It hurts. You asked for it. If you won't be quiet, this scarf'll fucking shut you up, bitch. Look at me now. *Bitch!* At me, not the ceiling. Aaah, Janine? *Janine?* What's the matter? Janine, talk to me. Say something, please, for God's sake! Oh, no. No! *No!*'

He thought of those portraits which were so cleverly painted that wherever he stood the subject had always seemed to look at him. Janine was the exact opposite.

He was still erect when he disengaged after climaxing, but whimpering. He cradled her in his arms like a baby, wiped her dishevelled hair off her face and closed her eyes. 'I'm sorry.' Tears streamed down his cheeks. He kissed her lips and her exposed breasts and lay on top of her, shaking with remorse.

What have I done?

'Stupid question, like you don't know.' The voice in his head got louder. 'Don't you fucking dare cry.' The face saying it all screwed up, thin blood-red lips drawn back into a snarl, teeth bared, and what he saw was the burning eyes and ugly, hate-compressed mouth going, 'You ain't got no fucking right to do nothing no more.'

Wonder what Janine's feeling? So quiet, why won't she tell me?

Hours passed. Footsteps on the stairs, hammering at the door, and the face vanished into thin air, pff, just like that, and there was only panting, shallow breathing and screaming panic, but no time. He was still knocking.

Randy. Through the peephole. Out for blood. Obviously been looking for her. Knew this'd be the first place she'd come. Think fast. Pretend I'm out. Mustn't panic.

Kurt panicked. The bell rang. And rang. His heart drum-rolled as he held his breath. Then Randy gave up and tramped down the stairs. Kurt remembered the penis.

It was his second wish, but he was going to have to go through with it. Time was against him. Randy would be back.

He extricated the still soggy penis from his pocket. Holding it as firmly as he could, considering how he was trembling, he said, 'I wish I was a woman.'

He didn't know why. It just slipped out but seemed the right thing to ask for. A sigh of relief escaped from his lips as the organ stiffened and thickened. He closed his fist tightly round it, unable to stop kneading it between his palm and fingers as if it were irresistible. He fancied he could hear the monkey yelp with pleasure as the thing shuddered and ejaculated, albeit weakly, its tiny blob of sperm from the foul mouth.

But nothing changed. Kurt was still a man. Dick in place. Deep voice. Facial hair. He put the member in his pocket and crept upstairs to Janine as if creeping lessened his guilt, his thoughts more and more fraught. Why wasn't anything happening? Perhaps it wasn't a genuine wish.

He'd end it all. He had some pills he'd take with vodka, on Clapham Common, leave a note and let the police work it out like on the telly.

He sobbed as he fingered the vodka bottle. He didn't deserve to wallow in self-pity and banged his head against the wall but stopped in case he alerted the neighbours.

He checked Janine. How was she now? Maybe she'd be OK

and none of this had happened. He stripped her naked and put her stuff in the washing machine. Then he took a shower, holding her body next to him, so she'd be completely clean and presentable and they could be together once more. He dried her, alarmed at feeling aroused as the towel chafed against her breasts but there was no time for that. Her clothes needed tumble-drying. He got dressed, his insides knotted.

When I wished I was straight, I never meant in ... that way.

He hurled the penis at the wall. It bounced back and hit him full in the face. Loose strands of fur entered his right eye.

'Fuck you!' he screamed as he tried to get them out, the lid of his stinging eye collapsing violently in on itself as if it were dissolving in acid. But while he was cussing, other tufts of urine-smelling hair got into his mouth.

'Agh! Pagh!' he tried to spit them out. The taste was as disgusting as the stench. He was praying he hadn't swallowed anything when he realised he was clutching it. His saviour, the slit mouth taunting him with simian whoops. 'You can't escape me.'

He howled in despair as it seemed to force his arm down, chattering all the time, triumphant.

The bell made him start. He closed the bathroom door and decided to say she'd gone. He had no idea where. That would give him time.

He checked the peephole, took a deep breath and opened the door with a fake smile. Facing him was Randy — a slim guy in his thirties with a dark widow's peak, whose small, mean blue eyes flashed with surprise as he smiled back and looked Kurt up and down.

'Hi, is Janine there at all?' His manner was distant as though Kurt were a stranger.

A shard of fear pierced Kurt's entrails and he raised his hands in defence. And that's when he felt them.

His boobs.

'My ...' he cried out, doubly shocked now. His voice was an octave higher, unbroken, swallowed up inside him.

Big tits and no time to enjoy them.

'I'm Janine's partner.'

He doesn't recognise me.

Kurt sighed with relief. 'You've missed her.'

Randy nodded and held out his hand. 'Randolph Marchant, but everyone calls me Randy.'

Kurt shook his hand. 'Er ... Brenda.'

Brenda? What kind of a name is that? Medical history's just been made, an act of sheer magic, and all dumbo can come up with is fucking Brenda!

'Haven't met you before, Brenda.'

'I'm Kurt's friend from work.'

'Right. Any idea where Janine went?

Brenda shook her head, irritated she didn't have time to adjust, to relish the changes and savour her new body.

Randy closed the door behind him. He hadn't been asked in, but invited himself anyway. Brenda turned, giving herself an opportunity to feel her crotch. No cock! Something else. It felt good.

Randy followed her into the living room. Brenda felt his hand on her tits. Hadn't Kurt secretly desired this long ago? But now they weren't the luxury he'd dreamt of. Brenda liked it, but began to be afraid. What did Randy want? She looked into his eyes for an answer but they were opaque, glazed with something she didn't comprehend.

Randy breathed out heavily, not smiling now. Perhaps he knew, or maybe ... Brenda was well aware what kind of man he was but now Kurt was no better.

The phone rang.

'Leave it,' snapped Randy as he stepped closer and embraced her.

It was uncomfortable. They were the same height but he was strong and wiry. As she tried to wriggle out of the bear hug, she heard Kurt's voice on the answerphone. The caller hung up.

'Can I get you anything?'

He didn't reply. His gaze was intense and he growled from the back of his throat when he breathed out. His face was flushed, cold eyes bulging from their sockets, sizing her up. Then his short, sinewy arms clasped her to him, like a crab seizing its mate.

'No,' she said, but he took no notice, and sneering, pushed her back onto the parquet floorboards. She banged her head and cried out.

I deserve this.

He mounted her, dropped his blue trackie bottoms and ripped her jeans open. Or rather, Tyler's jeans with the button fly. It didn't bother him she was in men's clothes. He just wanted her kit out of his way.

His hands were round her neck now, squeezing, choking her. She couldn't scream even if she'd wanted to. Then the beating started. First it was swipes across her face, but then came punches, real clenched power fists to head and body, much harder than the role-play blows Kurt had dealt Tyler.

But I don't deserve this. Kurt did it, not me. Randy didn't even recognise me. Let Kurt have it, not me.

But there was little she could do with him on top, punching and strangling her.

Pressing down on my new tits, slobbering over my nipples, no time to play with my new cunt, he's got there first, only been a virgin a few minutes ...

She heard herself yelling and gasping. When the violence ceased, he was inside her, jerking up and up and down and up and it hurt. Fuck, it fucking hurt! She conceived a hatred for him she never knew possible. Then she remembered what was in her pocket.

She still had one last wish.

He kept approaching his climax and easing off and restarting with renewed vigour.

What a boring fucker.

Her hand fumbled and groped. When it was in her grasp, she clutched it tightly like her mum's hand and mumbled, 'I wish he'd die of AIDS.'

He didn't hear. Too wrapped up in his own pleasure, desperate to come and punish this woman. It took what seemed like ages for the penis to swell and harden, and the fluid to soil her fingers as it reached orgasm, a few seconds before Randy finished and left his crown of runny icing-sugar round the rim of her brand-new vagina.

Sirens. The entire world is nothing but sirens, wailing out there and inside her brain. The worst headache. Should go in the Guinness Book of Records, but how do you measure that – throbs per second? There is no sleep. Only pain.

Sickly perfume. Not hers any more – *her* days are on hold now. Her friend's. The one with the sweet, lispy voice. Nosey. Took her in.

Pitied her when no one else cared. Found her on the street. Took her home. Bathed her. Fed her. Comforted her. Gave her new clothes. Shelter. Friendship. A job.

Steady work, and money. Lots of it. Expensive life. Rent to

pay. Commission. And constant fatigue. The friend's halo beginning to fade.

It was spring again. Leaves appearing on the trees. Light evenings. Bustle on the streets and a new sense of hope. Yet the work was relentless and she was always knackered. Then she started losing weight. Her clothes hung off her, and she only wanted to sleep, but her friend said, 'No.' She prayed for a rest, begged for a day off but her wish didn't come true.

And now the pain. She was expecting it. She asked for it, didn't she? Throb throb – the pain is blinding her and almost shifting her brain outside her head.

Burning. Fever. Sweat. She's a tropical rainforest, her skin eaten alive but she hasn't got the energy to scratch, or even stroke. It's more comfortable just lying down on the pavement, here, by the railings in front of Pizza Express, nobody'll notice or say anything. She won't be able to make it home anyway. If only she could sleep a bit. Maybe she's already asleep. Or dead, and in Hell. Feels *that* hot.

The hand on her. Ouch! She pulls her arm away, but weakly.

She hears the soothing voice with the lisp. Smells the cheap scent. Knows who it is.

The hands. Stroking her brow. She frowns.

Don't do that! Gotta open my eyes!

But she can't. No strength. Only endurance.

'You sad little bitch.'

It was Kira. 'You sad bitch this, you sad bitch that.' The first thing Kira had said when she found her wandering on Lavender Hill.

Got into a bit of an argument. 'Who you calling a sad bitch?' Well, she was drunk at the time and sleeping rough on Clapham Common. Had been for about a week. Didn't put up much of a fight, though. Any human contact was good.

'You're coming home with me.'

'I'm all right.'

What does the cow want of me?

'Get yourself cleaned up.'

Comfort is a great temptress. She ended up on Kira's spare mattress in Balham.

'I don't pry into anyone's past. That's your business.'

She wished she were far away, in another town or country. Or time. Yes, back in the past. If only ...

Kira went out to work every evening, dressed up. She didn't ask what Kira did. When she found out, it was too late. She owed her. TLC. Doesn't come cheap. Kind, Samaritan Kira had gone, and in her place was the real Kira.

The only way to pay her back was to work for her. The clients came in all shapes and sizes. She enjoyed it in the early days, but the non-stop pace was unbearable. Some of them hurt her, beat her up. Others made off without paying.

Kira got mad when that happened, but took it out on her. Sometimes, Kira also came home with mascara running down her face, slammed her bedroom door and didn't emerge till midday, having cried herself to sleep. Occasionally, she'd have a black eye or bruised arms and legs.

Paying off the debt was a slow business. As long as she stayed at Kira's, she had a rent bill, and Kira never took her eyes off her for a moment, so she dared not hide any cash.

When she started ailing, Kira told her to go to the doctor, but she didn't. Weeks passed, and apart from exhaustion and increasing emaciation, she developed a cough, which became a chest infection that wouldn't clear up. But Kira still made her work, although punters began to lose interest in a skeleton with skin.

'It's your fault if you won't get help, you sad bitch.'

Kira didn't speak to her any more, like she had at the

beginning when they were friends, before she found out what Kira was.

Kira had been doing it for years, although layers of make-up hid the truth. A yearning to turn the clock back was something they both shared, but when she started working for Kira, it was all they had in common.

Her lips part, but she can't speak. Too much effort. Should tell Kira to stop searching for money. There isn't any. Then the hands stop probing.

She can hear the question mark forming over Kira's head.

'What the fuck's this, you sad little bitch?'

The words are addressed to her, but Kira doesn't expect an answer, not straightaway. After all, she can't even open her eyes to see what she's talking about.

But she can feel it. Kira's stroking her fever-wracked cheek with something soft, like a long finger, but cold and coated in soggy fur. It leaves an irritating, wet sensation on her face and she so wants to wipe herself dry. Doesn't smell too good either – animal body odour and smegma.

'Ah!' she sighs, the first sound she's made for hours. She feels lighter now, almost free. Kira has the thing in her hands; she's taken it from her. It isn't hers any more, or rather, she isn't *its*. She smiles. Getting each word out is like lifting the heaviest weight in the gym above her head, and she can barely manage more than a faint murmur, but she's determined to explain.

At first, Kira scoffs, but keeps asking questions. It's so important to tell her how she got it and what she's learnt, but her voice is failing her now and her breath is needed for clinging onto life. The recent spark of energy has been extinguished.

Will someone shut those fucking sirens up!

She lies there, desperate to warn Kira, tell her about the

power of the penis, get her to promise never to wish for anything, but she keeps slipping in and out of consciousness and can't remember if she's already told her or not. This thought divides like a cancerous cell, the new one – wondering whether her third wish ever came true, and if so, how – distracting her from what she ought to be concentrating on, and so on *ad infinitum*.

They haven't expected her to make it through the night. So the junior doctor in intensive care is surprised she's still breathing when he finally signs off. It's almost 5.45 and just getting light. He's been on duty for twenty-four hours and is ready for an Olympic sleep.

'Most virulent case of AIDS we've seen for ages,' he remarks to his replacement. 'Nothing we can do now. Hope it's not a new strain. Remember that similar case in Belmarsh recently? Literally dropped dead in a few days.'

The other doctor recalls reading about it.

Without stirring or opening her eyes, the patient follows their conversation.

'That guy who murdered his girlfriend,' continues the less tired of the doctors, 'and her friend, whose body was never found. The police reckoned there must've been a struggle, a tug-of-war over the woman – they found both men's fingerprints on her, but DNA samples matched the boyfriend's. All a bit weird, but it couldn't have been the other bloke – he was gay. No one knew why he only hid one body, but a psychiatrist explained he probably felt his partner was his property so he hadn't done anything wrong. Anyway, he went mad. They don't know what got to his brain first, grief, guilt or AIDS. Funny name. Randolph something. Terrible tragedy. Strangled and raped her. Such a pretty woman. Denied it, of course. Claimed he was framed. Screaming he was innocent the whole time in court. Needed ten men to take him down to the cells. But it had to be him. Who else could've done it? She'd already reported him for abuse. He appealed, but then went down to five stone. Coughing up buckets of bloody sputum. Lesions all over him. Blind. Said he got it off some bird he shagged there the same day, but he'd obviously made that up. Police couldn't trace her. Never stood a chance.'

'Hasn't she got a surname?' he wonders as he looks at the patient's chart.

'Not that we know of. The woman who called the ambulance just referred to her as Brenda.'

Brenda no longer hears their voices. She keeps lurching from the South Pole to the Equator. And back again. She's spiralling far, far down the sweat-drenched sheets only to find herself at the top of the helter-skelter, terrified she'll not be caught before beginning the nauseating descent once more. Thrashing about like a fish being slowly poached alive, a volcano of mucus, erupting ribbons of phlegm.

Death is such sweet release. She enters the final phase of her life with the faintest smile on her cracked lips, remembering how she excused herself to go to the toilet as soon as she could slide out from under Randy's spent body. The widening of her grin is almost imperceptible as she recalls the blob of his cum she'd managed to scoop out of her new fanny with her index finger and then smear like ointment between the freshly cleansed legs waiting upstairs.

Crying. No consolation for the victim. Make-up running down her face, snot bubbling out of her bloodied nose. Sitting on the kerb, legs wide apart, wailing into the traffic. Nobody paying attention. She looks the type that asks for it.

She's lost a shoe, and her upside-down handbag is open, its contents strewn over the pavement. But not her money. He took that. Then smashed her teeth. And cracked a couple of ribs. Police don't care. Haven't got the time or manpower.

'You sad little bitch, *Kira*,' she whimpers to herself before white-hot fury consumes her.

'I wish a plague would wipe out every fucking man on the planet,' she screams at passers-by.

She's sobbing now, but stops, slightly surprised to feel the fluffy, sausage-shaped thing she has in her hand swell up and secrete a viscous substance onto her lap.

ALICE SWINGS
David Gee

Alice had read about swingers in books and magazines. A boy she'd dated in high school had showed her a movie – a mainstream movie, not porno – about wife-swapping. She wondered what it would be like to be a swinger, but married to a devout Jehovah's Witness there wasn't much likelihood of it happening; Mike wouldn't want to swap her for anything except maybe a snazzier Harley Davison. Next to God her husband loved his motorcycle more than anything – more than *her*, she sometimes felt – so it was kind of appropriate that when God called Michael home He sent a twenty-ton truck to knock him off his cherished old Harley.

After two months of wondering where her life was meant to go, Alice sold the house and rented a small third-floor studio flat in a London suburb. Within a month she met Ronald in the local corner-shop. Ron drove a delivery van; he wasn't a churchgoer; he had two ex-wives.

And he was a swinger. He took Alice to a party in the penthouse of one of Dockland's newest high-rises. Their hosts were a super-smooth litigator with a top law firm and his glamour-puss wife who wrote the society page in a fashion magazine. They served quality wines and a finger buffet. The background music was current West End show tunes. Ronald took Alice upstairs to a modishly-decorated bedroom with twin king-size beds; the sheets were the finest Egyptian cotton. Ron and Alice watched two other couples on the beds and then let the other couples watch them. Alice left the party feeling like a schoolgirl who's got away with something fairly naughty.

Next time the party was in a first-floor apartment above an

Indian take-away nowhere near the river. Their hosts were a fireman and his wife who worked on the check-out in Asda. They served beer and packet snacks. The hi-fi was playing yesteryear country hits. Their spare bedroom was not stylish; the bed was a scuffed mattress with no base and no sheets. Ronald watched while two other men took care of Alice and another woman. Then Alice watched while Ron took care of the other woman and the two men took turns taking care of Ron. The woman wanted to take care of Alice, but Alice said she wasn't ready for this. She left the party feeling she'd participated in something close to what the ancient Greeks and Romans were said to have done. Sodom and Gomorrah also came to her mind with a guilty flashback to her previous life with Michael.

'Do all the swingers do that?' she asked Ronald in the van, driving home. 'The gay stuff, the dykey stuff.'

'A lot of them do,' he said.

'Which do you prefer?'

'I like all of it,' Ron said.

'It's not what I was expecting,' said Alice.

'What did you expect?'

'Not that.'

Alice stopped seeing Ronald. She gave notice to her landlord and moved back to the country. She started going to church again and soon met a nice widower. His wife had died in a car crash and he'd given up driving. Alice didn't mind doing the driving in her little Toyota. She always drove – and now lived – within safe limits.

SEVEN HYMNS SET IN LONDON
Andrew Cheffings

1. DIFFICULT TIMES

The clouds glowed, orange, in the morning light;
All around, the dark streets of this fallen city,
Telling me of gentleness, all embracing,
In these difficult times.

I saw a stranger walk towards me –
Was he kind, or someone terrified, who'd hurt me?
But then he smiled, in gentleness, all embracing,
In these difficult times.

We pass each other on these fallen streets,
All around, the dark houses in the early morning,
Telling us of gentleness, all embracing,
In these difficult times.

2. BRIGHT LIGHTS

There are flowers opening, crushed beneath our feet.
The shops are full of shiny things and bright lights.

The rich throw us off the land,
Then sell us the food they grow on it;
Our will to thrive is sapped,
And we fall back on shiny things and bright lights.

No-one dares to listen to these hymns –
They remind us of what we've lost;
They are too painful,
And so we sing, instead, of shiny things and bright lights.

3. TINY ACTS OF KINDNESS

Thomas White, you terrify us –
Where are the tender kisses and poetry of love?
Screaming men and women beat and curse you;
We disown each other, hide, marry, and do church work,
Pray that our evil will not betray us,
Always watch our backs.

There are tiny acts of kindness
In this evil world.

4. NEW RIVER

I wandered around London with my gentle friend,
Along leafy, hollow ways and riverbeds –
Both, half-in-love with the same, unfaithful being –
His scars, in the mind,
Mine, in the body,
Both, deep within.

I taught,
He moved money, with pen and ink.
Money is treacherous –
When they murdered Thomas White, he was lost to me.
I was alone, with the moon and glowing sunrises and sunsets,
Over the New River.

5. SUNRISE

Don't mistake status and patronage for love
Love does not distinguish between male and female,
Different lands,
Rich and poor,
But status does.

The same glowing sunrise above palace and slum;
And compared to sunlight,
A palace is dust.

6. BLESSING

I loved you long ago,
But I didn't know your head could be turned
By wealth and glamour.

I followed you to London,
And thought you'd returned,
But didn't know your head could be turned, by danger,
To public safety.

I found myself in harmony
With him who'd taken you away before.

At times like these,
Romantics say,
They find you in the Universe,
But I know the Universe is empty,
And that is our only blessing.

7. THINGS APPEAR

Things appear and disappear;
The Universe is huge, and empty.

If we hold onto selves, through fear and hurt,
We cause blockages in Reality.
Yet still, it flows.

Let the fear and hurt dissolve
And flow downstream to the vast Ocean.

Reality flows through this changing shape
Which is temporarily, me.

I WON'T BE WRITING
ANY MORE NOVELS
Elizabeth J. Lister

... because the five I've written in the last eleven years have served my purpose, which was to introduce brave women who survive adverse circumstances like my characters Dee, Helen and Tracy (and their author). I'm reluctant to leave their company and that of their partners and family members but they have reached retirement age and can be left to live out their fictional life within their homosexual relationships (unlike their author).

My writer friends, Kathryn and Elsa, say, 'You could write a journal. Your daily emails are interesting.' But I can't see that details which make up the life of an eighty-one year old single woman who lives alone would hold much of interest for anyone. It's a different matter with the book I'm reading this week. Now that is a journal! It's written by May Sarton, a bisexual woman, much published as a novelist and poet. You see, she was born in Belgium to an academic father and wonderful embroidress mother and in my count that was a positive cultural start in life even if it meant her family had to escape from Belgium to live in America.

In the World War II years I lived in safe-ish places, in between Liverpool and Manchester. We never had to huddle in the air-raid shelter which was as well because it was always a foot deep in water. My dad did a good job of keeping the goods department of the railways running throughout the war. I hadn't begun to discover my mother's considerable talents (apart from her knitting. She was a Scot and I have inherited her love of Fair Isle knitting). She was just comfortingly there. It was a surprise, years later, to hear her say, 'My life was so empty; I used to stand in my bedroom and look out at the fields and think, "Is there to be no more to my life than this?"' And then she became Chair of this and Organiser of that and now we treasure her embroidery which she developed under tuition at afternoon classes. May Sarton writes a lot about desolation in the lives of married women. I quickly removed myself from my unhappy marriage situation by asking my husband to leave me. It didn't make for an easy life but it was one I steered myself.

I was jealous of May Sarton when I first started to read her journal but then she introduces subjects that concern me like 'loyalty'; the criticism one gets if one talks freely about people and money and things, like she did and I do. I defend my talkativeness in that I would never deliberately hurt anyone with what I say and May Sarton has the same approach and I like her a bit better. She met Virginia Woolf and says wise things about the enviable freedom the Bloomsbury Set had in which to be themselves. I admire and envy her literary success but I began to write at such a late date that success would probably exhaust me now. Could you see me travelling distances to speak about my novels like May Sarton did?

I am still alive. May S died in 1996. I'd like to have known her. I think I would not have been afraid to enter into a friendship with her. I am afraid of what some people think of me, less now that I'm surer of myself. She and I both love/loved flowers; she much more expansively and expensively than me. But here Elsa has made me laugh. I lent Elsa May Sarton's journal. 'Poor flowers!' Elsa says. 'They only have to show their heads above the soil and May Sarton whips them into a vase!' Don't we interpret actions differently?

Elsa is having a birthday today. She is so patient in her bed-ridden days and brave and helpful to me. Her sharp mind makes very interesting comments about the things I say or what she has read. This morning I threw away my Christmas cards but I kept the one from her in which she says how much she is enjoying reading my last book *Consequences*. Elsa has Kathryn. And that is something else that I won't experience in this lifetime, a loving relationship for more than forty years ...

May Sarton is disappointing when she talks about love. She calls her lover X but apart from going for walks she doesn't give any intimation of what she and her lover 'do'. I like details! The graphic sex descriptions in my stories please most of my readers ... but not one male musician friend who hasn't recovered from shock ... he never noticed that the sex was part of the story. He must have been colossally naïve; he daren't read my other books.

I do wish I had more friends with whom to talk books and writing and poetry and painting like I do with Elsa and Kathryn. My ex-lover best-friend, whom I had better call Y (if 'journals' are not to admit full names) listens patiently and suffered the long periods of my absorption in writing novels but she's glad now that I've stopped. There's just Jane in Manchester and Fran in Berwick who are interested. You can see why my emails every morning to Elsa and Kathryn matter so much to me. I tentatively mentioned my books and writing to friends a few times during my Christmas vacation with my daughter and her partner in Kent. I was told that I spoke too much about it. 'You've written five potboilers, get over it,' was the attitude. I allowed myself to be hurt. ('Always take responsibility for your reactions' my counsellor at Mind said.) I felt wronged and sad.

I seem to invite the 'put down'. Y thinks I exaggerate when I say this but there were teachers who took every chance to 'dress me down', make me feel small; no, worse than that, to crush me. It's very easy to crush someone who doesn't know who they are, who is a jumble of what she thinks she ought to be. The therapy would come years later.

Two horrible women have crossed my path; that's when I quote Christian advice to myself. Jesus said to his disciples that if they were not welcome in a place they must shake the dust of that place off their feet. I shook those two women out of my life. 'You'll have to meet up with them again to sort out the spiritual relationship between you,' one would-be Sufi priestess said to me. No fear! I uploaded a message to my Guardian Angel, 'Please make sure that never happens!' My Guardian Angel has a lot of work to do on my behalf. He/She (nicely androgynous like me) makes me smile. I ask a question and the answer is downloaded before I've finished sending it.

Then a guest at a Boxing Day party, a solicitor from Australia, said to me, 'Right, I've told you what I do. Now, what about you? I take it you're a writer.' I loved that! To be taken as a writer when I hadn't said anything about my hobby!

My elder daughter was seriously helpful in that she made critical studies of each of my scripts when they were in their elementary stage; my younger daughter says, 'I can't read your novels while you're alive, Mum. I'm embarrassed. I'll read them when you've gone.'

May Sarton's *Journal* was written when she was fifty-eight. That is so young! I hadn't even started to play an accordion when I was fifty-eight. Y bought me an old accordion and it opened up my life to personal achievement, playing in a band and a steamy love affair with a married man. It is interesting that one really does 'fall in love'. That terrific excitement when you wonder if the attraction is mutual. One night (I'd better call him Z) carried my heavy accordion out to my car after band practice and when I got home the love realisation flooded in. I couldn't go to bed, just stood feeling rapture and looking out at the full moon.

But then Y was enraged and I broke off the affair. I was ashamed. My experience as a rejected wife had been painful in the extreme. I shot northwards to live in Berwick-upon-Tweed, near my younger daughter.

I wanted to continue with my accordion playing but the folk music at Gatherings in Northumberland has to be Northumbrian. I was a bit pissed off that they were so precious about their heritage and thought, 'I live here now. I'll make my own heritage.' I wrote this song about my house.

THE WEE BITTIE HOOSE

There's a wee bittie hoose, it's in Berwick-on-Tweed, in
    a street that gangs doon tae the sea
Through a great big gate in the auld toon wa's (that
    Elizabeth's ramparts be)
And the wee bittie street is no' very straight and the
    hooses are a' diff'rent height
And the wee bittie winders they a' face north and they
    dinna let in much light
But ... the wee bittie hoose it is mine Ohooo!
The wee bittie hoose it is mine.

I've got copies of deeds of the purchasers frae nigh on
    three hundert year
And what were their names and how much they paid,
    a' scribed in Copperplate clear
And there at the top of each document is the reign of
    the king or the queen
And how much of land they ruled at the time (e'en
    France is there I've seen)
And ... the deeds of the hoose they are mine Ohooo!
The deeds of the hoose they are mine.

> Now all of they folk want to visit me in this toon of
>   Berwick sae auld
> 'Cos they ken I've a hoose wi' bedrooms twae and the
>   sea at the end of the road
> So, I walk them roond on the auld toon wa's and tak
>   them along tae the pier
> Then I sit them doon on my winder seat and gie them a
>   drink of guid cheer
> In ... the wee bittie hoose that is mine Ohooo!
> The wee bittie hoose that is mine.

The song won second prize at Alnwick, first prize at Morpeth and I was invited to sing at the winners' concert.

I like an opportunity to read to an audience or perform. I like the applause and knowing it's something I do well that is very much a part of who I am. It was enjoyable last week in London when I launched my last book, *Consequences*. The audience was small but friendly and it was great to TALK ABOUT MY BOOKS to those few interested people! A couple of glasses of wine made us cheerful. Also, Ellie was there. I don't see much of my daughters with the younger living in Berwick-upon-Tweed and the elder in Kent. One good thing about returning to live in Stoke-on-Trent, as I did in 2003, is that it's nicely half way between the two. Another good feature is that I live on a housing estate and I'm nicely anonymous, accepted as gay. 'You know the lesbian writer, the Love in the Modern World woman; that article in *The Sentinel*? Well, she had a half-hour interview on Radio Stoke recently.'

I told a neighbour that I was gay and she said her brother was gay and my other neighbour has a sister who is gay. Our Spanish teacher made us laugh this week. She was told when she was three that her uncle is gay and she thought it must be something wonderful. She says he was the light and life of any party but had to lie low in Franco's day. What a woman! Tall, long straight black hair, lovely bosom and wears very short skirts with black tights and boots. Y isn't doing too well with the Spanish but she goes to class to enjoy the teacher ...

No, I don't think I'll be doing any more lengthy writing. I've my knitting to finish and telly to watch and the gardening when the weather bucks up ... and I'm going to stay in Berwick-upon-Tweed after Easter and Y and I are going on a day-trip to Gloucester in April. And Ellie would like us to do the 'sherry triangle' in Spain. I say, 'Let's do it, I'm getting older! The next book of May Sarton's that I've bought to read has the title *At Eighty-Two*.

HUMAN EMOTIONS
David Reade

'There is no explanation for human emotions.' Alice said this deliberately, slowly and often, and I knew she was right. Alice had been a psychotherapist before retiring and becoming my next door neighbour, and she thought she knew a thing or two about the mind.

'Of course,' she went on, 'when it comes to divorce or separation or the end of the affaire – well, that's different insofar that different people react differently.'

'You're going off at a tangent,' I replied. 'Every divorcée feels awful, but awfully different.'

'This conversation isn't getting us very far,' Alice observed. 'What I meant to say is – or was – that when people behave in an extraordinary fashion because of their emotions we should not be surprised.'

'But you told me you were divorced twice, Alice.'

'Yes, that's true, but it was a long time ago. I'm better off by myself. I don't care for men anyway.'

'You never said that before,' said I, looking straight at her. 'Do you mean to say you don't fancy men?'

'You're right there, dear. But I don't fancy women either. I'm not Sapphic, you know.'

'You just don't like sex.'

'That's it, I don't.'

'Must be very useful for you, Alice,' I said, thinking about how much time and energy I devoted to finding a sexual partner.

'It means that I don't have to haunt the bars every night as some do. In any case, I can't take alcohol anymore.' Alice gave me a wicked grin as she said this. I grinned back and left to do my shopping.

Was it a problem, I asked myself, going out every night? Of course, I lived so close to the Boltons and the Coleherne near Earls Court – no more than five minutes' walk – and it was easy for me to pop into those bars and see people I knew. In fact, on one Saturday night two thirds of the customers turned out to be acquaintances of mine. As far as pick-ups went, these usually happened after the bar was closed and everyone hung around outside. There was also a street near-by, which the *News of the World* had referred to in a prurient article as 'the street of shame', where sex could be had if one persevered long enough, avoided the occasional police pres-ence and wore warm clothes. It was especially convenient for me since I lived so near to this street.

I came to the conclusion that it was only a problem if I wanted it to be. If I were old, like Alice who was nearly sixty, that would be different. Perhaps I shouldn't want sex then and would stay in my Redcliffe Gardens one-bed flat, perhaps having a dog for company and walking to Holland Park every afternoon if my legs would let me.

However that was a long time off as I was only just over thirty and might not even live that long, although I tried to live a healthy lifestyle.

It was about two weeks later on a Friday night at about eleven-thirty, and I found myself in the Gigolo Club in Kings Road, Chelsea, standing next to a promising looking guy of about twenty-four. After a few minutes, our hands touched and we started a kissing and cuddling session in the dark club. This continued for half an hour, when we left at my suggestion and went back to my flat, which was twenty minutes' walk away.

A most successful sex romp began which lasted a long time and continued again in the morning after the guy, whose name was Colin, stayed the night.

It was late when we left the bed, about eleven o'clock in the morning, and I prepared breakfast for my new-found lover, serving bacon and eggs at the kitchen table while gazing into his eyes.

At that moment came a knock at the door. 'Sorry to bother you, dear,' said Alice in her kindly way. She favoured everyone with the appellation 'dear.' 'I just wondered whether – oh sorry, I didn't know –'

'No, come in, Alice,' I said. 'This is Colin.'

'Hullo, dear,' said Alice, then the look on her face changed. I had never seen an expression change so quickly and in this way. Then I noticed Colin's handsome face had also changed: he was gazing at Alice in some consternation.

At last Alice spoke. 'Is your name really Colin?'

'Yes,' Colin replied.

'I swore I'd know your face anywhere, even after twenty years. My God!'

'Is your name really Alice?' Colin asked.

Alice nodded in the affirmative and they continued looking at each other.

Then Colin said in a strangled voice, 'Is it really you?'

Alice replied, 'Yes, I believe so.'

Colin jumped up from his chair and flung his arms around Alice, crying, 'Mother!' Alice hugged him back and I saw both their eyes streaming with tears. 'You are my son, my Colin,' she said, her voice breaking with emotion. 'What an amazing wonder!'

'I don't understand,' said I rather stupidly, although I assumed that Colin was Alice's long-lost son somewhere along the line.

'I had a son once,' Alice began, 'but when he was only three years old my husband divorced me and he got custody of the boy. I wasn't allowed to see him because I was in a psychiatric ward because of my alcoholism. My heart was broken and I thought I'd never get over it. That's what made me take up psychotherapy – to help myself as much as others really.' Alice tightened her grip on Colin. 'But I knew I'd always know him again if I saw him. Oh, my son, my son!'

'And I always knew I'd know my mum again if I saw her. I used to look for her on every street corner, and now –' Colin buried his face in Alice's shoulder and I saw his own shoulders shaking. This was an amazing scene to witness at breakfast.

'Let me look at you.' Alice broke out of the embrace and gazed at Colin's features. 'Why, you're a most attractive boy, you've grown up into a nice looking young man. You must have taken after me, not after your father.'

'You don't mind that I'm gay, Mummy?'

'Of course not, dear. You're entitled to live your own life as you want it, and I shall support you all the way. At least, I shan't be a grandmother,' she added mischievously.

'It was him,' Colin advised, pointing to me, 'who got us together. Isn't he marvellous?'

I replied to this, my eyes wet with emotion. 'I'm not marvellous, it's just a coincidence that I met you last night and that your long-lost mother happens to live next door.'

'Well, this is a most happy day,' Alice said, still clinging to her son. 'I certainly never expected the morning to become like this. It felt like an ordinary morning, then, without warning, ordinary morning became extraordinary day.' Alice was half singing and her voice was breaking.

Neither did I expect such a morning, but I felt so happy for them and it seemed that a new light was shining on our three lives and on the house in Redcliffe Gardens where Alice and I lived.

This new light continued to shine, and within a few weeks Colin had moved in with me, putting an end to my rackety life in the bars (except sometimes when he was away on business and I popped in). Naturally, we saw as much of Alice as we could, visited her in hospital and nursed her through her final illness.

All this happened years ago and Alice died, while Colin and I are still together. People refer to us as the Darby and Joan couple.

How I wish Alice could have been there for our gay wedding, she would have been so proud.

As dear Alice was fond of saying, 'There is no explanation for human emotions.'

How right she was.

BINKIE AND THE SNOWBIRDS
John Dixon

(A monologue to be performed with a Southern drawl)

Excuse me. Why are you staring at me like that? There's nothing wrong in looking good, is there? Haven't you ever seen a man wearing a bracelet before? New here, are you? Snowbird? Flown in for our winter. Well, we're hot all year round.

Oh, it's my dog you're looking at, is it? A lot of people do. Almost everyone round here has got a dog. A little dog. Wonderful ice-breakers. It's how we became such a tight-knit community. You can stroke it if you want. It won't bite. Can't you see? It's not real. Not anymore. It's stuffed. Runs on castors. A lot of people have their favourite dog stuffed. And then made up to look its best. My one's not actually my favourite. And that is quite unusual. There's a story behind it. Buy me a cocktail, and I'll tell you.

I got Binkie as a puppy. So I could train her. She didn't need it. From the start she had her own routines. She ended up planning my life! Always the same route for her walks. Always the same time. And always ending at this café. Binkie just loved it here. Ever the centre of attention. She showed up all the other dogs. Everyone made a fuss of her. She never went without. She had a really good life. All she ever wanted.

Not terribly adventurous perhaps. They say dogs walk three times as far as their owners. Binkie didn't. Most times when I let her off the leash she'd still trot along by my ankles, half the time expecting to be picked up and carried. It was the same routine every day. Out the apartment, down the stairs –

she hated elevators – over to the greenwalk alongside the swamp, then on to the bridge, where we'd look down on the alligators. And I'd cuddle Binkie and say, 'Be a good girl, or the crocs'll get you.' She knew I didn't mean it. 'You can't be too careful,' I said. Which was true. Because the alligators do come out – on the road you see them sometimes. They're no danger to humans. Adults, anyway. But they do take dogs. Quite frightening some of the stories you hear.

I actually thought of changing the route we took for our walk. Especially when building started on that apartment block overlooking the swamp. Too close for comfort for my liking. The apartments weren't cheap. They were advertised and sold before they were built. The dirt and disruption! And the thought of being spied on as you walked past with your dog. I tried another route, but Binkie wasn't having it. She was so set in her ways. The block got higher and higher, and some apartments were occupied before the garden surround had been properly landscaped. They just couldn't wait to get in and take over. Not likely to be the sort of people we'd want to know. Binkie and I hastened past the block and avoided eye contact. When we got to the bridge we'd studiously look at the swamp, and spot the alligators.

Well, one day as we were hurrying past I heard a peal of laughter. I thought it might be at my expense. I was not going to let that pass. I looked up and on the top floor, right in the picture window, was a couple, both young, both stripped to the waist, nice bodies, just fooling around. I have to admit they were the finest newcomers I'd seen that year. Take back all I said. Roll on the fresh meat. Made me feel younger just looking at them. They were so into each other, so pre-occupied they hadn't seen me. I couldn't take me eyes off them. Then they both waved, genuine, smiling. I thought, 'That's nice. Snowbirds fitting in so quickly.' I waved back. They tried to open the picture window, but they couldn't manage it and began tapping on the glass fit to break it – as if they were trying to get out, with a fire or something trapping their exit. I ran across the road to help. They started shaking their heads and pointing frantically. Then I realised.

They were warning me. I turned round and saw Binkie being tossed in the air by an alligator, and plunging headfirst down its open jaws. Before I could shout, 'Come back, that's my dog' the croc was underwater with hardly a ripple. Nothing surfaced. Not even a bubble. I ran to the bridge and looked both sides. There was nothing. It was so silent. I could hear my own sobs.

One of the regular dog-walkers saw me and ran up and I told him what had happened. He said, 'You've gotta get another dog. You mustn't let this put you off. It's like a car accident or a plane crash. You must get straight back in the driving seat. Get on the next scheduled flight wherever it's going. That's the only way. Promise me you won't leave it too long.'

I supposed this was right, but I didn't feel to do anything immediately. A week or so later I forced myself to the local pet store. It's a very good one. A comprehensive range of dogs. Little dogs. I saw one there. The spitting image of Binkie. I couldn't believe my eyes. Almost as if she'd come back. Unfortunately it was a He. But in everything else it could have been her. I just knew I had to have it. I didn't even ask the price. I said straightaway to the assistant, 'I want that one.' 'Certainly, sir,' he said. 'And is there anything else, sir.' 'Yes,' I said. 'Have it put to sleep and get it stuffed.'

I got the idea for the platform on castors from a lady friend. She had a dachshund, a sausage dog. I never liked them myself. Their back legs go. You can strap on a special trolley. Like a horse and cart, with the horse pulling its own back legs.

So there we are. Things haven't changed. I still take the new Binkie for a walk. We're here every day about this time. Most of the regulars think it's the original Binkie. If they look too closely between its legs I say, 'She had a sex change just before she died.'

The only difference is the dog leash. I bought one of those retractable ones. It works on the same principle as a hoover cable, but much more powerful. I keep it at a short length to pull Binkie alongside me. But when we get to the greenwalk, in front of the new apartments, I take Binkie down to the water's edge and rush back to the sidewalk unthreading the leash. In no time the alligator comes out and heads straight for Binkie. I push the catch on the leash and Binkie shoots across the grass faster than ever a living dog could run. You should hear the castors clatter on the sidewalk. And the alligator – it's the same one, I know, they're very territorial – goes without. Serve it right. It'll come to regret what it did. It's already looking thinner.

I do this every day. Just to taunt it. And I like to think that the pair of Snowbirds are still looking out the apartment block. I couldn't live like that. Stuck inside, top floor, viewing the world out a picture window. Elevator permanently out of order. Pretty sure I saw one of them recently. Close up he was nothing. And much older than you'd think. Hardly worth a second glance.

Go on, pat him if you want. It'll cost you another cocktail. You don't wag your tail anymore, do you, darling? Don't suppose the alligator does either. What did you say your name was?

SEVEN POEMS

Jeremy Kingston

LIVE LOBSTERS
DANCING NIGHTLY

(Sign above Fran's Restaurant, Toronto)

At half past ten the joint's really jumping,
We've been looking forward to this all day,
I mean it has to be something really special,
They don't have acts like this in Hudson Bay.

Jake says they train them in the Maritimes,
Salsa, ballroom, disco, even ballet,
Last week two of them did the jitterbug,
Nobody jitterbugs in Hudson Bay.

Look, here they come now. Seven, eight of them.
Oh, this is classic stuff! What a display!
All keeping step too, waving those pincers –
Flicking them, clicking them, snapping away!

Crazy! Fantastic! Who'd have believed it!
And there's no wastage either – downstairs they
Boil those who are past it, put them on sale:
We'll take some back with us to Hudson Bay.

FEELING THE PRESSURE

You're standing on this crowded Tube, become
aware of some hard thing against your bum.
You shift a bit but soon it's there again,
as if it knows you like it there. So then
you have to see who's doing this. – Oh. Right.
He winks. You wink. Your pants start feeling tight.
Then he says *Where you getting off?* You say
Same place as you. You're facing him. *OK?*
And so a few stops later you or he
finds himself where he hadn't planned to be.
Never know what can happen on the Tube,
one of you says, stretching for the lube.

ORCHIS ITALICA
(popular name: Uomo nudo)

If I'd in boyhood wandered
the Capri mountainsides
I could have stood and pondered
where each rare orchid hides.

The Monkey, Spider, Fly and Bee,
the Butterfly, the Wren,
and oh! look down there, do you see?
a field of Naked Men.

Regrettably, the Wren Orchid has yet to be discovered, although the 105 species of
European orchid include, in addition to the above, Bird's Nest, Bug, Bumble Bee,
Frog, Gander-goose, Lady, Lizard, Man, Saw-fly and Woodcock. A convenient rhyme
would have been the Fen Orchid but its southern limit is northern Italy and, anyway,
there are no fens on Capri.

MOONLIGHT RAMBLE

A few weeks into each year Dad
threw out the old year's diary.
His last survives (of course), no entries after March,
and just one other, sixty years its elder,
the year he engaged himself, so eagerly, to his future
    wife.
He writes, with the finest nib, *Tea with Kitty,*
Dinner with Kitty,
Walked back across Heath.
He notes his monthly salary (painfully meagre),
cigarettes smoked (Kensitas, De Reszke).
In March he reads *Antic Hay,* in April *Bliss,*
He plays chess every Friday.
The entries are brief and comment-free.
Did he enjoy *Antic Hay*, *No, No Nanette*, *From Morn to*
    Midnight?
He sits an examination in the week the
Great General Strike begins and fails.
But did he mind this? He doesn't say.
And then, overnight from Saturday the 26th of June,
thirteen months to the day before the wedding,
he goes with two friends on a *Moonlight Ramble.*
They catch the last train (11.45) to Loughton,
halt for refreshments at 2 and at 3
when *Mrs Rossett lights candles*
(they are now in Epping Forest).
The first bird sings at 4.29,
at 4.59 he is harpooning sticklebacks,
5.10 a corncrake croaks,
at 5.29 the sun is observed.
Again he says nothing of any feeling though
I like to think he enjoyed his early morning breakfast
Sat on corner Buckhurst Hill in the sun.
It's the detail, the times precisely noted

5.11 *Gnats*
that make me decide he relished every moment,
even the gnats.
And there's never a mention of Thérèse of Lisieux
or the Curé D'Ars or Rose of Lima,
saints who fatigued my childhood.
4.59 *Harpooning Sticklebacks*
I could have loved him then.

SCHOOLBOY'S PRAYER

Edney, Kite-Powell, Bellenger and Schmidt –
Dread Lord of Vengeance, sentence them to stand
Up to their eyeballs in a lake of shit.

First let them kneel and I'll have braziers lit,
I want to smell the fiery irons brand
Edney, Kite-Powell, Bellenger and Schmidt.

Then let them plunge into that stinking pit
thrust down further by your infernal hand
up to their eyeballs in a lake of shit.

Impale them upon pokers, hit and split
their balls to pulp, now let them be unmanned!
Edney, Kite-Powell, Bellenger and Schmidt

cockless in Reigate, just a dribbling slit –
that's even better than to watch them land
up to their eyeballs in a lake of shit!

O gorgeous vision of the biters bit,
with each slow, screaming death minutely planned.
Edney, Kite-Powell, Bellenger and Schmidt,
up to their eyeballs in a lake of shit.

PANTIES AND BRA

Let us pretend to be somebody quite
Different, quite other than what we are.
How does it feel to be wearing her high, tight
Yellow embroidered shoes, panties and bra?

EXIT FROM EDEN

You mean we must leave?
Say goodbye to the garden?
OK, then, let's fuck.

LOVE AND HATE
Alice F. Wickham

When the parents moved to their one-bed bungalow by the sea, I had the stark impression that I was no longer required. It was no fun sleeping on the sofa in the living room, dressing in the bathroom and trying to avoid eye-contact with those two bozos, so I moved out.

My friend K had found this place; it was the first floor conversion flat of a narrow Georgian terrace in a grey Dublin suburb. At eighteen years of age, our expectations were low. We had a door knocker, a set of stairs, a kitchen, a bathroom and somewhere to lay our heads. Our bedroom glanced out over a patch of garden, a bald patch, but a patch nonetheless. The bare floorboards were dollied up with brown varnish lending a respectable appearance. A thin, see-through rug and faux-leather sofa completed the House and Garden décor and K placed a wispy little fern on the windowsill; it gave the place a homey touch.

K was large, and I was lean, but we managed to manoeuvre around each other in the cramped kitchen space. K would put the kettle on, and I would fetch the cups, and then I would move to the sink while K would edge toward the larder. It was a study in movement and dance, like miniature theatre.

If we argued, it was over silly things like butts left in saucers, or towels crumpled on the floor. Once, when my face broke out in spots, I discovered that K had been using my face towel to wash her bits. We didn't speak for days. I wasn't about to have a face like a prickly pear for the sake of keeping the peace. That was a seminal moment in our friendship. After that, K kept her hands off my towel.

At night, we tramped off to a bar on Nassau Street that

sold imported lager. It came in tall brown bottles with a canary yellow label, and HOLSTEIN drafted in big bold letters; seriously strong shit. If we scraped our pennies together, we could get wasted on three or four drinks. One night, we drank like sailors, having persuaded a couple of Libyans to buy us drinks all evening. They probably thought they were going to shag us rotten. Well, that never happened. We flew out of there at around midnight and caught the bus back to Fairview, giggling our arses off.

We passed out back at the flat. At around 4 a.m. I woke up and saw maggots crawling up and down the wall. I screamed and K woke up, rubbing her eyes.

'What's wrong?'

I pointed at the wall, 'White maggots! They're coming down from the ceiling!'

'Go back to sleep, Alex,' K said.

After a while, my eyes adjusted to the flowered wallpaper, and what I thought were maggots was a pattern of leaves and branches. Only then, I realised I was lying in K's bed.

'Why are we sleeping together in this bed?' I asked.

Then I dropped back down on the pillow and prepared to conk out again.

K took my hand and placed it on her thigh, hot and damp with sweat.

'K, what are you doing?' I asked, puzzled.

K slid my hand up along her thigh. I pulled away but K held on fast.

'Oh, Alex,' she moaned.

I felt queasy. 'K, what the fuck is going on?'

She took my fingers and placed them in her wet vagina.

I felt embarrassed. 'K, this is not a good idea, you'll regret this in the morning,' I told her.

K moaned.

Then it all came together in my head, the delirium I felt,

K's moaning, the feeling of her warm, wet open pussy, the strange exhilaration at hearing her cry out, the feeling of joy when K moaned with pleasure. I plunged into the wetness and K came all over my fingers.

The next morning, when I awoke, the room was ablaze with disgusting white light. I got up and closed the curtains. K was still asleep, snoring like a walrus.

I got up and went into the kitchen to make tea. There was one teabag left and still a scrap of milk in the bottle, so that was good. The one thing we always had was a bag of white, Tate & Lyle sugar. But there was no bread for toast; we'd run out.

K and I lived on air. The only time we ate was when K invited me home to her mother's house for Sunday lunch with her siblings who were all large and lusty like K. I liked that, and the kitchen stove was always groaning with gigantic pots full of beef and potatoes, marrowfat peas and good green cabbage. On those occasions, I ate like a horse. The rest of the time I had a gnawing hunger.

While her Ma dished out the food in the kitchen, K's Da sat in the front room reading the bible and bemoaning his fate. He despised his progeny and loathed his wife for producing them, but he accepted it as God's will.

I took the tea into the bedroom and poked K awake. She woke grumpily, like a bear coming out of hibernation. I handed her the watery cup of tea and she sipped quietly with a sheepish look on her face. Finally, she looked at me with those large, velvety, come-to-bed eyes. 'Alex, did we ...?'

'Yes, we did,' I said, grinning from ear-to-ear.

I looked at my best friend, sitting up in the bed, stone cold naked. She was no longer the fat, funny, feminine, slightly cookie character I had grown used to; she was a beautiful exotic goddess, as round and ripe as a melon. 'It was wonderful,' I said.

K looked down at her cup. 'Alex ... I ... we ...'

'Don't be ashamed, K,' I told her. 'I have to admit, it was gross at first but ...'

K splurted in her tea.

I felt alarmed. 'K, what's the matter? Do you want an aspirin? Some liver salts maybe?'

This new concern I felt for my friend took me by surprise.

'I'm fine, Alex,' K said.

'K, you've opened my eyes, I never felt this way before.'

K put her tea down on the floor by the bed. 'Listen, Alex, I know we had our bit last night, but we mustn't ever do that again.'

I was dumbstruck. Surely K couldn't mean what she had just said. 'Huh?'

'We were drunk, Alex,' said K. 'It was a mistake.'

'No, it wasn't,' I said.

'Yes, it was,' said K. 'And, Alex, I'm a full-blooded, heterosexual woman.'

'So, am I,' I said. 'But what's that got to do with anything?'

K looked at me, pityingly. 'You're gay, Alex, and it's not that I've got anything against lesbians, but I'm not one myself.'

She got me there. So, I was a lesbian and she wasn't. What the fuck did that mean? I was too much of a gentleman to remind her that she had seduced me, not the other way around.

'If you say so, K.'

'I'm still your best friend though. That hasn't changed.'

Later that day my face broke out in nasty red spots. This time it wasn't to do with K using my face towel on her undercarriage. It had more to do with K using my paw on her pussy.

All day long I puzzled over the incident, but K being a 'full-blooded' whatever, didn't worry me unduly. It was a case of 'the lady doth protest too much' and I felt certain that in time, K would confess to the fact that she was head-over-heels in love with me, as I was with her.

The word 'lesbian' bothered me, a lot. It was not a title I relished. When I was a young kid, there were two oddball women who used to stroll through the neighbourhood holding hands. The other kids used to laugh and call them names, like 'freaks' or 'lesbo', but I found them fascinating. I liked the way they seemed to exist in a world of their own, drifting like spectres through the housing estate, totally unconcerned with their surroundings. I didn't see myself that way; a hand-holding freak.

Weeks later, I acquired a new boyfriend, P. P's father was a big-wig in Guinness and they lived in a posh villa in Ballsbridge. P had been to Trinity College and shit, whereas I had left school at fifteen. P told me he was an 'intellectual', but that I was not a bad looking girl, and so that evened us out.

When P climbed on top of me with his huge red throbbing penis, I felt a muted panic. It took ages for me to adjust to the idea of having that thing inside my vagina. Luckily for me, I had broken my virginity with a man of slender means, who would ask, 'Can you feel it?' over and over again, as he slipped back and forth with his knitting needle penis. He broke my intact hymen with nary a murmur. But P made up in cock, what he lacked in body mass. It was as if all of his muscular attributes were concentrated between his legs. It was shocking.

One night, to stimulate my sex buds he introduced me to porn. I waited in anxious expectation as he inserted the videotape into the machine. Figures appeared before us on the screen. P removed his wire-framed glasses, put his arms around my shoulders and began fondling my breasts.

'This is great, isn't it?' P said.

I didn't know what to say. I felt sorta numb, sitting there watching two naked white bodies doing gymnastics on screen. There was a lot of pulling and shoving going on prior to the sex act.

'It's boring,' I said.

P laughed. He had a sense of humour; I'll give him that. 'Wait,' he said. 'It gets better. I promise.'

'OK,' I said.

I waited. Eventually, the man put his penis inside the woman and moved back and forth, mechanically, like a marionette. I saw the penis going back and forth. Then the woman sat astride the man, and I saw his balls and cock swallowed by her vagina. Their pink and white nakedness repelled me.

'Are you getting excited yet?' P asked, his breathing faster than before. 'Because I am.'

His hands squeezed and kneaded my breasts like putty. I remembered my cookery nun, Sister Consuelo, instructing me to roll and squeeze, roll and squeeze the dough.

Eventually, P got up the courage to unzip his fly and let his thing pop out. He took my hand and placed it atop his manhood, whereupon I squeezed and rolled, squeezed and rolled.

'Not so hard,' P said.

'Sorry,' I said and lightened my touch a little, which pleased P.

'You have a great set-up here,' P said through his hot breath. 'What with that fabulous body of yours, and this place, nice and private, you and I can have a lot of fun together.'

'I suppose so,' I said, stroking away.

When P came, he seemed displeased. 'What about you?' He asked, accusingly, 'Did you enjoy that?'

'It was OK,' I said, noticing P's acne scars again.

The relationships foundered after that event, and I returned to my emotional obsession with K.

One night, drunk as skunks, K and I repeated our love-making. The next morning it was the same as before.

'Did we do something naughty last night?' K asked.

A ray of sunlight came through the open window of the bedroom, catching K's curly blonde hair and lighting up her face, she looked like a Botticelli angel.

'I'm in love with you K,' I told her, opening my heart at last.

K lit up a Silk Cut and blew smoke into the room. 'Alex, I know we had our bit, last night.'

'Why do you call it that?' I said, trying not to show my annoyance.

'What?'

' "Our bit." It sounds so pathetic.'

'That's all it is, Alex,' K said. 'It's just a bit of sex.'

'It's more than that K,' I said.

'No, Alex. It's not.'

She repeated her mantra about being a full-blooded hetero-sexual woman strictly into men. She said we had to stop doing what we were doing.

'We're not doing anything wrong,' I pouted.

'Yes, we are Alex.'

'But we're in love,' I protested. 'How can we stop, and why should we?'

Even as I said the words something inside me was rearing up against K. Didn't she realise what a bitch she sounded? Surely, she couldn't mean what she said, she was just difficult, or worse; maybe she was trying to hurt me. I mean really hurt.

'It was a mistake,' K said.

'Well, we keep making it,' I said.

'So we have to stop,' K said.

An engine screeched to a halt outside. I got up and went over to the window, butt naked.

'Alex! Get away from the window!' shouted K. 'Someone will see you. They'll think this is a brothel.'

'So what,' I said, watching the red van screaming away from the lights. I turned to K. 'Maybe it is a brothel, and maybe you're the whore.'

We didn't speak to each other for a week. Then the bickering began. K accused me of stealing her weight-loss tablets, I accused her of leaving her sanitary napkins on the bathroom floor. She said I left the door unlocked when I went out, I said she left her filthy cigarette butts everywhere except the ashtray. We avoided being in the kitchen together and tip-toed around each other in the one shared bedroom. I got a job downtown and left K to carry on working at the Hotel where we had both worked as barmaids.

That helped a lot. I didn't have to see her chatting up customers and she didn't have to see me glowering during our shifts.

My new job in a city café restored my self-esteem. The manager liked me, and pretty soon I was given a promotion. I got to open and close the café and see to it that the customers were served well. It made me feel good about myself.

I rang P to tell him the news. 'Hey, guess what, I've got a new career,' I told him.

'What's that?' P asked, who had just become a TV producer for RTE.

I told him about my responsible new position in the café.

'Hardly a career, now is it,' said P. 'More of a 'job', wouldn't you say?'

But back home, K was impressed. 'They made you into a manager?'

'Assistant manager,' I said.

'Wow, that's so cool.'

It didn't make a blind bit of difference. K still acted like a full-blooded bitch, going out with guys, coming home drunk, and avoiding me all over again.

One evening, K said. 'Alex, our friendship is suffering.'

'What friendship?' I asked.

'Oh Alex, I really want things to be the way they were before,' K said. 'Let's try and make it up.'

My ears pricked up. 'What does that mean? "Make it up." '

'Let's go out on the town this weekend.' She suggested. 'Have a few drinks and a laugh the way we used to do.'

I felt a smidgen of hope. K and I would be like old times, get drunk, get wasted and have a giggle and a laugh. Nothing complicated.

We decided to do a pub crawl along Capel Street and then head over to The Brazen Head near Christchurch so that we could score some dope from the Trinity eggheads who drank at that worthy establishment.

When we got there the pub was empty. I said to K, 'Let's get out of here, it's a desert.'

Then an old hippy raised his glass and grinned at us from the bar. K waved back at him, and for once I didn't mind.

'Encourage him,' I said. 'Maybe he'll come over and buy us a drink.'

To our surprise, he was one of the poets. Someone introduced him to the crowd, Donal Duggan, and we watched him get up on the mic and read his stuff. He was dressed in a white vest and a black leather waistcoat. He wore his hair long and in a ponytail, and his greying beard came down to his chest.

'Do you think he might stand us a few drinks?' I asked K.

'I'm not sure,' said K, sizing him up. 'Does he look like he has any money to you?'

'I'm not sure.'

We listened to the dude reciting his poetry about old mother Ireland, with references to the time of the troubles and shit. Most of it went over our heads.

'He keeps looking our way,' I said.

'Yeah, I know,' said K, batting her eyelids.

K did her magic and after his recitation the dude came over and joined us at our table.

'Would you ladies care for a joint?'

'Sure.'

We watched as he rolled the joint, his long, careful fingers sprinkling the brown powder across the tobacco like a magician, not losing a crumb. He took a few hefty tokes then passed it around. It was good shit and we got stoned right away.

'Where's the music in this place?' asked K.

'There's no music tonight,' Donal said. 'It's a poetry evening.'

Our hippy friend got up and left us holding the joint. We didn't mind. I looked about at the old pub with its lofty, Gaelic-speaking patrons and its stone and oak surrounds. All of a sudden I felt like a fish out of water. 'Let's go,' I said.

As we were getting up to leave, the hippy dude came back over to our table. He asked us where we lived. We told him, Fairview.

'That's a long way away,' he told us. 'Why not come back to my pad? I only live around the corner. I have a house in the Liberties.'

K and I looked at each other. Was he inviting us for a threesome or what?

'We don't do threesomes,' I said.

'Who said anything about threesomes,' the hippy said. 'I'm only offering you a place to crash for the night. How are you going to get back to Fairview at this hour?'

K looked at her watch. 'Jesus Christ, Alex, it's past

midnight. The buses are finished.'

'We'll walk,' I told her.

'I'm not walking all that way in the dark,' K said. 'Not at this hour. We'll get mugged!'

'Don't worry,' I said. 'You're with me.'

The hippy intervened. 'Ladies, ladies, don't be silly. Come home with me, I have a spare bedroom, and you can get a good night's sleep.'

'How many beds?' I asked.

'Well there's one in the spare room,' he said, 'And then there's mine, of course, a nice big king-sized bed ...'

All of a sudden the proposition seemed very attractive. If we kipped at his gaff, K and I would wind up sleeping together in the spare room, and the chances were she would try seducing me again, her being so pissed and stoned.

'Alright,' I told him. 'We'll stay over at yours, but no monkey business mister.'

He held up his hands. 'Scouts honour,' he said.

He drove us back to his house in a yellow Volkswagen Beetle. True to his word, he had a tiny, terraced house in the Liberties with two bedrooms one upstairs and one down. His bedroom was spread out over the whole of the upstairs floor, and he had an adjoining bathroom. There was no toilet downstairs, so I figured K and I would have to enter his bedroom to go to the toilet. What was more, we would have to climb the stairs in the middle of the night just to go for a pee. It sucked.

The three of us went into the kitchen.

'Listen,' Donal said, his long sensitive fingers rolling another joint. 'Why don't you two ladies sleep in my room? It will be much nicer if we all sleep together, I won't lay a finger on either of you, I promise.'

K looked at me. 'What do you think?'

I looked at Donal and then at K. It sounded OK, I thought.

The guy was gentle, not pushy, and he seemed lonely like he just didn't want sleeping alone. Perhaps that was all he needed, some company. All of a sudden, I felt sorry for the dude. 'OK,' I told him. 'We'll all sleep together, why not?'

'Suit yourselves,' Donal said.

Upstairs, there was a life-sized painting above his bed. He said it was a self-portrait of his ex, who had been a model. Another, tasteful charcoal of the same lady was hung in the hallway. K and I undressed and lay nervously in our knickers and bras on Donal's king-sized bed, watching him undress. He had a pale, skinny body. Tufts of hair sprang out from under his armpits and on his chest. He climbed naked into bed, his soft white penis swinging this way and that.

I drifted off to sleep and woke before dawn to the familiar sound of K, moaning in her sleep.

Sensing movement, I turned towards my friend. I saw Donal's thin rump, moving backwards and forwards, and I heard K cry out in ecstasy as he climaxed violently on top of her body. I bolted upright.

'You whore!' I screamed. 'You bloody fucken whore!'

K leapt out of bed and pulled the sheets up around her body.

Donal told us to leave.

'I'm sorry, girls, but I can't have bad vibes in my home.'

In the dead of night, he ejected us from his house. We walked back to Fairview in stony silence, me striding ahead, and K struggling to keep up, terrified of the menacing darkness surrounding us.

By the time we reached Fairview, morning had broken, and the milk delivery truck was out doing its rounds.

I turned the key in the lock and pounded up the stairs to the flat, two at a time. Once inside, I pulled my haversack down out of the wardrobe and began packing.

'What are you doing?' K asked, in a trembling voice.

'I'm going,' I said.

'But Alex, you can't leave, what about the rent?'

I shoved my things into the backpack.

K pleaded with me to stay.

'But Alex ...'

'Goodbye, K,' I told her and ran downstairs to the hallway.

FRED'S RETRIBUTION
Joseph Hucknall

Fred Grundy climbed the stairs to the back bedroom, took out his binoculars from the top drawer and scanned the house opposite. In a good light he was able to see into the rooms if he focussed the binoculars correctly. Nothing untoward appeared and he felt a twinge of disappointment until he saw a man in what appeared to be a white dressing gown, looking out from an upstairs window. He hadn't seen the man before and the room had not been occupied for some weeks which suggested to Fred that he was a new resident of the home. He looked to be surveying the scene but he caught Fred off guard when he quickly looked in his direction making Fred hide for cover behind the curtains.

Why the man should be in his dressing gown at two o'clock in the afternoon made Fred wonder, but he hadn't seen anyone else in the room so perhaps he was alone. As Fred peeped out from behind the curtains he saw the man draw the curtains together, an action which at that time of day, aroused his suspicions even more. Ever since the 'Residential Home for Gentlemen' opened, Fred had been consumed by curiosity of what went on inside. During his surveillances, which were several times a day, he had only seen men go in and out of the house and some of them were young and rough-looking and by no means could be described as gentlemen. Their frequent visiting fired his imagination and added to his suspicions of it being more of a home for homosexuals.

He heard his wife returning home and quickly put the binoculars back into the drawer, reminding himself to keep watch on that room. His wife, Minnie, was also obsessed by the establishment of the Home, but for different reasons. She raised objections on the grounds that it was a business in a residential area and would set a precedent if allowed, and had joined the campaign against it being opened, despite open hostility from her husband. 'Nothing to do with you,' he would say vehemently. She had even spoken out against it at a Council meeting, but as the house retained its residential status, the application had gone through.

Minnie and Fred Grundy were in their late sixties and childless and not in a happy marriage. They had both been celibate when they married in their mid-twenties and it soon became apparent that Minnie preferred to keep it that way. She had given in to his overtures on their honeymoon despite her headache but at breakfast had opined that she didn't know why such a thing as sex was made so much of. She had insisted on him wearing pyjamas she had bought for him, garments he had discarded in his youth, and Fred's attempts to smooth her acceptance of his manhood met only with disdain and excuses and the few occasions when she grudgingly acquiesced to his advances were devoid of emotion and immediately followed by visits to the bathroom to 'wash herself down'.

Fred eventually reconciled himself to the fact that he would have to forego his marital rights for the sake of peace and continue to find relief by occasional masturbation as he had done since his youth and any brief risky encounters in public toilets. Now he no longer considered having sex with his wife and their abstinence was never mentioned by either of them. After finding dissatisfaction with her marriage, Minnie had found religion and had long since moved into her own bedroom while Fred despised religion and slept alone often dreaming of having sex with men he had known.

Minnie had a long-standing school friend who had never married, who she shared confidences with and who was a willing listener of Minnie's recounting of her limited sexual experience.

'I could never do with it. All that humping and messiness. You would think that God would have devised a more savoury way of populating the world. Perhaps he did when he created Adam and Eve and then it was those two who got up to it. No wonder he banished them from the Garden of Eden. He obviously didn't approve of it either.'

Before retiring from her secretarial job where her typing skills were no longer needed, Minnie had to accept a demotion in fact if not in name to the Invoice Department, filling in for absentees and holidays generally, which ended her working life feeling bitter and resentful. Not having children to fill her days, she was consumed with other people's business, churchgoing and helping out at a charity shop when called upon, and harassing her husband. 'Looking after him', she called it. Not that Fred could not have looked after himself, but in her mind he could never manage on his own and as she often asked her friend, 'What would he do without me?'

Fred would have led a very different life without her and often thought of the sacrifices he had made to live the respectful 'normal' life his wife expected. Fred had been ambiguous about his sexual orientation before he married but never admitted to being homosexual, not even to himself. Rarely did he hear the word used and the euphemisms he did hear, such as queer, gay, poof, pansy, repelled him. At school he had fumblings with other boys and occasional masturbation in the toilets, but beyond these brief and guilt-ridden encounters he had controlled his urges.

When it became known that the house opposite was a residential home exclusively for men he became envious of the residents. It conjured up a companionship of men he had not known since he was in the army years ago. He had enjoyed the companionship of other men then and, although he had not indulged in sex with any of them, there had been occasions when he regretted having abstained. Then it would have been illegal and he was never one to risk being caught and possible prosecution, let alone imprisonment. Now, when sex with other men was permissible, and it was only in the pub and at work where he enjoyed the fellowship of other men, he felt he was paying a heavy price for his abstinence. The realisation made him question the continuance of his marriage. Thoughts of divorce increasingly surfaced in his mind and he knew he had good grounds for securing one, but the house was in both their names and, knowing his wife, she would not settle for half of it without pursuing him for half of everything else, including his company pension and modest savings.

Thoughts of divorce eventually turned to thoughts of her demise and how much better off he would be. He would own the whole house and everything else and, more to the point would be a free man again, free to follow his natural sexual inclinations. He had been a fool all these years to put up with her coldness and the restrictions she put on him. Yes, he thought, he would put an end to his marriage and to her. Minnie had warned him often enough that her heart would give out and she would die before him. She was something of a hypochondriac making frequent visits to her sympathetic compliant doctor who seemed all too ready to give her prescription pills. How could he put an end to her so called suffering, he wondered?

Fred looked up various drugs and chemicals on the websites and found that potassium chloride could produce signs of cardiac arrest and be fatal if an overdose was taken. He bought it over the counter without any questions being asked and next morning crushed one of the pills into her tea before he took her the cup in bed and waited for her reaction after drinking it. All she said was that she was still tired and was sorry that he had awakened her. The next morning he made the tea stronger and put two pills in. Minnie complained that the tea was too strong and later complained of having palpitations and feeling confused and that she would stay in bed until lunchtime. Fred said he would make her favourite soup, fresh tomato and basil, and would bring it up to her.

As he prepared the ingredients that morning he deliberated on his intensions and was having second thoughts until he began to envisage his future without his wife. He would be able to be his true self, free from her bickering and constraints, free to have his own life and sex with other men and be financially better off. With these thoughts strengthening his resolve, he added more tomatoes and basil and a good helping of sherry. At twelve o'clock he looked into the bedroom and saw his wife was awake.

'Are you ready for your soup, dear?'

'Yes, I feel quite hungry.'

'Then I'll give you more than usual. I've made it quite thick anyway.'

Arriving back in the kitchen, he hesitated momentarily in the realisation of what he was about to do but dismissed his apprehension, and with a shaking hand, finely crushed six of the pills and stirred them into the bowl of soup. On reflection he poured more sherry into the bowl, placed it onto a tray with a slice of bread and took it upstairs. His wife was sitting up in bed looking happy at the unusual solicitude shown by her husband.

'It looks good,' she said as he laid the tray on her lap.

'Yes. I have made it thicker than usual and I've added sherry to it.'

She took the first spoonful.

'I can taste it, but you have put too much salt in it.'

'I will bring you more if you want it. I'll have mine and then come back.'

He felt a pang of guilt on leaving the room and nearly turned round to take the soup back but with resolve that the deed was done he went into his bedroom, sat on the bed, and listened. He had not long to wait before he heard his wife gasping and convulsing before crying out for him. He covered his ears with his hands and steadfastly remained on the bed until the noises ceased.

He tentatively put his head into the bedroom and saw his wife lying unconscious, her eyes staring accusingly at him, her mouth wide open and her tongue hanging out. He bent over her but she was not breathing and he closed her eyes and mouth and left the bedroom. Downstairs he poured himself a large whisky and sat contemplating the finality of his action. No room for remorse now, he told himself, just think of what you have to do next. He decided to wait until the following morning before calling for the doctor and after looking into the bedroom to confirm that his wife was in fact dead he spent a sleepless night, burdened with guilt and worry over whether there would be a post-mortem.

The doctor came in the afternoon and after examining the body concluded the death was caused by a cardiac arrest and, as she had been on medication for her heart, a post-mortem would not be necessary. There were few mourners at the funeral, just her long standing school friend, two women from the charity shop, a woman who used to work with her, and Fred. The women commiserated Fred and agreed that her death had come as a shock but her long-standing friend said that Minnie had often complained of a weak heart and it was no surprise to her. After the cremation, Fred invited them all to have a glass of sherry or two with him at a pub, which in remembrance of Minnie and in sympathy to Fred, they readily accepted and, after they each recalled incidents in

Minnie's life, they all agreed how fortunate she had been to have such a devoted and loving a husband as Fred.

After the bereavement it did not take Fred long to put his house on the market, nor too long for it to be sold. With the date for the transfer agreed upon, Fred crossed the road to the Residential Home for Gentlemen and knocked on the door to make enquiries about residence there. He was received kindly by an elderly man who welcomed him into the hall. It was dimly lit and windowless but Fred could make out a crucifix hanging on the wall.

'I have just suffered a bereavement,' Fred explained. 'My wife, you see. Yes, very unexpected and now I'm looking for a residential home to live in. This one appeals to me, being for gentlemen only,' he added, risking a tentative smile.

The man looked at Fred curiously.

'Are you of the cloth then?' he asked.

'The cloth?' queried Fred in surprise.

'Yes. You don't have to be, but most of us are. We are known amongst the fraternity as the White Fathers, you know. Retired now, of course. Most of us were missionaries in Africa. We started in 1868. Not heard of us?'

'Oh, I didn't know,' Fred floundered. 'My wife never said that.'

'We chose the name, "Retired Home for Gentlemen", to be inclusive of others as we were informed that if we had called it "Retirement Home for White Fathers", as we wanted to, it would have been misinterpreted and deemed to be racially discriminating. But, of course, if you are not of the faith and don't mind prayers and grace, etcetera being said, your application can be considered by the committee.'

Fred suddenly felt weak and his optimism drain away.

'But what about the young men who come and go?'

'Young men? We have no young men living here. Oh! You must mean Dez and William. They come to work in the garden and Dez gives a hand in the kitchen. Do you know them? No? They are young offenders who have to do, I think, twenty hours a week community work. The probation officer asked us to find work for them. I don't think they have long to do now. They are very good workers and we shall miss them, but why am I telling you all this?'

'Well, I do appreciate the information,' Fred stuttered, looking round the gloomy hall. 'I will not be coming. It's just not what I thought it was.'

HAPPY BIRTHDAY
Ramon Gonzalez

Today
is your birthday
one year has past
since the last
and with this earth you've done
another orbit around the sun
the carousel of life goes round and round
the seasons come and go to time they are bound
we hitch a ride so brief however
but then nothing goes on forever
and so today let's celebrate
another year lived to date
let's sing and dance feast and be merry
dream of love and drink some sherry
let our hair down and not forget
a life not lived is but regret
laugh have fun and not feel sorrow
today we live not yet tomorrow
and though we know life is unfair
let there be hope and not despair

A NIGHT ON THE RACK
Tim Blackwell

The posters in front of the Piccadilly Circus news theatre, read '30 Minutes of the Latest Pictorial Events & 1950, Review of The Year'.

Ray hovered around outside. He stayed as close as he could to the doors, because every time they opened, a waft of warm air billowed over him. He kept to the left of the entrance, so that he remained unseen by the commissionaire, who, tonight, was staying inside and close to a radiator on that side of the foyer. The newsreels were attracting a sparse audience. Perhaps, being so close to Christmas, people wanted something more than reality.

If Ray looked inside, as the occasional patron came and went, the first thing he saw was an advertising picture on top of a small display case of confectionary; a cardboard head and shoulders of a fleshy-cheeked schoolboy, beaming and licking his lips, after having taken a bite of Fry's Chocolate Cream. The last thing Ray wanted to think about was the taste of chocolate, but he couldn't avoid glancing at the cabinet every time the door swung open. He'd spent the last of his money on Tuesday morning, and the only thing he'd eaten in the three days since then, was a single can of condensed milk.

Ray favoured his weight onto his good leg, but his lower back was aching and there seemed to be no adjustment he could make to relieve it. And besides, he had little control over his muscles because they were locked tight in an attempt to dissuade his shivering from becoming too intense. The slush on the pavement allowed him to slide his artificial foot to and fro. This provided some distraction from the relentless itching in his stump. Ray knew better than to give way to scratching, but sometimes, especially when he was trying to sleep, he couldn't help himself.

Eventually, Ray judged it was safe to return to Piccadilly.

But halfway across Regent Street, he saw the policeman waiting for him on the far curb. Ray put his head down and carried on, thinking it would look more suspicious if he were to turn around and go back the way he'd come. Ray had been aware of the patrolling policeman all evening, that's why he'd left his spot on the rack to wander Leicester Square. But now, the constable, by fixing him with a malevolent glare, was making it clear that he'd also been aware of Ray. A narrow gap in the railing was the only access to the pavement, which meant Ray couldn't veer very far off course. He held his breath as he stepped off the road, fully expecting a hand to grasp his shoulder. But he was allowed to pass. The officer stood solid and still, maintaining the stare, until Ray had skulked away into the mist.

Ray walked down Regent Street to Pall Mall, and then cut across. He was heading for a corner of Trafalgar Square, where he'd noticed a chestnut seller, earlier. He thought, maybe, that if the man looked friendly, he would ask if he could warm himself by the brazier.

The Christmas tree towered in the centre of the Square. It should have been dwarfed by Nelson's Column, but it wasn't. The mist hazed the lights on the tree into glowing orbs that seemed to float about the branches. Ray thought that it looked like a huge transmitter of some kind.

From a distance, Ray detected the aroma of the chestnut stall. It didn't smell of food particularly, more of a log fire, but still it stimulated his appetite. His mouth began to fill with saliva.

'Horrsheznus, horrsheznus ...'

The call sounded muffled, like the man was shouting into a

pillow. Ray wondered what the word was meant to be. Surely
you couldn't eat horse-chestnuts? But then he realised that
the cry was 'hot chestnuts'. The burning coals in the brazier
cast a hellish glow up into the vendor's face and the vapour
surrounding it. As Ray approached, he fancied that the chest-
nut seller was a gatekeeper to the Square, guarding access to
the powerful Christmas tree.

Cautiously, Ray shuffled forward. The man saw him,
scraped a small shovel across the grille and dropped the
chestnuts into a paper bag. Ray leant over the fire, feeling a
wave of heat hitting his cheek. 'I didn't put no change in my
pocket when I came out, I'm afraid.'

'On you go then, I'm not a public heating service. Horr-
sheznus ...'

Ray stepped back.

He trudged around the edge of the Square, crossed the
road, and disappeared into the backstreets behind St
Martin's-in-the-Fields. He couldn't bear to be seen by any-
body else for a while. He wanted to be invisible.

The fog was thickening. That would be in his favour if he
returned to Piccadilly. But perhaps he should just go back
home to Lamb Street. There was still a little paraffin left in
the stove. He could wrap himself in the eiderdown he'd
bought from the rag and bone cart, and hold on until
morning.

But it was the hunger. Hunger. Ray had spent all day
trying not to think about it, but he hadn't been able to control
his mind. He just kept picturing one plateful after another,
and cups of tea with lots and lots of sugar. These thoughts
began to feel as though they were causing him harm. In a
strange way, it seemed that the imagined food was eating
him, scraping away at the inside of his stomach, making it
emptier and emptier. There had been no escaping these
thoughts. They had compelled him to take action, to get up

and go out and find food.

The mist began to smell very greasy; hot dripping with a needle of vinegar. He was passing a fish and chip restaurant. A 'closed' sign was suspended on the inside of the window, above a poster of bells ringing in a snowy steeple, and the words *Merry Christmas* written across the bottom in old fashioned writing. The front part of the place was dark, where the wooden tables and chairs were, but there was still a light on over the fryers. A middle-aged man with funny, sticking-up hair was dragging a big, slotted paddle through the fat, skimming out burnt bits of batter and banging them into a pail on the counter. Ray stopped and watched. He positioned himself at the very edge of the window, so he wouldn't be noticed. After the man had finished with the paddle, he emptied the remaining things from the hot cabinet. There were only three or four pieces of brown food – small, the size of a cigarette-box. Ray presumed that they were Spam fritters. The man took a bite from one of them. But it can't have been very nice, because he dropped it, half-eaten, into the pail.

Ray wondered what would happen to the food.

A door opened at the back of the shop, and more light shone through into the restaurant. An old woman came out, with a big tin-can and a cloth in her hand. She started to go around the tables, emptying the ashtrays. Ray didn't want the woman to catch him looking, so he retreated into a side-passage.

There was a narrow courtyard at the end of the alley, with an iron fire-escape zigzagging up the back of the buildings. Light was coming from a couple of windows. There, next to some dustbins was one of the huge, galvanised pig bins. Ray went up to it and lifted the heavy lid. It stank, as these bins always did, a flyblown farmyard sort of smell. There must have been a collection today, because, as far as Ray could see, the bin was empty. The posters always told you to make sure that no metal, glass or paper got into the pig bins. But Ray thought that if he could find newspaper to drop into the bottom, he might be able to salvage the fritters when they were thrown away. He could take the newspaper out again afterwards, so no harm would be done.

He began to search the area.

A few wooden crates were stacked under the iron steps. Would they work? The scraps of batter would fall through the slats, but the fritters would probably be saved. Ray started to drag one out, but they were bigger than he thought, and clearly wouldn't fit into the bin. Ray checked the dustbins, but there was no sign of newspaper. The shop would use it all to wrap fish and ...

A back door opened, light flooded the courtyard.

Ray spun around and looked for somewhere to hide, but it was too late. The man from the restaurant had seen him. There was no way for Ray to get back to the street without passing him. The man didn't say anything. He stood with the pail in his hand, holding the door open. Ray looked to the ground and began chewing his cheek in shame. The man called back into the shop, 'Florrie'. The woman appeared. The man said to her, 'stay there' – then he took the tin can from her, and emptied the cigarette ends and ash all over the top of the food. He marched up to the pig bin, clattered aside the heavy lid and emptied the pail, banging it loudly against the side. Ray was sure that he made this noise as a warning. The lid was crashed back on, and then the man and the woman went inside, and Ray heard keys rattling in the lock.

Violent images fired into Ray's mind. He pictured himself rushing at the door, grabbing the man by his stupid hair, frogmarching him through to the fryer and ramming his head down into the boiling fat. He saw the hot dripping, smoking, bubbling away around the man's ears, frying them to crisps. He saw his own hands turning scarlet, blistered ...

Ray began to shake.

There was nowhere for this fury to go.

He daren't move. He was terrified that if he did, it would be the first step in turning this atrocity into reality. He hated these thoughts. They came from nowhere. So clear and compelling, that they demanded to be made real – like the thoughts about finding food. Oh God! What was to stop him? What was the barrier between thought and action?

Ray forced himself to stagger backwards, to the far end of the courtyard, where he crouched down under the fire escape steps. He wedged himself into a corner and pressed his fingers up into his hair. He dug his nails into his scalp and concentrated on the pain. He was angry. They were only thoughts. Just thoughts. He could never really do something like that ...

Of course he could. Anyone could.

God knows, the war had taught him that. Ordinary brothers, sons, uncles, fathers, had stabbed, shot, raped, bombed. They had not been monsters from a different species. They were just men who'd been told that the rules had changed, that they were allowed to do these things, that God and their country expected it of them.

Ray's stomach hardened, his breath quickened. His body was preparing for crisis. Hold on, he thought.

* * *

Guinness, Schweppes Tonic Water, Bovril. Bovril, Guinness, Tonic Water. Ray tried to slow his mind to the rhythm of these advertisements, alternately illuminating the fog in Piccadilly Circus. He'd returned to the rack some time ago. It was late. The policeman had gone. Those left on the street edged along the pavement staying close to walls, only becoming visible in the form of shadows when they were within three or four feet of him.

At last, one such shadow paused at the railing nearby.

Moments passed.

The man turned. He approached. His face materialised from the mist. He stood before Ray, fumbling for longer than necessary in a trouser pocket. Then the cigarettes were produced and offered. But, while offering, the man's expression was not encouraging, or nervous, or friendly; he looked appalled, as if he were holding out the remnants of a sandwich to a filthy beggar. Ray took the cigarette, though. It was his first offer, over three nights of waiting. A match was struck. The bargain was made.

Ray began to walk, doing his best to disguise his limp.

They stayed some paces apart. They didn't talk. Ray had noticed that the man had good shoes. He wore a bowler hat, so he probably worked in a bank or something. But he wasn't rich; his collar was dirty.

Ray heard the footsteps behind him pause slightly, at the slope down to the underground car park of the Savoy. So, Ray thought, the man had taken this walk before.

Even though Ray was a solitary and occasional member of the trade in Piccadilly, he made sure that he observed the rules. He knew that the car park beneath the Savoy was reserved for the boys who worked outside the Criterion.

Ray continued down towards the river. The man seemed impatient, but he was following. At the bottom of Buckingham Street, Ray turned right and headed for his spot. There were very few streetlights down here. Back yards of premises on one side, and park railings on the other.

Down a small bank, on the edge of the ill-kept gardens, stood a strange building that didn't seem to belong there. It looked a bit like Marble Arch in miniature. It comprised three arches, a crest in the stonework topping the central one, and reclining lions sitting over those to the left and right. It was as if it should be an entranceway to somewhere old and grand. But there was nothing all around it. It was stranded. The structure was in a bad state. Thick, black branches of buddleia grew out of cracks in the grey stone. Two iron poles had been braced under the left arch to support it, and wooden builders' boards closed off the space on that side. But no work had been carried out, not in all the time that Ray had been bringing customers here.

There was no-one around on the path, so Ray coughed, and waited for the man to catch up. Ray whispered that he would go first, and when the man was happy that it was safe, he could follow him in.

Ray entered the archway from the front, went behind the boards, and found himself in the familiar, few square feet of privacy that seemingly only scrawny roosting pigeons knew about.

He waited.

Presently, the man joined him in the shadows.

It wasn't ideal to kneel down here because of all the bird droppings, but Ray was used to it.

They'd been started for a few minutes. But it seemed that Ray was getting it wrong; the man kept tutting. Ray glanced up briefly. The man's face, as much as Ray could see of it, showed no sign of pleasure, or even interest in what was going on below his belt. The man just looked angrily left and right, perhaps listening out for approaching footsteps or watching for a policeman's lamp. Ray gathered as much saliva as he could and spat subtly on the floor to his side, hoping to rid his mouth of the sour taste that was making him gag. The man wasn't clean. It tasted like he'd already had sex that evening. Ray went back to work on him.

'Hurry up!' the man hissed.

Ray used his hand to try and speed things along. Seconds later, the man knocked it away and took over the job himself at furious speed. With his other hand, he grabbed Ray's hair at the back of the head and held his face in close. Ray put a tempering hand on the man's arm, but the grip on his hair didn't loosen. Ray closed his eyes and held his breath. Mercifully, it was over quickly enough; but Ray was unable to avoid the spray.

At last, the man released his hold. And Ray stood swiping a hand across his forehead. The man was already buttoned up and ready to leave. Ray snatched at the back of his coat. The man didn't look at him, but threw a crumpled bank note to the floor. And then he was gone.

Ray left it for a few moments. He listened as hard as he could. There was distant conversation, but it sounded like the voices were getting further away.

After he emerged from behind the boards, he looked all around, and then headed back up the bank, crossed the path and stepped into a dim gateway. He reached his left hand into his coat for a handkerchief – but it was in the other pocket, and his right hand was the one that needed to be wiped. So he reached awkwardly across his body, got his handkerchief, wiped his face again and then his other hand. He wanted to throw the handkerchief away – but he could rinse it later. He folded it up tight and put it into his back trouser pocket.

It was strange, and vaguely alarming; now that he had money, he found he no longer had an appetite. His intention was to head for the all-night tea-stall, in the arches beneath Waterloo Station. If he couldn't eat, at least he could drink. But he worried that the stall-owner would not want to change a ten-shilling note for the price of a cup of tea. Ray didn't know where to go. All he knew was that he wanted to be warm – to be alone – to be still.

He left the gateway and re-entered the fog.

A face from the war, that Ray knew he would never forget, belonged to a young French girl with red hair, who was about to be raped by members of Ray's company. Her face had looked to him for help. Ray hadn't been able to help at the time, and it tortured him to know that now he would never be able to. Her face was as permanently printed onto his brain, as the bluebirds and bleeding hearts were tattooed onto arms of the other soldiers. He often saw her when he was walking away, after a customer had finished with him. He sometimes wondered why this should be so, and was always disgusted with himself for wondering. There was no similarity between him and that poor girl. He knew what he was doing. He was the one who sought it out. But all the same, some nights, with some men, a question formed in Ray's mind; was it possible to rape yourself? To do something to a part of you that another part didn't want at all.

He heard a shout. He tried to run.

A DOG'S LIFE
Kathryn Bell

'I don't like it,' Reg said.

'What don't you like?' his drinking companion George asked.

'That Millennium Dome, I *said.*'

'You been in it, then?' asked Stan.

'Course not. I meant, the look of it. Like a big ugly bug on its back with its legs in the air. You been in it?'

'Nah. I don't like it neither,' said Stan. 'Tell you what I do like, though. Canary Wharf. No matter where you go, you can see it. You could walk for miles and never get lost, you can always see Canary Wharf.'

'Won't catch *me* walking miles,' said George, 'not with my legs. Anyway, our Rick says it ain't the Millennium yet, not until two thousand and one. And he's an accountant, he knows them things.'

'Oh sure,' said Reg, 'your Rick's right and everybody else is wrong. One way or the other, I still don't like it. Another thing I don't like is yuppies.'

'Right there,' George agreed, 'hate yuppies. Moving in where they don't belong, putting up prices, putting out *clean* milk bottles on the doorstep, can't stand 'em. How about you, Stan?'

'Dunno, never thought about it really.'

'Well, you should, you've got a pair of them living next door to you.'

'Yes,' said Reg, 'and not just yuppies neither, a couple of *queer* yuppies, hell, I hate queers as much as I hate yuppies.'

'Don't know about that,' said Stan, 'don't have nothing to do with them and their daft little hairy dog.'

'Best way. Another round?'

'Not for me, Reg,' said Stan reluctantly. 'Got to go now. Madge likes to be home by eleven, and I can't afford to get up her nose. Don't know what I'd do if she stopped minding Dad and I was cooped up in them four walls the whole time, I'd go bonkers.'

'All right, Stan, mind how you go.'

'Yeh, don't turn your back on them yuppies!'

Three evenings a week, Stan paid Madge to sit in with Dad while Stan enjoyed a couple of hours with Reg and George and their other cronies at the Duke of Wellington, an old-fashioned dowdy pub patronised mainly by men of Stan's age, pensioners who liked a quiet drink with no music to annoy them. Few women visited the Wellington, and no young people; they drank in the Frog and Newt two blocks away. The rest of the time, Stan stayed home to look after his father, who was getting increasingly senile and could only be left long enough for Stan to hurry to the corner shop for the groceries, or take his small terrier for a quick walk round the block.

He let Skipper off his lead while they walked home. The dog might as well enjoy himself while he could; Stan's little outing was over for another two days. He wished he could afford a minder for Dad every evening. Damn it, he wished he could afford to put Dad in a home. A decent one, of course, not that Council rat-hole where the old people slept eight to a room, and the really gaga ones went around pulling other people's blankets off them and shouting and going on all night so's nobody could get any sleep, and then all day they sat around the walls of the big day-room waiting for death. The only bit of excitement was when one of the poor buggers sat, by accident or malice, in another one's chair, and then there was a mother of a row. Stan had seen it all when he used to take Dad up there to visit one of his old mates, before the old mate died. No, Dad would go into that place over Stan's dead body. But a nice clean private nursing home, where he would have his own room, and attractive young girls to look after him and joke and flirt a bit, that would be all right. Dad would be better off there, and Stan would have his freedom. Out to the Wellington every evening, long walks with Skipper every day, and peace and quiet when he got home, with no grumbling babbling wreck of a man sitting by the fire demanding tea and snacks, needing to be dressed and washed and taken to the toilet. Not that Stan minded these chores; he would have done them gladly for a father who was in his right mind, who would be a bit of company, with whom he could have a conversation. Conversation with Dad was like talking to a three-year-old, except that the child would be improving every day and Dad was getting worse. Stan pinned his hopes on the Lottery. Well, somebody had to win it, why not Stan?

They were nearly home when a breeze got up, blowing litter about, and Skipper, seeming to think a plastic carrier bag on the other side of the road was something worth investigating, trotted across after it. Stan called him. Skipper hesitated, then started back over the road just as a car came too fast round the corner. It hit the little dog then went speeding on without stopping. 'Bloody maniac!' Stan shouted helplessly.

Skipper was hurt badly; he was bleeding a lot and Stan couldn't see where the blood was coming from. He was afraid to poke around in case he made the injuries worse, but he couldn't leave Skipper there, and he didn't know what to do. He knew about the animal hospital which was open all hours, but he also knew they charged a lot of money, and he would have to take a cab there, if he could find one that wouldn't object to carrying an injured dog, and he didn't have that much cash, and was by no means sure that Madge would agree to stay on with Dad for however long it took Stan to get to the hospital and back, even if he could afford it, which he couldn't. He could run back to the Wellington and try to borrow money from his friends there. Skipper could die meanwhile. Stan crouched miserably in the road, patting the dog's head and wondering if it would be any use at all appealing to the police for help.

Another car pulled up. 'Ooh, what's happened here?' a voice called excitedly.

Stan looked up. It was one of the yuppies from next door. Stan didn't even know their names. When they first moved in, they used to greet him and try to chat with him over the garden fence, but Stan had responded with morose grunts, not wanting to get involved with these people who weren't his sort, and the yuppies had given up their attempts at sociability.

'Been run over, has he?' the yuppie asked.

Stan nodded.

'It doesn't look good. Quick, Nigel, go inside and get a blanket, we'll take him to the hospital,' said the yuppie.

The other got out of the car and hesitated, looking at the dog.

'Get on, Nigel, hurry up. Just think, it could be Hop Sing.'

Hop Sing was the yuppies' dog, stupid-looking thing with a squashed-in face and long hair trailing to the ground. Stan knew the dog's name from hearing them call him.

Nigel went into the house and came out with a khaki blanket. Gently the first yuppie eased the dog on to the blanket, then lifted him to the back seat of the car, gesturing to Stan to get in with him. Should he tell them he hadn't enough money, Stan wondered. No, get help for Skipper first, worry about the money later.

A young woman vet examined Skipper carefully, then smiled at Stan's worried face. It wasn't as bad as it looked, she explained, there was a lot of blood but nothing was broken. 'He was hit by something sharp, probably a torn edge of mudguard, and ripped up here, look. He'll need stitches, and we'll keep him in overnight so we can keep an eye on him. Phone tomorrow to find out when he can go home. We'll give you some antibiotics for him, in case there's any infection, but he should be fine.'

Jeremy paid with his credit card, Stan looking on anxiously.

'Don't worry,' Jeremy said, 'you can pay us back in instalments. Whatever you can afford, there's no hurry.'

Nigel raised his eyebrows, but Jeremy hissed 'Supposing it had been Hop Sing?'

Luckily Madge was fond of Skipper and calmed down when she heard he had had an accident. 'Bye, then!' she called as she hurried off home. 'Hope the little chap'll be all right!'

Stan set about the task of getting Dad undressed and ready for bed. He couldn't expect Madge to do any of that, it wasn't as if she was a nurse or anything. Some things you couldn't ask a lady to do, even if she had been married three times like Madge. Stan had never been married, never had a girl-friend, never been in love, never even fancied anyone much. He supposed he had loved his parents, but his mother had been dead forty years, and his father might as well be. Stan remembered the father he had known as a child: a noisy, laughing, singing man, full of jokes and games, throwing Stan in the air, carrying him on his shoulders, playing football and cricket with him. He was never too busy, always had time for his boy. Then the war came, and Dad joined up, and when he came home on leave he was different, quiet, and after the war he was quieter still. Stan had looked forward so much to his homecoming, but he wasn't the same man. No more laughing or singing, and the jokes had become sarcastic, and there was no time to kick a football about with Stan. There was just going to work, coming home, sitting reading the paper and going to bed. He had got worse after his wife's death, and over the years deteriorated to a state of mindless senility. Stan couldn't honestly say he loved him now, but for the happy memories of the man he had been, he determined to do his best by him. 'You looked after me, Dad, and I'll look after you,' he said. 'What's that?' the old man mumbled.

'Nothing, come on, it's bedtime, a nice cup of tea before we go.'

Jeremy and Nigel were on Stan's doorstep at noon the next day.

'I phoned the hospital,' said Jeremy, 'and they say Skipper's doing very well, and we can fetch him at two today. Would you like to come with us, or shall we bring him for you?'

'I'd like to come,' said Stan, 'poor little chap will be missing me, and he'll be frightened if he doesn't see me. I can leave Dad for an hour or so, he'll be all right.' Stan had explained some of his problems with his father while fretting about Madge the night before.

'No, no, Nigel'll be glad to stay and look after your father, won't you, Nigel?'

Nigel smiled feebly.

'That's settled then, see you about half one.'

That left Stan time to go to the corner shop for his Saturday shopping. When the shop had been taken over by an Asian family twelve years before, Stan had thought he would never go in there again, but now he laughed to think how silly he had been. Mrs Mukerjee was far more pleasant than her predecessor Mr Jones, and the prices were no worse, considering inflation and all. While Stan was buying his few groceries, Mrs Mukerjee filled him in on how her sons were doing at school, and gently teased him about his purchase of a tin of curried lentils. 'We will make a vegetarian of you yet,' she laughed.

By the time Stan had finished his chores that evening, and made Dad comfortable in front of the telly, and sat down with his own sandwich and bottle of beer, and Skipper asleep in his basket, he was just in time for the National Lottery draw. Stan always used the same numbers, a sequence based on his own and his father's birth dates. He had never had more than two numbers right, and you don't get anything for two numbers. He sat back in his armchair, thinking about seeing Reg and George and the others on Monday evening, and how he would tell them about the yuppies. Queers or not, he would say, they were good Samaritans to me and Skipper.

Suddenly he was on his feet, frantically searching in his pockets. Jacket – hanging on the back of the door – nothing. The carrier bag he'd brought his groceries home in – nothing. Not in his wallet either. Then he realised: in his haste and anxiety about Skipper, he'd forgotten to pop into the newsagents after shopping at the Mukerjees. *He hadn't bought a Lottery ticket.* All six numbers had come up, and for the first time since the Lottery had started, he hadn't bought a ticket.

He sat down again, the television voice saying something about indications being that there were no jackpot winners. Stan had thought a person would go crazy if something like this happened. In fact he had read of men who topped themselves because their numbers came up and they had forgotten to buy their tickets. Stan would never do such a thing, but he did think he might just go barking mad. But now that it had happened, he didn't feel like that at all. He wasn't sure what he did feel. That sort of money – what was it this week, nine point four million, and it would all have been his – wasn't real money; a couple of thousand would have been nice, but people like Stan didn't get to be millionaires, it was against nature.

Nevertheless he allowed himself to fantasise a little. With that amount of money, he wouldn't need to put Dad in a home, not even the most expensive in the country. He could buy a big house, and hire a private nurse. Two nurses, working in shifts, so that they could attend to Dad's every need round the clock. Pretty, friendly young girls. No, perhaps with the lifting and the toilet and all, men would be better. Two handsome muscular male nurses. They would have their own flat at the top of the house, but when they'd settled Dad in bed of a night they'd come down to sit in Stan's kitchen for a beer and a chat and a laugh.

The fairy money dissolved and Stan came back to earth.

'Another week and we still haven't won,' he said. Dad looked blank. 'So we soldier on a bit longer,' Stan added.

'Soldier,' said Dad. 'I was a soldier, I went away to the war, and they wished me luck, but I never came back.' His eyes filled and tears rolled down his cheeks. 'I never came back from the war.'

'Well, that was a long time ago,' said Stan. 'No need to fret about all that now. How about a nice cup of tea?'

RIMBAUD

A SONNET SEQUENCE

Zekria Ibrahimi

MOTHER

You are creatress. You are nemesis.
Do I thrill to your slaps and to your blows?
You are my priestess, and in your cruel kiss
I call you 'mother' as my anger flows –
My anguish gushes – into your abyss;
You are my friend of friends and foe of foes,
God's slut, whose deep vengeance will never miss,
Shafted through me, and my wounds do not close,
And you must lick my never ending pus
With a self-righteous malice that I dread,
Yet also welcome, for the word is 'Us' –
We are not separate; linked till we are dead,
We share our hatred, over which you fuss
Like Heaven's busy whore, up from her bed.

TEACHER

Arithmetic rams into me, and Greek,
And Latin, the sensation of a crash,
Of hurt that knowledge always has to wreak,
Each page I go through hurting like a gash –
Maimed by learning, I, prodigy – or freak –
'Please the teacher', for each essay is flash,
Is arrogant instead of being meek;
I look down on the usual schoolboy trash –
'Amo, Amas, Amat', rubbish by rote,
And explore all the pain of puberty,
My voice like savage venom in my throat.
What is more vindictive than poetry?
And Izambard surveys my rhymes – takes note.
Does teacher fear this pupil as – too free?

COMMUNE

Paris, less pretty than the vicious sore
Upon the vulva of some diseased whore –
Paris, usually a mad prostitute,
Used to the bribe – or blow – of any brute –
Paris becomes, so suddenly, as pure
As gold refined from what was dirty ore –
Corruption, in the end, is sullen, mute;
Now Paris sings, sweeter than harp or lute.
The Commune, like fever at a star's core,
Explodes, a supernova, born of war –
Born of blood, and of anguish, at its root;
But it, an angel, as cruel soldiers shoot,
Caresses silenced martyrs amidst gore,
With Paris, silenced Paris, raped once more.

TOMB

I wish to be a far from divine flower,
A plant in fact, growing on Rimbaud's tomb,
Not able to feel or sense hour by hour,
Not aware of time, in the light or gloom,
A small shoot over which the Sun would tower.
And, *most of all*, as noon, its rays, might loom,
I *could not love* – oh, I would not seem sour,
Not show the faintest perception of doom,
No, as such a gentle non-entity,
I would mock love as something to avoid –
For *love* tortured Rimbaud so callously;
It is through *love* that poets are destroyed.
But ... the plodding sap would not be in me
His disturbed blood that God and gods *enjoyed* ...

MURDER

All poetry means murder in the end –
Thank Hell, it kills that curse, 'belonging', *kills* –
To be a stranger is its thrill of thrills,
To be an alien, to be dream's friend.
Gun down reality, too maimed to mend,
Like a shot corpse from which the gore soon spills.
The task of verse needs the outsider's skills.
Please, welcome such slaughter as must descend
Like deadly lightning through the humdrum dark,
And, if I perish – thank Hell – the delight!
More than an ember, and more than a spark,
Murder, a million volts of it, its might,
Cracks the sky apart, and its fingers arc,
Like a strangler's, round shadows of life's *spite* ...

GUN

The revolver, with its own soul, must aim
Itself at me. Verlaine – the would-be thug!
The gun, the bullet, and hate are the same –
Is he enraged as I just sigh, and shrug?
His shot – hits me – the gun is never tame,
And nor is poetry, and, on the rug,
Mingled repellently with shock and shame,
My blood descends, and pain – which is death's tug –
Jabs into me, and, in this drab hotel,
Verlaine, playing the hooligan before,
Starts now to weep – yes, all tears are from hell,
And a nurse wipes away the ugly gore,
But no one can bandage betrayal well –
I lie. Verlaine lies. The weapon lies more ...

CAGE

Can even poetry be like the bars
Against which helpless captives will protest?
Rhymes must be the equivalent of scars,
And the 'Muse', that whore, seeps gore at her breast,
From which I suck, still singing of the stars
Even as I lick and chew slime, at best –
There are no violins now, flutes, guitars,
Just screeching rats that, with teeth of lust, wrest
One more chunk out of me, mute and afraid.
And verse is vermin, with its need for lies,
And I want every sonnet to degrade,
And alexandrines are traps in disguise,
Pretending to be cosmic, while, betrayed,
I feel the gutter's nothingness rise, rise ...

HARAR

The slaves – just eunuchs now – laze in the street;
There are the spices sold, then excrement
Lingers, with its humdrum stench, at my feet –
I trade in malice, the equivalent
Of castrating the soul; the slaves I meet
Seem so otherworldly in their content.
I buy one more whore, each of us a cheat,
And 'love' – that is, the way life is misspent –
Becomes simply the path to syphilis,
And my sores, hideous, engrained with pus,
Are like this town, its paths of shit and piss,
Its dirt that always is confronting us.
And who are we? Not citizens of bliss,
But of Harar, where con-men feud and fuss ...

MARIAM

'My native woman' – and she has a name –
Mariam – and we must fuck every night.
She cleans up the house, and is there to blame
When cushions are dusty, stained, not quite right ...
And I shag her blackness, and spit on shame,
And she is domesticity, held tight
By me, as though she and I are the same,
Made twins by 'love' – but 'love' proves only spite,
And I give her some Thalers, say 'Get Lost',
And do not want her nearness any more –
For I am white, with skin the hue of frost,
And let me be cold, cold to my deep core!
She has been very used to being bossed –
'Love', like the rest of life, turns out a *bore* ...

SLAVES

I trade in guns and slaves, in slaves and guns;
I am an accountant of misery –
I measure up all of the blood that runs
Along my hands, grown used to cruelty.
The African Sun, the worst of all Suns,
Must look down, purged of pity, upon me.
I am the dark sinner that the priest shuns –
And what is there left of me now to see?
It is like cancer, money, in the end –
It cuts through me, with very zealous claws –
It has no time for faith, freedom, or friend;
The pain of it in me lacks any pause.
And money's blind anguish chooses to send
Eyes to Hell without kindness or applause ...

THE TELEPHONE
Michael Harth

If they had just chosen a sensible new modern telephone, none of it would have happened, Richard rather suspected. But Janice was a collector of what he privately considered horrible old artefacts, and she had pounced on this particular item with enthusiasm, paying what Richard considered a ridiculous price for it. Then once she had got it home, of course she expected Richard to install it. She had bought it because they wanted an extension phone in his study, but he flatly refused to use it, taking the one in the hall for himself and replacing it with the monstrosity. Janice accepted this re-arrangement happily, since it meant her new purchase, with its grotesquely over-ornate features, would be on display to any visitors.

In fact, Richard had a spot of trouble getting it to work: there seemed to be some sort of crossed line, and he kept getting connected to someone jabbering away in a foreign language. However, he managed to sort it out fairly quickly, for Janice regularly indulged in long chats with one or other of her female friends – mercifully, from Richard's point of view, since he paid the bill, during off-peak hours – and she had been tapping her feet impatiently while he installed it, the usual prelude to one of her outbursts of temper.

A few days later, when she answered it, a voice she didn't recognise said, 'Your order is on the way, madam,' and promptly rang off. She couldn't think what it referred to for, to the best of her knowledge, she had no order outstanding, but as she had no idea who had rung, all she could do was wait to see what should arrive. She supposed it must be something Richard had ordered for her: perhaps it was to make up for being so rude about her new acquisition, she decided – unless, of course, it was a wrong number, and the order was actually meant for someone else.

But no: a little later the doorbell rang, and when she opened the door a strange-looking creature was standing there with a large box which he had obvious trouble in carrying. He looked hardly human, but she supposed he had been hired through one or other of those rehabilitation schemes the government was so keen on.

He handed her a form and a pencil, and she scrawled her name where he indicated, impatient to find out what the box contained. When that was done, she tried to take it inside, but found it much too heavy. However, the creature pushed her aside and brought it into the hall for her, after which he left, pulling the door to behind him.

When she opened it, she saw to her utter and complete astonishment that there was a nude man inside. Not only that, but he was sporting an erection of a magnificence never before encountered even in her dreams. She found herself blushing at the blatancy of it, but at the same time she couldn't drag her eyes away.

'Surely he can't have been sent by Richard?' she thought. He was not the world's most exciting performer, but she hardly thought he would admit to his shortcomings by sending her this stud. But if not Richard, who could it be? She couldn't believe for a moment that any of her women friends were responsible: if they had come across something like this, the last thing they would do would be to pass it on to her: they would have dragged it into their own bedroom without delay.

Realising that she was wasting what might well be precious time – she didn't imagine this object was hers to keep: probably he would only stay an hour or so – she took him by the hand and led him upstairs. There he performed in a very satisfactory manner, and she was more than a little sorry when the doorbell rang again and another creature, just as strange-looking, was there to collect him.

Over the next few days she racked her brains as to where the delivery could have come from. The problem was she didn't want anyone to know about it, so when talking to her friends she could only refer to it in a roundabout manner, but so far as she could tell, no one she knew had any connection with it.

It was a memory to cherish, far and away the most exciting and outrageous event of her whole life: the only downside was that she couldn't tell anyone. She would have liked to be able to boast about it to one or two of her friends, particularly Sheila, who was always recounting tales of her latest amorous escapade. Most if not all of them, in Janice's opinion, were figments of her imagination, but all the same they were irritating to hear about.

It made Richard seem even more dull than he was, and she fielded his suggestion, that evening, of their indulging in a spot of marital activity, by having one of her headaches. Eventually, she knew, she would be reduced to putting up with him again: lightning didn't strike the same spot twice, but while the memory of that one glorious hour was still fresh in her mind, she didn't want it diluted by his inept fumblings.

Now every time the phone rang she would feel a stab of hopeful excitement, even though she knew she was being wildly over-optimistic. It was never what she hoped, just a gas company wanting to tell her about their new tariff, somebody trying to sell her double glazing, or one of her friends in the mood for a chat.

It was an effort to be civil to them, but gradually she reconciled herself to her boring normal life, and ceased to hope for another glorious interruption. So her excitement was un-contained when, just over a couple of weeks on, she heard the well-remembered voice announcing another delivery, and a little later answered the door to find the same odd delivery man with the same giant box.

Her hand was shaking so much she could hardly scrawl her signature on his form, and when he had brought the box into the house and departed she stood there and gazed at it for a little while with a rapt expression on her face before she fetched a knife and undid the string. Inside was indeed the same sort of goods: he was different from the last one, but just as welcome, and possibly, she thought as she looked him over, even more interesting. There was no time to be lost: she intended to savour every moment of this second gift from the gods, and so she led him straight upstairs.

She had no idea how long he actually spent with her, but the time flew by all too speedily. It would have been wonderful if he could have stayed all night, but on the other hand Richard would be home in a while, and she didn't think he'd be too impressed at her visitor. The trouble was that she now had no idea when she might receive another delivery: if only it had been the same day of the week, it would have been easy for her to make sure always to be in on that particular day, but as it was she had no idea.

It had actually been seventeen days between deliveries, she worked out, so she checked on the calendar when the next seventeenth day would occur and waited in all day hopefully, but nothing happened. She was so disappointed that she couldn't help being unpleasant to Richard when he arrived home, so that he asked gruffly what had got into her.

In fact it was more than a week after that fiasco that she got her third call, by which time she had begun to suspect gloomily that the glory had departed out of her life. When she undid the parcel as it stood in the hall, the fellow inside was brown-skinned: she couldn't tell his ethnic background, but he was as impressively built as the other two had been, so she wasn't going to worry about a little thing like that.

Then there was another long interval. She had resigned herself to the unpredictability of the deliveries, but, though she didn't go out as much as she had before it happened, the firm managed to pick one of her infrequent absences. But as it chanced, Richard was at home, taking a day off in lieu of some overtime he had done recently, so it was he who answered the phone when the caller rang, announcing the arrival of the next parcel.

Knowing nothing of the previous deliveries, he assumed that Janice had been in one of her extravagant moods, so he waited in, instead of going out as he had planned, so that he would see exactly what she had been up to. When the delivery man arrived, he signed the form abstractedly, fearing the worst when he saw the size of the box. He had had to lecture her only a couple of months before about being extravagant, so he decided to open it so that he could confront her with the evidence.

When the box-sides fell away and he saw what they contained, he was thunderstruck, but somehow he found his eyes continually returning to the physique on display. Richard had never before felt any interest in his own sex, but this was something different and, he had to admit, pretty much irresistible. With an effort he recalled that this was extravagance on a much worse scale than he had suspected. He thought about sending the fellow away, but then he decided the most suitable punishment for her would be to make use of her tame stud for himself – if the fellow was agreeable, that was, though he imagined these types were pretty much adaptable. And sure enough, the man made no bones about following Richard up the stairs, while the session that followed was unique in Richard's experience in more than one way. Certainly it made the tepid encounters between him and Janice even more boring by comparison.

When the fellow had gone, he spent a while trying to decide whether to confront her with the evidence of what she had been getting up to behind his back, and brazen out the fact that he had taken advantage of this latest arrival as a matter of sauce for the goose, or to say nothing and let her wonder what had happened to her order. It was a difficult decision, but eventually he decided to keep mum and see what she had to say. As she of course didn't know that a delivery would be made on that day, she had no suspicion that anything had happened during her absence, and Richard was somewhat taken aback by her lack of any reference to it.

But then, just a few days later, the phone rang again, and the same by now familiar voice, though with a more unpleasant edge to it, reminded her that their account was overdue, and unless it was settled within the next forty-nine hours the appropriate penalty would be imposed. It was distinctly worrying: the services she had enjoyed could well come in at a pretty expensive figure, and not having any idea how to pay for them, even if she could afford whatever it might be, was even more worrying.

She was expecting their debt collector to call round, and spent the next couple of days in an agony of uncertainty. She knew she would have to own up to Richard, since she could hardly hide the financial arrangement, whatever it might be, from him, but it took her quite a while to screw up her courage sufficiently. Richard replied to her confession with one of his own, which she at first found it difficult to believe, but once she had accepted it she felt slightly better.

When the doorbell finally rang, they debated for some anxious moments whether to answer it, but having decided it was better to know the worst, they opened the door. This time there were two of them standing there, and they immediately stuffed Richard into a canvas bag with the speed of light, while Janice watched, horror-struck but unable to intervene, as he was taken away.

She felt dreadfully guilty: it seemed as if Richard would be paying the price for what were mainly her indulgences. What would his employer say when he didn't turn up, she wondered. Most important of all, would the monthly pay cheque still come through?

Richard, meanwhile, was loaded into a van and driven off. He had no idea at all where he was when he was finally taken out of the bag and locked in a little cell along with, he presumed, other defaulters. He was too demoralised to ask any questions, just waited for around a quarter-of-an-hour in miserable contrition, until he was collected and taken into a room that looked more like an operating-theatre than anything else he could think of.

There he was made to strip off, and strapped to a contraption uncomfortably similar to an operating table. A machine unlike anything he had ever seen before was swung over him, a light shone in his eyes, and he lost consciousness. When he woke, and was helped off the table, he noticed with shock that his figure was much improved. The telltale signs of middle-aged spread had disappeared: his skin was bronzed and firm, some inches had been taken off his waist, and others added where they would impress most. He realised with amazement that he looked better than he had even in his youth: it seemed a strange penalty for not settling a bill.

But then he was taken to some sort of waiting-room, where he saw half-a-dozen other men all waiting around, each one of them in the same sort of peak physical condition: all of them, he realised with a sinking heart, a sight to gladden the heart of any customer, and he now understood how he was to pay off his debt. As the day wore on, one after another the men were collected, while others joined them in the waiting-room. He was almost glad when he was taken out, to find himself being put into a familiar-looking box, and then delivered to an address, where the lady of the house was ecstatic when she opened it up and saw him.

He had been worrying that in no way would he be able to come up to the standard of the one that had been sent to him, but it seemed that nothing essential had been neglected, for he found himself able to perform with an ease, energy, and enthusiasm which were completely new in his experience. Afterwards he was taken back home, where Janice was so relieved to see him that she was nicer to him than she had been for years. Then, at intervals during the next few months, he was again collected, transformed, and delivered to another address, where he was always able to delight the customers.

Unfortunately the enhancements seemed to have an anaesthetic effect so far as he was concerned, but even so there was satisfaction to be derived from the pleasure he was giving, and he was quite sorry when his term of duty was over. He even toyed with the thought of volunteering to continue, but since no words of any kind had been exchanged during his hours of duty, he didn't know how to.

It was disappointing that the enhancements only stayed while he was on duty, but he cherished the memory of how he had gladdened the hearts of his clients, male and female, when they opened the box he arrived in to feast their eyes on what he had to offer. He would have been happy to run up another bill, but that particular caller never rang again.

THE MAN ON HAM COMMON
Rex Batten

It had to be the same man. The framed photograph on Richard's sideboard had to be of the man I met on Ham Common. I met Richard through a mutual friend. He was always good company and we had quite a lot in common – sex didn't come into it. He was going through a bit of a rough patch and I seemed to be able to help. He would unload his problems. He needed someone to talk to. The fact that I listened I am sure made him feel better. On the evening in question he was giving a little dinner party. I had been to his flat on a couple of occasions but hadn't noticed the photograph; now I couldn't stop looking at it. It had to be the same man I had met on Ham Common. To say I had met him could be a little ambiguous. We had exchanged half a dozen words but nothing more. Nothing happened. I didn't ask him his name and he didn't offer. I simply remember him as the man in the blue-striped suit. That was what was so incongruous, or ridiculous – a man in an obviously bespoke tailored suit on Ham Common on a hot summer's afternoon looking for all the world as if he had just come from the office. One thing I did notice: even though he wasn't smoking, he kept flicking what looked like cigarette ash off his suit.

Perhaps I had better explain about Ham Common. Until a couple of years ago I had never heard of the place. I knew that Ham was on the Thames up river from Putney. I had even been to Ham House, a National Trust property, but I was not aware that no more than a ten-minute walk away was a five-star cruising ground. Acres of public open space covered with scrub trees and bramble, criss-crossed with a maze of footpaths and dotted with little clearings in the bushes often occupied by nude males basking in the warmth of the afternoon sun.

But to get back to the man in the photograph – the man in the blue-striped suit. Why he stopped and spoke to me I have no idea. It wasn't as though he was trying to pick me up; in fact I don't think he was trying to pick up anyone. I am not sure he was really cruising, but that was true of a lot of the men there who seemed to be hurrying to catch a bus except they couldn't find the bus stop, or maybe the right pick-up spot might be a more accurate phrase.

I had been lying on some grass at the intersection of five paths, suitably unclothed, when the man in the suit walked purposefully past. He did look, but that was all. Ten minutes later he came back. This time he nodded and I smiled and on he went wherever he was going. Since it was my first visit to the Common I wasn't at all sure how it worked. I had been told the place was so cruisy you couldn't go wrong but I had been there for well over an hour showing everything and the only person who had even given me a second glance was the man in the suit, who I really didn't fancy, so I thought I would pack it in and go home. Anyway the clouds were building up and it looked like rain, so there was no point in staying.

I was just about to sling my bag on my back when the man in the suit came along again.

'Going?' he asked.

'Looks like rain,' I said.

'No, it won't, not today.' He sounded so sure of himself I almost laughed. Anyone who could be so sure of the English weather has to be a bit of a nutter.

'Enjoy yourself,' was my parting shot.

'Do come back,' he said, and gave me the most engaging smile. 'Do come back and I am sure you will enjoy yourself. I'd like to help you.'

I started to walk away. 'You are on the wrong path,' he called. I turned and he indicated the path I should take, and then he said, 'It's important not to be led up the wrong path.'

He was right. I would have gone the wrong way. He was also right about the weather. It didn't rain.

That was nearly a week ago.

I took the photograph off the sideboard in Richard's flat. It had to be the same man. The suit wasn't the same and he was a lot younger in the photograph, but it had to be the same man. Richard had been pouring a drink whilst I'd been looking at the photo and thinking of the incident on Ham Common. He brought my whisky over, saw what I was doing, took the photograph out of my hand and put it back on the sideboard before he gave me my drink.

'Friend of yours?' I asked.

'Why do you ask?'

'I'm sure I saw him,' I said.

'Where?'

'On Ham Common.'

'You couldn't have done. Your whisky OK?' Richard asked.

'Fine. It's very good whisky. I could have sworn it was the same guy.' The man in the suit had seemed so incongruous the day before I just couldn't get him out of my head.

Richard was dismissive. 'I assure you, you didn't. He left me some time ago.'

It was obviously a touchy subject so I thought it best to sip my whisky. The other guests began to arrive and nothing more was said, but when I looked again the photograph was gone.

Ham Common was not a subject for that particular meal even though Harry who had told me about the so-called 'premier cruising place' was one of the guests.

I don't have a regular job, which leaves me free during the

day so when a couple of days later it was sunny and warm I got in the car and thought I would try my luck again. The grassy patch at the junction of the five paths was vacant and I was just about to lie down when the man in the blue suit passed. He smiled and said, 'Welcome back.'

I smiled, trying to think what to say. I did think *this guy seems to inhabit the place* and then I understood Richard's attitude. If your partner or boyfriend spends all his time cruising it can't be much of a relationship, particularly if he does it dressed for the office. That is being a bit too kinky. Keep away from him was my reaction, so I took one of the paths not knowing where it would lead. I decided that afternoon was to be the test to find out if Ham Common was what I had been led to believe.

After wandering up and down paths and in and out of bushes for possibly half an hour and passing a number of men again in a hurry to catch a bus, I decided it was not the place.

I caught one glimpse of activity through the bushes but as soon as I got near they stopped and fled like naughty schoolboys.

I believe the Common is a designated nature conservation site and I came to the conclusion it was certainly conserving one aspect of nature. It was then that I realised I was lost. I had no idea how to get out of the maze. The first path I took led me round in a circle. The second came to a dead end.

'What a waste of an afternoon.' I must have said it aloud because a voice behind me said, very gently, 'Not necessarily.'

It was the man in the suit. Richard's ex-friend. I was about to say 'Piss off!' but his smile was so disarming, so I said something like, 'This place isn't cruisy or nobody fancies me, but it's all a bit of a waste of time.'

'As I said, not necessarily.' And he went on to explain that he wasn't interested in sex. His sex life had died but he did like to keep an eye on things. He did make me feel a little uncomfortable when he said he had taken to me when he saw me lying nude at the meeting of the paths a few days earlier. I thought it only tactful not to mention Richard. My intention was to get away from the place and not come back.

It was then the suited-up gentleman gave me explicit instructions on how to get to the spot where things were going on – 'or coming off,' he added with a camp flick of his eyes.

'Now off you go.' And he waved me away.

He had been right about the path to take and the weather, now he was more than right about the cruising ground. How he knew what was going on and where, I have no idea. It couldn't be seen from the path and his suit was so immaculate he could not have climbed through the bushes, though that may have been how he got the ash or dust on his clothes.

His instructions were very precise. Left after a particular tree and you'll see a piece of rag hanging on a bush. The path is not obvious but follow it and you'll land on your feet – though feet may not have been the right word. If I go into detail of the next ten or fifteen minutes I shall be accused of writing porn, but try to imagine being dragged into a group of five horny males ranging from a handsome twenty-year-old to a big hairy bear, with those in between getting nine out of ten in any attraction rating.

One by one they came and went. The last to leave was well-built, to say the least; he put his arms around me and thanked me, when it was he who deserved the thanks. He waited for me to make my getaway before he collected his clothes from behind a bush. He must have thought I couldn't see. It wasn't jeans or a tracksuit that I expected him to pick up. It was a policeman's uniform.

I wandered slowly back to the five-path junction. This time I had no difficulty in finding my way, but my benefactor in the suit was not to be seen.

I do belong to a gay swimming group. Our sessions are on a Friday and it was two days after the Common incident when I was doing my usual unenergetic breast stroke that there was one great splash. It had to be Harry who had told me about the Common. He always held his nose and jumped in right in front of me.

'Do you always have to make a splash?' I asked, trying to get the water out of my eyes.

'Have you been to Ham Common?' he asked, then added, 'I meant to have asked you when we were at Richard's last week.'

I told him I had.

'How did it go?' he asked.

'Are you in a hurry to get away after swimming?'

He wasn't. So we arranged to meet after the session.

We sat in his car and I told him what had happened, including Richard's reaction. Harry listened; he was a very down-to-earth guy but said nothing. He let me finish and then told me I had got it all wrong. He had known Richard for years. The man in the suit could have had nothing to do with the photograph. The man in the photograph had been a close friend of Richard's. They might have been lovers once but for more than twenty years had lived separate lives. They had always been very close and mutually supportive. It was the way they made their relationship work. In any case his friend had died a year ago. Richard had arranged his funeral. So it could not have been him.

That was obvious. There was nothing more to say, so I said 'Good night,' got out of the car, closed the door, and walked towards my car.

Harry caught me up. He began to speak then shook his head. 'No, that's stupid.'

'What's stupid?' I asked. 'I told you what happened.'

'I know. I believe you. Richard's friend, I know you didn't

know anything about him, but he's dead.' He paused and looked at me. 'But I know he would have wanted to show his appreciation of your support for Richard. He was that kind of guy.' He turned to go back to his car, stopped and said, 'I went to his funeral. Oh, this is crazy. He left strict instructions he should be cremated wearing his best blue-striped suit and that his ashes should be scattered to the wind. That was what Richard and I did. We threw them to the wind. I was with him. My god! We did it on Ham Common. It was a sort of joke. Richard often accused his friend of haunting the place. This is crazy. He knew everything that happened there. I think he knew every bush and where anything was happening. Nothing escaped him.' Harry stared at me. 'No. There has to be another explanation.'

What could I do but agree? I closed my eyes and could see the man flicking ash off his suit.

THE REUNION
Ross Burgess

'Not too bad for 45,' I said to myself, adjusting my bow tie in the mirror. At least I've not put on too much middle-age spread. I don't get too many black tie invitations these days, but my suit still fits me, just about. I hope the style won't seem too old-fashioned.

'Very smart, dear,' said Barbara, brushing a speck of dust off my shoulder. 'Just don't get drinking too much with your old school chums.' She kissed me on the cheek. We're still on affectionate terms, even though we have separate bedrooms, and she seems to prefer the company of her little group of women friends.

Andrew Booker was already in the hotel bar when I arrived. Like me, he still lived locally and we'd been in touch from time to time. 'Thanks for suggesting this,' I said. 'It's been years and years since I came to one of these reunions.'

'Glad you could come,' he replied. 'Our year in particular has been under-represented recently, so I decided to encourage everyone I could think of to come along. By the way,' he added, taking me to one side, 'you may have heard that I've been elected Chairman of the Conservative Association. Just between you and me, we're looking for new people to stand at next year's Council elections, and I'd like you to consider it. I know we're supposed to be politically correct these days, but someone like you, happily married and a respectable businessman, would really appeal to our potential supporters.'

I was taken aback by this. I'd never had any real interest in politics, although perhaps that made me a natural Conservative. I told him I'd think about it, but decided not to mention that my marriage was no longer what it might seem. Andrew moved on to chat to people who'd just arrived, and I said hello to some of those I recognised from our year, trying not to reveal that I'd forgotten most of their names. Some seemed hardly changed in twenty-odd years; others time had not been so kind to.

We were called in to the function room and Andrew organised those in our year to occupy the end of one of the long tables. He sat on my left, and another old classmate, John Carter, on my right. The meal proceeded as these events generally do, with chat about family, mortgages, and life in general. I revealed that my two children had now left the nest, and that the business was trundling along. There was a toast to the old school, and a mildly amusing speech from an old boy who'd had a successful army career.

We'd got on to the after-dinner drinks when someone said, 'I see old Bimbo's died. Well, he won't be touching up any more boys.'

I knew what he meant, of course: there'd been repeated rumours about our late music master. Boys were invited to extra choir practice, and things had supposedly happened. Having no musical abilities myself, I was never involved in the choir, let alone as one of his favoured soloists; I was never sure whether to be relieved or disappointed to have missed out on this extra attention.

John nudged me and added, 'Well, I think even Bimbo would've been surprised at what we got up to behind the pavilion.'

Andrew looked across at John and frowned. I was starting to get uneasy at the way the conversation was going. Yes, of course, I remembered those incidents after games, or coming back from a cross-country run – the secluded spot behind the pavilion, conveniently shielded by bushes, the exploring hands, the shorts pulled down. Nothing really, perfunctory and pretty innocent, and the activities only continued for a few terms, but they fuelled my fantasies for many years afterwards. John's willingness to recall them suggested that he regarded all this as just part of growing up. By all accounts he'd moved on to a very active heterosexual life.

'So how come I missed out on all this activity?' The speaker was sitting diagonally opposite me, and I'd been trying to work out who he was. But as soon as he entered our conversation I knew the voice. It was Mark Davis, one of the more academic and studious boys in our year, who'd always seemed shy and awkward with other boys and avoided games as much as possible. I wasn't surprised he'd been left out of our activities – we wouldn't have thought he'd have any interest in sex. But he was very different now: the mousy hair had become the sort of grey that's described – accurately in this case – as 'distinguished', the unbecoming spectacles had gone, and altogether he seemed much more confident and relaxed. His suit fitted him very well, and could those be diamonds in his cufflinks? He went on to tell us about his life. He'd gone to Cambridge, taken a year out, and then got a job in the media. And he was gay, currently single after the break-up of a long-term relationship. Andrew, his political instincts aroused, commented on how good it was that gay people were so accepted these days, and how the Conservatives were to thank for same-sex marriage. I nodded, but found it difficult to respond.

A little later some of us felt the need for a smoke, or at least a breath of fresh air, and went out on the balcony. It was quite dark after the bright lights of the function room. Mark caught up with me, and led me to a sort of alcove behind a pillar. 'Well,' he said, 'you've not changed much – you're looking pretty good compared to some of these old farts. Did you know I rather fancied you in those days?'

This came as a complete surprise. I could only stammer in reply, 'You're ... you're looking good yourself – I, er, didn't recognise you at first.' Somehow this seemed a totally inadequate response, and I was feeling more and more embarrassed.

'You kept very quiet, when they were talking about what happened behind the pavilion,' he went on. 'Maybe all that meant more to you than you're letting on.'

'Maybe it did,' I said, 'but, of course, I'm a married man. Er, perhaps we'd better be getting back inside.'

'Perhaps we should,' he said, '... or perhaps we could enjoy the night air a bit longer.'

I tried to think of a reply, but the words wouldn't come out. Gently he slipped his hand inside my shirt and started stroking my chest. All of a sudden it seemed that some of my fantasies were coming true. I kissed him on the lips and held him close. He began to undo my flies. In my married life with Barbara, sex, such as it was, had always been of the 'missionary' variety, and this first experience of oral sex was quite a revelation.

After we'd adjusted our dress, we went back into the function room. Andrew caught sight of us coming in together, and maybe picked up something from our body language. At any rate he seemed distinctly unamused. I concluded that my chance of becoming a councillor had taken a sudden turn for the worse.

FOUR POEMS
Pat Dungey

STARK SUNDAY

Sun streams through the slats.
Distant radio ditties.
Far off joyful sounds on the breeze.
That damned cheerful summer blackbird.

With all the volume
Of a falling wall of bricks,
Fear, terror, throaty ache,
Emptiness
All shudder about me.

In my bed,
Embryonically curled
At the one end
Avoiding the other
Empty side.

Hell, it's only 7.30
Too early to ring ... Anyone.
Alone
Marooned in my claustrophobic darkness.
The stark truth.
On a stark Sunday.

BOX NUMBER XYZ

Who is she ... ?
What is she ... ?
A mockery of love she makes.
A CV of attributes she wants.
Love to order.
Sex on tap.

Tick off what's wanted.
What's there?
Going somewhere
or going nowhere?
That elusive advert woman
Beware!
Box number XYZ

COMING OUT ... AGAIN AND AGAIN

Coming out ...
Of what?
Into what?

Like a 50s coming out ball.
Of all the stupid confusing phrasals,
Coming out is queen.

Coming off ... The street
Into that first bar, alone.

Pulling it off.
Chickening out.
Passing by.
All more apt.

I'm still coming out
After 20 years ... finding me
In love, happiness and pain.
And often going in again, on myself, to rest.

MENOPAUSAL MUSINGS

Bony outcrops
Fleshy mounds
Hairy patches
Scaly pads
Menopausal Misery

This room or that one?
Can't remember
Why I am here?
It's there, at the back of my mind
Tip of my tongue
Menopausal Miasma.

Saturday nights in.
Wine, feet up, music, TV
Pleasure from so much more
Menopausal Miracle.

FACING UP TO PAEDOPHILIA
Donald West

Paedophilia is a psychiatric term for excessive sexual attraction to immature children. Legal statutes define sexual offences against children by actual behaviour (not mere attraction) and by the calendar age of the child, avoiding any mention of 'immaturity' or 'paedophilia'. Laws to protect children from sex have expanded from rape, sexual assault, and indecent acts, to encompass grooming, spying and the production, possession, distribution or viewing of inappropriate films, drawings or computer images of children. The perpetrators of these diverse offences are not all incorrigible predators working together. I am using the term paedophilia loosely for any adult sex behaviour linked to a child.

Adultery, homosexuality and kinky sex have become less shocking. In 2012, a male prostitute, on trial at Southwark Court under the Obscene Publications Act for supplying his clients with pornographic videos, was acquitted when the jury found them not legally obscene. They included graphic images of a forearm thrust up a man's anus. Women having intercourse with under-age boys used to be thought to do them an educational favour. Today, any hint of paedophilia is abhorrent. In the past kids were less chaperoned, touching up choirboys was a joke, and children being molested in their homes was not so often in the news. We are wiser now. Appeals to former victims to come forward have put an overwhelming demand on police investigators. We should not have been surprised, remembering historic revelations of impoverished parents selling their children for prostitution. Recent exposures of media celebrities, politicians and priests show that no class is immune from child molesters. Research using plethysmograph measurements of penile swelling shows that a significant percentage of men have a degree of erection while watching child porn. In surveys, including my own, questioning adults about their experiences, a high proportion of women and a substantial number of men recall sexual contacts with older people when they were under sixteen. Most were considered not very serious at the time and were said to have had no appreciable long-term effect. When homosexual attraction was a taboo topic, people did not know that it was quite common and not invariably harmful. The same might be said of sexual attraction to the young.

Sex abuse cases coming before the courts are generally serious, some of them truly horrifying, and mostly against girls in their family home. The offenders are usually hetero-sexual males: fathers, stepfathers and mothers' lovers, visiting relatives, temporary child minders or family friends. Im-proper behaviour by women, under the cover of intimate motherly child-care, avoids suspicion. Women are rarely identified as offenders against children, and then usually in association with a man. Two notorious and uniquely dreadful examples are the multiple murders by Myra Hindley and Rosemary West.

Within their family, children can be trapped in repetitive sex abuse. Unless it is painful, very young children may not know something wrong is happening. As they learn better, they feel guilty and ashamed. Much abusive behaviour is simply inappropriate, persuasive rather than aggressive, but when force is used, especially if there is sexual penetration, it is both immediately traumatic and linked to psychological damage that can be permanent. Girls who complain risk being initially accused of lying. Later, they suffer police and courtroom interrogations on embarrassingly intimate details. An offending parent is likely to be imprisoned and the family broken up and impoverished. On release, an offending father is forbidden to return home to the children. Many victims are effectively orphaned. If the offender has been in other respects a caring parent, the child feels bereaved. I have seen pathetic letters from children to imprisoned fathers. The child may have wanted no more than that the abuse should cease. Victims' hesitation to report abuse is understandable, given the heavy cost of doing so. Situations may become known only when the offender is discovered in the act, or when unexplained irritation or infection of the genitals triggers an inquiry. Establishing a case against a suspect family member is complicated, especially when faced by conspiratorial family denials, making action by social workers seem dilatory.

Young girls are generally chaperoned outside the home. Problems arise when older girls, not yet ready to make mature choices, find contacts on the internet or elsewhere with men they regard as lovers, who soon become exploitative. Notorious are the predatory gangs of immigrants, having scant respect for young European girls, with their liberal manners and revealing dress. They seduce their victims into guilty sexual relationships, preparatory to propelling them into drug dependence and coercive promiscuity. Some of these girls are further victimised when dealt with by the police as delinquents.

Sexual abuse of boys in their homes is less frequent, if only because fathers are usually heterosexual. Some paedophiles target young children of either sex, but they are not likely to be fathers living in families. Boys' encounters are more often outside the home at amusement arcades and other places popular with children, or sometimes with adults with whom they have regular contact, such as youth workers and sports coaches. The experiences are less traumatic; the boys are usually free to walk away and it may be just a one-off event. Reporting may lead to prosecutions and publicity, exposing the boy to accusation that he was acquiescent and therefore gay. Continuing anxiety about their own sexual orientation is common among boys. Whereas premature exposure of girls to heterosexuality appears to provoke inhibitions in adult heterosexuality, exposure of boys to homosexuality is said to seduce them into becoming gay.

It is with the connivance of parents or carers that children are induced to adopt lewd poses, or participate in sexual acts in front of cameras for child porn producers. Although unaware when it is happening, they are further abused as their images are distributed to all and sundry. Pictures of infants in the nude taken by their parents, a once popular practice, can be technically criminal, if shown to others. Much behaviour now defined as criminal remains unknown to the children concerned. Children at play on the beach are unaware when their pictures are being taken secretly by paedophiles with cameras embedded in spectacles or with telescopic lenses. Youngsters sending nude pictures to friends on the internet may be behaving illegally, but the activity is mostly innocuous, although it can become a vehicle for blackmail or embarrassment in later life.

There is no obvious connection between minority sexual interests and personality. Only a tiny minority of paedophiles are the violent, psychopathic monsters highlighted by the press. Paedophiles can be successful in professions and in personal friendships despite their guilty sexual life. Although many offenders seem bent on their immediate sexual pleasure, with little regard for the consequences, others form ongoing relationships and are genuinely concerned. Relationships can even blossom into a platonic attachment continuing when a boy grows into a heterosexual adult and later a married family man, although more often they come to an end when, disappointingly for the boy, he reaches beyond the age the paedophile finds attractive. Romantic features in such relationships have been depicted in literature, from the Greek classics and ancient Persian poets to Shakespeare, *Lolita* and *The History Boys*.

There is no settled scientific view on the causes of paedophilia. Some men can respond sexually only to children and are incapable of sex with adults however much they try or whatever punishment they suffer for touching children. As with exclusive homosexuals, they may have a genetic predisposition or an innate peculiarity of the hormonal and cerebral mechanisms of physical sexuality. Although modern neurological techniques have identified a variety of subtle abnormalities in selected paedophiles, no coherent explanation is yet available. Many detected offenders say they have been sexually abused when they were children. Whether this is cause and effect is doubtful; it is a convenient excuse. Criminal justice purists have no sympathy with the plea that paedophiles suffer temptations most of us do not experience. People can abstain from sex if they want to, as some do for religious reasons. As with gay orientation, the paedophile orientation is not all or none. Some men are attracted to both adults and children and some, the hebephiles, are predominantly attracted to adolescents. Gerontophiles, fixated on the elderly, certainly exist, but do not excite the same public attention because their acts are usually consensual.

Widespread sexual attraction to legally under-aged youth is evident from the prevalence of youthful images in commercial porn (not to mention commercial advertisements). The legal age of consent at sixteen, and in some circumstances eighteen, does not tally with the variable age when a young person starts to want sex and may be ready to initiate it. Under-age girls can be angered when disapproving parents or Local Authority carers secure the prosecution of their boyfriends. Sexual behaviour with a willing, or even eager, young person does not deserve the same punishment as a real sexual assault, especially when the age gap is small. The arbitrary way examples attract prosecution is unjust.

Paedophilia may be unchangeable, but Home Office criminal statistics for sexual offences against children show a low reconviction risk compared with ordinary crimes, although the risk persists to a relatively late age. Potential offenders can be trained to control their behaviour, avoid situations of temptation and, if needed, use sexual suppressant drugs.

In some cultures there is much less concern than in the UK for the protection of youngsters from sex, especially boys who are free from risk of pregnancy. I recall a man awaiting a prison sentence for indecent conduct with a boy, who told me he planned to move to India on release. He described a night in bed with a boy in his caravan in India, when a police officer called him to open up. He showed no interest or surprise about the boy, but warned the vehicle was unwisely parked. We do not need to emulate other cultures, but such differences suggest that the practical consequences of paedophile behaviour are culture-bound.

Fear of an ever-present 'paedophile' menace is harmful. Exaggerated response from parents to minor incidents makes matters worse. Touching and fondling is not physically harmful, but psychological damage can be exacerbated by the assumption that terrible effects are inevitable. Over-protection of children denies them opportunities to develop self-reliance and independent socialisation with peers. Children kept at home, spending time in their bedroom, glued to the internet, can still have sexual contacts. As an only child in the thirties, my happiest recollections are of frequent rides with a friendly milk deliveryman in his horse and cart, and lone cycle trips along a canal towpath into the countryside, activities that would now be suspect. Today, passers-by, especially elderly men, must think twice before befriending a lost child or intervening in naughty behaviour. Parents no longer dare to let their children walk to school.

GAY MEN'S PAEDOPHILE REPUTATION

The risk to boys from 'grooming' into adult homosexuality looms large in Russian anti-gay propaganda. Although unsupported by evidence, the belief lingers that gay men are more likely than heterosexuals to be attracted to children. When the scandal of priests molesting boys was gathering momentum, Cardinal Bertone declared that it was not celibacy, but homosexuality and its link to paedophilia that was responsible. The activities of the banned Paedophile Information Exchange, campaigning for law reform to allow consenting children to have sex with their elders, seems to have fed belief in this link. The movement's leaders were gay males, and some of them were subsequently convicted for sex contacts with boys. The civil libertarian politicians who supported PIE at the time were much criticised years later. PIE's public condemnation had the effect of discouraging proposals for reforming the law on consent to sex, on the grounds that they were a cover for homosexual paedophilia.

Gay men's bad reputation persists and appears supported by the number of convictions for offences with boys, which is larger than expected in comparison to convictions for offences against girls, considering the much smaller proportion of gay men in the population. However, homosexual offences against boys occur mostly outside the home, making detection and conviction easier, and inflating the statistics. Murders of children in a sexual situation by strangers receive maximum publicity, but they are minuscule in number compared to other murders of children, which are mostly by their parents. Rather than sexual sadism, panic, when a child molester has reason to believe he faces a fate worse than death should the child betray him, can be a motive for killing.

Teachers unions have complained about the large number of accusations of sex abuse of pupils and the devastating effect on teachers' careers, even when the accusation is unfounded or malicious. Gay male teachers are particularly vulnerable. Children have become better informed about sex, and malicious pupils know their power to damage by alleging sexual impropriety. The effect on the recruitment of male teachers, especially in primary schools, has been dismal. Tight regulations about any physical contact or one-to-one relationships between pupil and teacher deter what might otherwise be helpful influences. Old-fashioned hugging and comforting small children who have hurt themselves is out of the question, and the holds used to restrain violent kids are limited.

WHAT MIGHT HELP?

Children's welfare should come first. Social workers used to avoid the sometimes dire effects of police intervention by managing privately some cases of misbehaviour within a household. When an unaggressive offender admitted his guilt, was deeply shamed and willing to collaborate in supervision, it was a practical and often successful policy; but today social workers must notify the police immediately of any suspicion.

The differing age of consent in otherwise comparable countries points to the problem of a fixed cut-off. It might be better left to judges and prosecutors to take account of age, maturity and circumstances.

Parents and teachers, who are alert to unexplained changes in a child's behaviour and mood, facilitate disclosure of abuse at an early stage and reduce the number of victims coming forward years later complaining of post-traumatic disorders from unchecked childhood abuse. These traumatised adults often come from families with multiple problems of marital conflict, drug abuse etc. They are not helped by psycho-therapists attributing all their troubles to real or presumed past sexual abuse. Therapists in the US have been sued for implanting false memories of abuse by suggestion.

Both research funders and research workers are put off the topic of paedophilia by the angry reaction if findings conflict with received wisdom. I was a joint author of a book that included doctoral research by a clinical psychologist who interviewed convicted paedophiles and obtained useful information about their attitudes and the circumstances in which offences occurred. When the book was re-published in the US, it was denounced in the press for promoting paedophilia, the opposite of the author's intention. He was reported to the British Psychological Society and was for a time under threat of losing his NHS employment.

Free speech is not for paedophiles. In 1980, when Tom O'Carroll, one of the Paedophile Information Exchange activists, published *Paedophilia: The radical case*, he was invited to talk at a seminar at the Cambridge Institute of Crimin-ology where I was working. Following cautionary advice from a judge, the event was cancelled. In 2010, under the pseudonym Carl Toms, O'Carroll published *Michael Jackson's Dangerous Liaisons*. It was the fruit of many years of research, documenting the singer's close relationships with and lavish patronage of young boys, their parents profiting from the situation, and the bad effects on the boys themselves. It was no advert for paedophilia, but when the original publishers were told the identity of the author they declined to distribute the book.

Another paedophile author, Eduard Brongersma, was a distinguished Dutch lawyer and sometime senator, who was influential in lowering the age of consent in his country. In his huge tome *Loving Boys*, he researched the varied attitudes and practices in different cultures, both contemporary and historic. I visited the archive he amassed and was struck by letters from prisoners, serving long prison sentences in America, still worrying about the welfare of their former boyfriends. He submitted a paper to the *Howard Journal*, but the editor would not accept it unless I contributed a 'balanced' commentary. He committed suicide in 1998, disillusioned by the stoning of his house and the growing hostility to his ideas. He left his archive to a university for research purposes, but the authorities' first reaction was to try to use it to pursue self-confessed paedophiles; they were frustrated by Dutch laws limiting the prosecution of historic offences. Dispassionate study of the writings of well-informed paedophile authors would be more helpful than denouncing them unread.

The punitive provisions of the criminal justice system, besides swelling the already large prison population with a dramatic increase in sex offenders, discourages the development of more effective evidence-based policies for their management and treatment.

Greater investment in sexological research and the dissemination of its findings would inform social policy and public opinion, but there are obstacles. Most paedophiles are not known to the police, and it is very difficult to recruit a representative sample or to estimate how many there are. Men fear to be frank with research inquiries in case their identity is leaked. Researchers have to take steps to ensure that they are legally safe in preserving confidences. Important questions remain unanswered. For example, does viewing erotic images of children avoid or promote actual contact? Are paedophiles mostly lone offenders? How many know and collaborate with others in locating, grooming and sharing victims?

Imprisonment is an expensive means of control, destroying whatever place the offender has held in society. It used to be said that sending homosexual men to prison was like confining alcoholics in a brewery. It is equally unsuited for treating paedophiles. Those who are unrepentant, and resist treatment proposals, argue that their activities are harmless, they are befriending children, and being persecuted unjustly. Placed in segregated prison units for protection from violence, they soon find others of like mind to plot ways to thwart therapists, find victims, and avoid detection.

Worthy attempts are made to treat prisoners by 'cognitive behaviour therapy' (mostly discussion of the adverse effects of their behaviour on themselves and their victims and how to avoid temptation) but the punitive prison ethos is unhelpful. Men are disinclined to reveal their problems for fear of prolonging their detention, and limited provision of therapists means that not all receive help, even among the genuinely cooperative. Despite these difficulties, treated offenders show slightly fewer reconvictions than the untreated.

Whereas aggressive rapists of women are often criminals in other respects, offenders against children are often otherwise law-abiding social conformists who could be held in specialised institutions, more like medium-secure hospitals, where treatment is the primary purpose and outcomes likely to be better.

The sex offender register and the provisions for control and supervision of ex-prisoners by a probation officer are fine in principle, but can become counter-productive if too oppressive. Announcements of an offender's presence in a community can mean refusal of employment and shunning by neighbours. Newsworthy murders of persons wrongly identified as paedophiles highlights the danger from vigilantism. Unemployed offenders, alone, frightened, rejected by their families, with nothing more to lose, are liable to abscond and comfort themselves with a child. While control is essential, so is an appreciation of the obstacles and temptations each offender faces. A not very bright patient of mine, on probation for indecency with boys was living alone in a Cambridgeshire village, where his reputation was too well known. He was being continually pestered by boys knocking on his door wanting treats in return for sex play.

My final pleas: Acknowledgement of the huge grey area between sexual impropriety and grossly abusive behaviour. More and bolder research. A humane and child-centred approach to all affected by paedophilia.

FIVE POEMS
John Dixon

NOT QUITE FITTING

I wear loose clothes
that range from the back of the chair
to the washing machine
never the wardrobe or dry cleaners
still less the ironing board.
Comfortable, casual
a size too large
elasticated waists, open neck
and wide-fitting slip-on shoes.

Then came
a black-edged envelope
with a card inside
with a name I knew
and a date I had to attend.

I tugged at the wardrobe door
to check the formal clothes
I hadn't worn for years
but never had the heart to throw.
They didn't fit. I'd put on weight.
And in the chain-store fitting room
the angled all-round mirror spoke
'You're no longer off-the-peg.'

The modern delay
between death and despatch
gave me and my new tailor,
much-needed extra time.

I chose a sombre cloth
and was measured with discretion.
Will he pad the droop?
Loose fit the gut?
Did it really matter now which way I hung?

The chalking-up began before I left.
Mute as an undertaker
the tailor's only words
'Be ready for fitting next week.'

THE LAMENT OF QUIMMY-LAURA

I long for a sunbathe like the other girls have
and not get white lines on my breasts
but the moment I loosen the straps of my bra
butterflies land on my nipples
and flatten their wings like moths.

I watch girls lining up for a quick skinny-dip.
I resolve to join in and begin to strip
but the minute I take off my swim-suit top
butterflies land on my nipples
and flatten their wings like moths.

I'm OK in the bedroom and bathroom
and by day with the front curtains drawn
I tried the back garden with tall trees all around
I stripped to the waist and threw bread to the birds
but
butterflies flew to my nipples
and flattened their wings like moths.

FANCY THAT

To think
that little boy
I used to tickle
under the chin
is now the grown man
I'm tickling under the balls.

Ah, Time! Ah, Change!
Same finger action.

GAY ARCHIVES

Liber scriptus proferetur

Doesn't have to be in book form.
Hand-written'll do
in code undeciphered
leaves from a diurnal
in need of re-assembling.
Photos qualify, tapes and films
and mock officialese
clandestine minutes
indelible ephemera,
and graffiti itself defaced.

Unthread with care
the pseudonymous confession
less proferred than deferred.
Ease out the bilharzia worm
and spool it round a twig.

In quo totum continetur

Surely no one thing contains the lot!
But should such a claim be made
beware explicit boasting.
Much is omitted, destroyed, suppressed.
There are lines to read between
invisible ink to call back to visibility.

Unde mundus judicetur

From which the world can judge us?
Not any more.
Thanks to Facts. Stored. Accessible.
An acknowledged discipline
literature, history, copious bibliography.
Growing.
Alumni put right past misconceptions
elucidate the impetus behind the persecutions
strive to oppose their re-occurrence.
Get beyond that judgmental
mentalità.

Liber scriptus proferetur, In quo totum continetur, Unde mundus judicetur is a section from the medieval dog-Latin Requiem Mass. The usual dog translation is – 'Lo! The book, exactly worded, wherein all hath been recorded, thence shall judgement be awarded.'

THE WEDDING RING

I always wanted one of those.

Mother had one.
She used soap to get it off
before she did the washing-up.
Almost lost it once down the plug.
In later years
after her husband died
she never took if off
more from gout than grief.

Don't know what happened to it when she died.
She always said it's not 9 carat gold, it's 24.

Our one is – or rather our two are –
not up to that.
I hope we'll share the washing-up
and not get gout.

AN ENCOUNTER IN THE PARK
Joseph Hucknall

A walk in the park is almost a daily routine for me. Not only do I benefit from the half-hour exercise, but it also invigorates the senses and frees the mind from worries. I have enjoyed this exercise for over twenty years and have seen many changes in the park. Saplings that have grown into mature trees; shrub borders overtaken by brambles; increasing deposits of litter; energetic joggers appearing for a few days, then mysteriously seen no more. It is not a much frequented park and often I have been the only person in it, but there is a children's playground fenced off with swings, a roundabout and a slide, which on some days attract a few children, usually with a parent.

Recently the Council erected three exercise bars, of varying height, and also a circular exercise platform, all outside the children's fenced playground and, judging from their size and height, intended for use by adults. I had not seen anyone use them, which seemed a shame, and out of curiosity, I tried the bars but quickly gave up. I did not have the strength to lift my body weight. Out of passing interest I then tried the circular exercise platform, and standing on it, I started to twist my body round, as the instructions stated, when I noticed a policeman approaching. I remained on the platform.

'Good morning, Sir.'

He was a young policeman, but they all are now. Good looking too. He looked at me apprehensively.

'I have not seen anyone using this before,' he said, pointing to the platform. 'We have been informed that someone has been loitering around the children's playground area. Do you mind if I ask you a few questions?'

'Not at all'

'Do you live in this area?'

I did and wondered what difference it would make if I didn't.

'Do you have any children yourself?'

Now, what would his reaction be if I said that, being homosexual, it would be unlikely?

'Do you come here often?'

'Most days,' I said. It had been many years since I was asked that question.

'When were you born, Sir?'

Should I refuse to tell him, I thought, but I did.

'Are you sure?' he asked.

Did my looks belie my age, I wondered? I hadn't thought of bringing my birth certificate with me on the walk. How remiss of me.

'Have you any identification, Sir?'

No, I had not.

'Could you give me your name?'

I duly obliged, and thinking he was being overzealous, asked him why he was so suspicious. He gave me a withering look and ignored the question.

He then spoke into his radio and gave my name and asked for it to be checked. Obviously they did not have my name on their records and, with a look of disappointment, he said that if I wished to make a complaint, I could do so at the police station, turned on his heels, and walked off.

My walks in the park are less frequent now. I go out of my way to avoid passing the children's playground, and the exercise platform remains unused.

SEASONAL HAIKU
Jeffrey Doorn

buds burst on branches
       tree trunks go green and ooze sap
         my sap rises too

garden colours clash
       flowers turn to face fierce sun
         its rays crisp my skin

red leaves on the trees
       soon to be falling to earth
         like my once red hair

frost covers hard ground
       locking germs of life within
         will I be reborn?

AUTHORS' BIOGRAPHIES

REX BATTEN was a student at RADA in the same class as Joe Orton. He eventually took up teaching. He has written plays for radio and produced several local history publications. He became a gay activist and wrote *Rid England of this Plague*, based on personal experience of the 1950s purge when simply being gay was a crime. The book became a set book at Gender Studies courses and led to several television appearances.

CHRIS BECKETT grew up in Ethiopia. He won the 2001 Poetry London Competition and second prize in Chroma 2006. His collection, *Ethiopia Boy*, came out from Carcanet/Oxford Poets in 2013 and he is now trying to write about hunger in an Ethiopian context, and not just the Live Aid kind! Meanwhile, he is collaborating with his partner, the artist Isao Miura, on translating Bashō's *The Narrow Road to the Deep North* into visual and textual images. The first 'outing' of this work, *Sketches from the Poem Road,* was shown at the Poetry Café, 2015, and the book from Hagi Press was shortlisted for the Ted Hughes Award. A much larger *Sketches* exhibition was held at the Glass Tank Gallery in Oxford Brookes University, summer 2016.

'Lemon for Love' was previously published in *Ethiopia Boy* and also in *Ambit* No. 208, April 2012.

KATHRYN BELL was born in Glasgow and went to work in Africa where she met Elsa Wallace. She has been writing for about 25 years. Her stories have been published in *Sappho, Capital Gay, Gazebo, The Green Queen* and *Queer Haunts*. She produces the quarterly *GAW Newsletter* and edits *The Green Queen*. She would like to write a novel but – so she says – lacks the stamina. She enjoys folk music, chocolate and arguing.

'A Dog's Life' was first published in *The Green Queen*, No. 6, May 2001. A version of 'Hetty Garbage' was first published in *The Green Queen*, No. 15, July 2010.

TIM BLACKWELL lives in North London with his dog, Olaf. He trained as an actor at The Webber Douglas Academy, and has wide experience performing in theatre and film. Tim writes prose and drama. Several of his plays have been produced at venues including The Young Vic and The Crucible Studio, Sheffield. A collection of his short fiction, *The Bingo Caller and other stories*, is published by Connaught Books.

LES BROOKES is the author of *Gay Male Fiction Since Stonewall: ideology, conflict and aesthetics*. He published his first novel *Such Fine Boys* in 2013 and is currently at work on a second. He has twice been a prize-winner in the Cambridge Writers Short Story Competition. www.lesbrookes.com.

ROSS BURGESS lives in Purley with his husband, Roger, volunteering with LGBT groups and creating online articles for the UK LGBT Archive, www.lgbtarchive.uk. Before retirement he worked as an IT consultant and technical author, and produced books on computer subjects. Having edited *Out of the Shadows* (Bona Street Press, 2010) and *Diverse Performances* (Paradise Press, 2014) he became commissioning editor for *Amiable Warriors*, the history of the Campaign for Homosexual Equality (Paradise Press: Volume One published 2015). Encouraged by Gay Authors Workshop, he's recently started writing fiction for the first time since leaving school.

ANDREW CHEFFINGS writes: I am a Buddhist, practising Soto Zen and Pureland traditions. I have had OCD for 45 years and am currently having EMDR therapy. My writing is an important part of my healing journey and I have written hundreds of hymns called *Hymns of Change* in which I am working on the spirituality of moving from a very difficult mental outlook to, hopefully, a calmer one. I have been with my partner, Ian, for 26 years.

DANIEL CLEMENTS lives in Cambridge as close as he can contrive to be to his office to save on bleary-eyed morning walks. While he now works in IT for the NHS, in the past he has dabbled in archaeology, education and cookery. Writing has always been a private affair, a way of organising different thoughts and feelings by pinning them on a piece of paper. This is, therefore, a terrifying experience for him. His interests outside of writing include board games, computers, science and anything else that can have the word 'nerd' ascribed to it.

SIMON DESSLOCH studied Creative Writing at Birkbeck College. His stories have appeared in *Nthposition*, *Faster than Life*, *Rouge and Mr X* and in *People Your Mother Warned You About*.

'The Worm Boy' was previously published in the horror anthology *Worms*, edited by Alex Davis (Knightwatch Press, 2014).

JOHN DIXON has had poems in *Envoi*, *Chroma*, *Iota*, *Orbis*, *Nomad*, *Gazebo* and *Haiku Quarterly*. His first volume was *Seeking, Finding, Losing*. His short stories have appeared in several anthologies and his volume of short stories, *The Carrier Bag*, includes the Bridport Prize-winning title story. The story 'Comrades' included in this volume won a prize at the Chorley Writer's Competition. His novel *Push harder Mummy, I want to come out* is due for publication shortly.

He has edited *Fiction in Libraries*, and a volume of Ivor Treby's unpublished poems. He co-edited the poetry anthology *Coming Clean*. He is at present drawing up an inventory of the stories and song lyrics by the late Michael Harth.

JEFFREY DOORN was born in New Jersey, and now lives with his civil partner in South London. His work has appeared in *Gawp and Gaze*, *Queer Words*, *The Quarterly Review*, *Mandate*, *Gazebo*, *Queer Haunts*, *People Your Mother Warned You About*, plus the poetry anthologies *Slivers of Silver*, *Oysters and Pearls* and *Coming Clean*, all of which he co-edited. He is active in his local civic society and Library Friends group, and also contributes to local history publications.

PAT DUNGEY writes: I was born in Luton, Bedfordshire. I came out at 31. I have recently stopped full-time teaching and am focussing on writing about my experiences and researching 1920s and 1930s women in London and Paris. I enjoy giving talks and visiting London galleries and museums for inspiration.

Writing these poems has got me through some difficult times. I hope the reader recognises the feelings in these words and feels less alone, at such times.

STEVE FERRIS writes: I am not a poet, I am a painter. It controls and colours everything I do. I have, despite that, written many poems including several sequences. Poems have appeared in the anthology *Coming Clean*. I am currently devoting my time to artwork, getting ready for summer shows and competitions. I recently had to move house and shifting the 10,000 finished paintings caused me no end of trouble: perhaps it will lead to another sequence?

DAVID GEE has worked in London, Bahrain and Qatar. His first novel *Florence of Arabia* (under the pen-name David Godolphin), republished as David Gee's *Shaikh-Down*, anticipated the 'Arab Spring' by ten years, with a gay banker and an air hostess kick-starting a spicy revolution on a Persian Gulf island. He has published two dark social comedies set in his native Sussex: *The Dropout* and (from Paradise Press) *The Bexhill Missile Crisis*. Coming soon to Kindle, *Howl and the Pussy-Kat* features a soap-stud and a porn star cast in a remake of a Bette Davis weepie. Website and blog: www.davidgeebooks.com.

RAMON GONZALEZ was born in Galicia (Spain) and has lived in London since 1971. He studied art first at Chelsea School of Art and later at Wimbledon School of Art where he obtained a degree in Fine Arts in 1982. One of his paintings was used to illustrate the book cover of *A Life's Tales* by Joe Hucknall, his partner. Apart from the combined activities of painting and poetry, another main interest is philosophy on which subject he is writing a book (now near completion) which he intends to publish in the near future.

MICHAEL HARTH, who died in April 2016, was a founder member of GAW and a prolific writer and lyricist. He early gave up a conventional life and for many years was one half of a piano duo, performing original lyrics set to newly-composed music. He was editor of *Lightning Fingers,* a symposium on the British composer-pianist Billy Mayerl.

His short stories appeared in various gay magazines, going back to one of the first, *Quorum*. He produced three volumes of short stories, and edited two short story anthologies, as well as editing the GAW in-house magazine, *Gazebo*. He wrote three novels and at the time of his death was preparing for publication a trilogy about a gay priest.

Michael gave unfailing support and encouragement to other members of GAW and it is only right that his considerable volume of unpublished work be listed and prepared for safe-keeping in a gay archive, and an interim selection of unpublished work be published by Paradise Press.

JOSEPH HUCKNALL was born in Cumbria and educated by seven siblings who came before him, then drafted into the army before drifting south as a protégé of Woolworth. Joe worked the system until he was found out and paid to take early retirement. He travelled extensively in comfort, picking up and dropping relationships until, late in life, he met his soulmate, Ramon Gonzalez, and handcuffed him into a civil partnership.

His first work, *A Splendid Book for Lucky Children,* written at fourteen, never made it into print. Joe has contributed to *Gazebo* and defunct minor poetry publications. For greater insight and revelations from boy to man read his memoir, *A Life's Tales.*

ZEKRIA IBRAHIMI writes: I am a schizophrenic – someone always in fear of being sectioned. The psychiatric establishment is about middle-class conformity. I am doubly-disadvantaged – mentally disabled, and swarthy and ethnic, under a racist British society that cannot accept difference. Being categorised as elderly, I have grown scared of ageism everywhere.

JEREMY KINGSTON is a poet and playwright, the author of two novels and two children's books, and for many years he was a theatre critic, for *Punch* and then for *The Times.* His most recent plays have been *Oedipus at the Crossroads* and *Making Dickie Happy.* His two poetry collections are *On the Lookout* (2008) and *Who is he, who am I, who are they?* (2013); a third, *Risking It,* is planned for 2017. He has recently completed a sequence of linked short stories, *Eye to Eye,* tracing responses to homosexual love down the centuries.

V. G. LEE lives and writes in Hastings, East Sussex. She is the author of a collection of short stories, *As You Step Outside,* and four novels. Her fifth novel, *Mr Oliver's Object of Desire,* will be published in September 2016 by Ward Wood Publishing. In 2014 she won The Ultimate Planet award for Best Established Author. In her sixtieth year, she decided to become a stand-up comedian and is a regular performer at Laughing Cows comedy nights in London, Birmingham and Coventry. www.vglee.co.uk, www.facebook.com/val.g.lee, twitter.com/vglee_lee.

ELIZABETH J. LISTER began to write seriously after her seventieth birthday. Her aim to create suspenseful stories, in which her characters live comfortably with their homosexuality, has resulted in short stories and five consecutive (stand-alone) novels in which women tackle real-life problems like prison sentences, rehabilitation, single parenthood, unfaithful partners and homophobia. Love interweaves the plots! 1: *Prisoner 537*; 2: *My Life Outside*; 3: *Nothing Stays the Same*; 4: *Tracy Manners*; 5: *Consequences*.

DREW PAYNE has had work published in *Chroma, Velvet Mafia, Creative Week, Out in the City, Gay Flash Fiction* and *ImageOut Literary Magazine*; and in the anthologies, *The Monster in My Closet, Eros at Large*, and *Boys in Bed*. He writes regularly for *Nursing Standard* and *NRC* magazines. His sketches have been performed in the *News Revue*, the longest running satirical review show.

CHRISTOPHER PRESTON is a playwright and dramaturg/director. His first play *The Davids* played to sell-out audiences for the London New Play Festival in 1999. His development of *Underbelly* (LNPF 1998) and *Babel Junction* (Maya Productions 2006) are favourite projects. *Twenty-two Eighty-four* was published by Paradise Press in 2014 and he is currently preparing an anthology of his plays. After working in UK theatre for 35 years, Christopher now lives in New Zealand, writing fiction and blogging about travel and the arts on www.christopherprestonwrites.com.

DAVID READE was born during the Second World War and grew up in Chelmsford before settling in London for 30 years. He now lives in Thailand. He has always distrusted all kinds of authority, including his father and his headmaster. He has composed many short stories, several appearing in the *GAW Newsletter* and the anthologies *People Your Mother Warned You About* and *Eros at Large*. He has written four novels and many poems.

IVOR TREBY, who died in 2012, was a poet, early gay activist and member of Gay Authors Workshop. He produced five volumes of poetry between 1988 and 2000, but virtually abandoned writing to edit the poems of Michael Field, the pseudonym of two lesbian poetesses of the late nineteenth century. He resumed writing in 2006 and until his death wrote over sixty poems. A handful of these were published in small magazines, and a few surfaced at readings he gave to gay groups. These unpublished poems 2007–2012 were edited by John Dixon. The poems are generally short, genial and formally constructed. It seemed appropriate that his early un-published poem *Another Gay Anthology* should be included in this volume.

LEIGH V. TWERSKY lives in London, where he was born. While he has had poems and short stories published before, he is delighted that this is his first for Paradise Press. He is currently adding the finishing touches to a gay-themed novel set in a dystopian Britain and working on a couple of novellas in what he recently learned could be described as the 'gay insect horror' sub-genre.

ELSA WALLACE lived in Africa for the first 30 years of her life, and has been writing for 40 years, mostly short stories, which have featured in several anthologies. Her collections of short stories include *The Monkey Mirror*, *Ghosts and Gargoyles* and *Kissy-Face*. She has written a novel *Merle* and the novella *Lord Hyaena*. Her favourite authors are Dickens and Ivy Compton-Bennett.

DONALD WEST studied medicine and specialised in psychiatry and sexology. He has authored eleven books on psychiatry and crimin-ology, including the pioneering *Homosexuality* (1955, rev. ed. 1968); *Sexual Crimes and Confrontations* (1987): *Male Prostitution* (1992) and *Children's Sexual encounters with Adults*. His memoir *Gay Life, Straight Work* was published by Paradise Press in 2012. He has had several short stories published in anthologies. He was thrice President of the Society for Psychical Research and is now an Honorary Vice-President of CHE.

ALICE FRANCES WICKHAM is an Irish writer, living in South West London. She edits the popular blog site, newlondonwriters.com, which started out as a street zine in 1998 and featured such luminaries as Bette Bourne of Bloolips and the late, great Quentin Crisp. Alice works as a Medical PA and in her spare time, writes, blogs, edits, runs writers' workshops, and occasionally acts as a literary scout for London-based literary agencies. Alice has been published in *Litro* Magazine, *Edge* Magazine, and one or two other slipstream outlets. Currently working on a humorous novel set in Dublin about the problem of her non-binary identity.

GREGORY WOODS is the author of five poetry collections from Carcanet Press, the latest being *Quidnunc* (2007) and *An Ordinary Dog* (2011). Peter Porter called him 'the poet with the sharpest technique for social verse in Britain today'. Sinead Morrissey called him 'probably, the finest gay poet in the United Kingdom'. His non-fiction includes *Articulate Flesh: Male Homo-eroticism and Modern Poetry* (1987), *A History of Gay Literature: The Male Tradition* (1998) and *Homintern: How Gay Culture Liberated the Modern World* (2016), all published by Yale University Press. He was the first professor of gay and lesbian studies in the UK. www.gregorywoods.co.uk.

INDEX BY AUTHOR

(Titles of poems are shown in italics)

Gay Authors Workshop,
founded 1978, is a co-operative of
LGBT creative writers – poets, drama-
tists, fiction and non-fiction writers. It
provides opportunities to meet, read,
discuss and develop work in progress.
Some advice can be given in preparing
books for possible publication – editing, proof-
reading, art-work and getting printed.

Monthly meetings are held in different venues: mainly
in the London area, but GAW is a national organ-
isation. Our quarterly Newsletter keeps members
informed of meetings and events, while our bi-annual
magazine, *Gazebo,* provides an in-house outlet for
members' short stories, articles and poems.

Membership is open to all LGBT writers, from begin-
ners to experienced and published authors. There is a
modest annual subscription.

Paradise Press was set up in 1999 to get our work
published in the face of indifference by mainstream
publishers to lesbian and gay writing. It is run by a
collective within GAW.

The collective provides editorial and
practical support for individual authors
publishing through Paradise Press, in-
cluding a process of collective discussion
and review.

For a full list of titles, and how to join
GAW, see www.paradisepress.org.uk.